TALISMANO

**OTHER WORKS BY ABDELWAHAB MEDDEB
IN ENGLISH TRANSLATION**

Tombeau of Ibn Arabi and White Traverses
The Malady of Islam
Islam and Its Discontents

TALISMANO
ABDELWAHAB MEDDEB

TRANSLATED AND WITH AN INTRODUCTION BY JANE KUNTZ

Dalkey Archive Press
Champaign and London

Originally published in French as *Talismano* by Éditions Sindbad, Paris, 1987
Copyright © 1987 by Abdelwahab Meddeb
Translation and introduction copyright © 2011 by Jane Kuntz
First edition, 2011

Library of Congress Cataloging-in-Publication Data

Meddeb, Abdelwahab.
 [Talismano. English]
 Talismano / Abdelwahab Meddeb ; translated and with an introduction by Jane Kuntz. -- 1st
ed.
   p. cm.
 ISBN 978-1-56478-629-6 (pbk. : acid-free paper)
 I. Kuntz, Jane. II. Title.
 PQ2673.E34T313 2011
 843'.914--dc22
                             2011002777

Partially funded by the University of Illinois at Urbana-Champaign, as well as by grants from the
National Endowment for the Arts, a federal agency, and the Illinois Arts Council, a state agency

Ouvrage publié avec le concours du Ministère français chargé de la culture – Centre national
du livre

This work has been published, in part, thanks to the French Ministry of Culture – National
Book Center

www.dalkeyarchive.com

Cover: design and composition by Danielle Dutton, illustration by Nicholas Motte
Printed on permanent/durable acid-free paper and bound in the United States of America

It would spoil nothing to reveal that, in the epilogue of Abdel-wahab Meddeb's willfully cryptic novel *Talismano*, the author admits to having "confided through writing, but without giving you a foothold, having strained your eyes with our arabesque of words." Though the novel's project undoubtedly involves intentional disorientation, arabesques at both sentence and structural levels, as well as a dizzying number of obscure cultural references, there is method to Meddeb. The eponymous talisman is the book itself, at times inscrutable to the reader, as talismans are meant to be, yet instilled with the kind of magic power that makes one delight in bewilderment.

Meddeb is himself a product of the bilingual, bicultural education available to Tunisians of his generation, who knew their Arabic and French classics with equal fluency. His erudition in Islamic and European art history, architecture, and literature is on impressive display at every turn in this novel. His ideal reader would almost have to be his intellectual match, someone well versed in the Koran and the Bible, in Islamic and Christian doctrine and culture, not to mention in the politics of one-party governmental regimes and the sprawling multigenerational households of the southern Mediterranean. Readers who catch his references will experience the pleasure of recognition, but the less well-versed need not be discouraged; rather, they should surrender to the strange place-names, the riddles posed by layers of digression and flashback, the startlingly bawdy scenes of sensuality and carnal love, and the sheer proliferation of events and anecdotes mapped all over *Mare Nostrum*.

A native of Tunis, Tunisia, ten years old at the time of that country's independence in 1956, the author/narrator is writing his text from his walk-up apartment in Paris, the exile of choice for so many Maghreb intellectuals disenchanted with the single-party regimes that came to power after national independence. In this case, the regime belongs to Habib Bourguiba, enlightened national hero in the Atatürk tradition, self-declared president for life. Indeed, figures of authority of all kinds—from fathers to clerics to the landowning bourgeoisie—are all targets of collective wrath in the carnivalesque, almost nightmarish popular revolt at the heart of this novel. Proud of his own genealogy (hailing from Andalusia on his father's side, Tripolitania and Yemen on his mother's), Meddeb nonetheless satirizes the noble families of Tunis, Fez, and other cities as they struggle with modernity and with the long-suppressed underclass.

The basic frame of Meddeb's story involves the narrator as prodigal son, imagining his return to Tunis, particularly to the city's old Arab core, or *medina* (the Arabic word for "city"), where he was born and raised. Unlike the new rectilinear town that sprang up around it during the French protectorate (1881–1956), the centuries-old medina is a maze of winding, narrow streets and alleys where the uninitiated are easily lost and led into seemingly endless digressions. Meddeb coins the verb *médiner*, to "medinate," or stroll through the labyrinthine streets, medina-minded, thus setting the pattern for the novel's plot: the narrator's account of his aimless amble through the old neighborhoods where every place-name is a weighty signifier for any readers familiar with the city, or a spur to the imagination for those who are not.

Over the course of the book, the narrator comes upon an assortment of colorful characters, from Jewish alchemists to hirsute prophets of doom in the midst of fomenting a popular rebellion—here, more like a hybrid of festival and orgy—that culminates in the medina-dwellers' mass exodus from the city into the backcountry, a hinterland that still retains the essence of a pre-modern, even pre-Islamic past. The narrator elsewhere qualifies his countrymen as "falsely sedentary," no longer nomadic in spirit, so that this uprising amounts to a kind of return of the repressed. And here is one of Meddeb's central themes about contemporary Arab-Muslim culture: the combined paralyzing effects of undemocratic political regimes and a narrow, legalistic interpretation of Islam have stifled the people's creative energies, rendering them both helpless and resentful. On the other hand, Meddeb's many nods to Sūfi Islam, defined as the more inner, mystical aspect of the religion, clearly indicate where his own religious sympathies lie. The great Sūfi mystics Ibn 'Arabī, Hallāj, and Suhrawardi, to name only three, provide subjects of reflection throughout the narrator's many digressions.

Though this basic frame spreads over roughly twenty-four hours (not unlike Joyce's *Ulysses*), time gets amplified many times over, as events move backward and forward in countless discursive asides and set pieces on the part of the narrator, whose memory is triggered by the sights, sounds, and smells of his familiar childhood surroundings. And what he unfailingly remembers are other walks in other cities, whether in Europe, the Maghreb, the Middle East, or all around the rim of the Mediterranean—Fez, Cairo, Venice, Rome—cities that the narrator captures via a chance encounter, an architectural detail, or a literary reference that, more often than not, gives way to yet another aside, all of which eventually find their way back to our narrator's medina madness, in the company of his intrepid companion, Fātima, who will prove the more resourceful of the pair.

Writing with his feet, then, the peripatetic narrator also frequently strays into self-referential commentary not only upon the act of walking but the act of writing itself. He muses upon the difference between Arabic and Latin scripts, on the frustrations of the manual typewriter, on the calligrapher's art, and of course, on the writing of talismans, which in his part of the world once consisted of esoteric inscriptions and pictograms on a paper to be folded up and kept on one's person to ward off the evil eye or other imagined threats. The wearer of the talisman need not understand the inscription for it to have an effect. Reader, take heed and take heart! Indeed, a re-production of a talisman is included in the book, a little past the midpoint of the novel, one written by the narrator himself on the banks of the Nile, at the request of a local café owner attempting to rid his café of evil spirits. The narrator claims to have received the message to be inscribed one star-studded night in a single burst of revelation, without fully comprehending its meaning—a potentially blasphemous play on "revealed" religions in general. That parts of this novel might escape the reader's grasp is therefore a recursive feature, not a flaw.

Nevertheless, readers should be armed with some basic distinctions regarding the traditional North African, or Maghrebi, city, notably the difference between a mosque (*mesjid*, in Arabic) and a *zāwiya*, or shrine, two religious landmarks where much of the novel's central action takes place. The mosque, in this case primarily the great mosque of Tunis, called the Zitūna (eighth century AD), is the official house of worship where practicing Muslims come to pray, particularly on Fridays when prayer is led by the imām, who also delivers the weekly sermon. The Zitūna, along with Cairo's Al-Azhar mosque and Morocco's Al-Qarawīn, was a very early center of learning, comparable to the universities of medieval Europe. Meddeb is descended from a line of theologians who taught there.

Mosques are found everywhere in the Islamic world. The zāwiya, by contrast, is typically North and West African, and is a site of more popular, less officially sanctioned forms of religious expression, notably of Sūfi mysticism. Zāwiyas are often shrines to the founder of a religious brotherhood. In the case of the zāwiya Sidi Mahrez, whose shrine features prominently in the novel, the shrine celebrates the patron "saint" of the city of Tunis. The zāwiya is often the site of ecstatic dancing and singing, ritual sacrifice, and praying for the intercession of the saint in some personal matter or collective need, such as for rain or a good harvest. They are often pilgrimage destinations, more steeped in superstition and folklore than official Islam recognizes, and depending on the size of the zāwiya complex, they can provide overnight accommodation. Meddeb violates this distinction between mosque and zāwiya by camping throngs of boisterous and bawdy townsfolk in the otherwise solemn house of prayer that the Zitūna represents, turning it into a hotbed of popular dissent and worldly pleasures.

The novel's most iconoclastic, even shocking violation involves one of its more gruesome and memorable scenes, the assembling or "re-membering" of body parts from disinterred cadavers to create an idol temporarily installed in the great mosque. For not only does Islam condemn idolatry, but most adamantly outlaws any desecration of human remains. This act of pure imagination on the part of the author—nowhere in Islam does anything even remotely similar ever take place—is carried out by a sorceress and her crew. The desecration involves unearthing and dismembering bodies, then stitching together assorted parts that are then mummified, paraded through the medina, and finally incinerated, marking a politically inflected ending to all forms of idol worship. The point is to "eliminate the saints, but divide up the spoils of sainthood: that each shall wear around his head a ray of the halo that one saint alone used to monopolize." But this is only the most outrageous rite in a night of erring and error, where all taboos are temporarily lifted and all hierarchies leveled.

A second distinction worth addressing is that of the two languages at work within the original text. Meddeb wrote his novel in French, but a French inflected by his native Arabic, which is itself a double language: classical standard Arabic combined with Tunisian dialect, the latter being a delicious mixture of Arabic, Berber, Italian, and French. The narrator takes pains to remind us that he is "describing in a language not [his] the insanity of a city." In addition to the countless transliterated Arabic terms with French equivalents in apposition (". . . our lord *Sidna*," "the *bendīr* drumbeat," "*barzakh*, isthmus," etc.), an equal number of terms leave the reader guessing. This estranging effect takes place not only at the lexical level, but at the sentence level as well.

Like many of his generation of Tunisian, Algerian, and Moroccan writers utilizing French, Meddeb refashions the language in a way that allows his native tongues to show through. Prepositions and articles disappear, subject/verb phrases get collapsed into a gerund or an infinitive, and strings of long noun phrases stand in for sentences, lending the text a randomness that suits the narrative forward motion of the haphazard stroll through the city. His language is "French on LSD," as one of my brave literature students once said, struggling through the novel as part of an assignment. Many of these stylistic features are too peculiar to French to be translatable, but all efforts have been made to conserve in English the strangeness of what Maghreb literary scholar Abdelkebir Khatibi calls *bi-langue*, texts written somehow in two languages at once in an ongoing mutual translation. Another Meddeb scholar,

Ronnie Scharfman, has called this effect "nomadic writing," and calls upon readers to read nomadically in turn, and not be too concerned by disorientation or ambiguity.

Geography is not always destiny, but Tunisia's peculiar cultural plurality that has emerged from the Berber, Punic, Roman, Byzantine, Arab-Islamic, Andalusian, Turkish, and French influences (to name only those) would seem to make a writer like Abdelwahab Meddeb and a novel as wildly eclectic as *Talismano* almost inevitable. Yet there is no one else in Tunisian letters, or in the modern Francophone canon for that matter, who quite matches Meddeb's scope and style in this, his first and most ambitious novel. With madcap philological erudition, the lustiness of Tunisian Sheikh Nafzāwi's fifteenth-century erotic classic, *The Perfumed Garden*, and an insider's glance at the plight of the post-colonial Arab-Muslim, *Talismano* can produce in readers a healthy derangement of the senses and an equally salutary corrective to any stereotypical notions of the literature being produced by today's Muslim writers.

TALISMANO

PROLOGUE

Bloodshot and tear-stained, if only in these hours dying everywhere; and the idea that dawdles and wavers between shores: the idea that sometimes locks itself away and paralyzes the fingers; the idea cast off, shattered, unloaded from one vessel to the next, pulverized, a refugee in the morning dew that drips sweetness from the foliage on the outskirts of so many cities. History is nothing but words and ghosts, sex restrained or intense, in all haste, borders reconciling the myths of a fleeting self.

Scent of pearl, of oceans, of seas, sonorous vibrations, salt lakes, lagoons, abandoned cemeteries; breathlessly adrift when irrelevant scraps of meaning happen to clothe me in a flash of insight: the body a jumble of spume, a glorified fragment, tipsy, rescued from near disaster.

We have experienced the crashing silence: the dead at rest; faced with the eyes, the shopwindows of pain, insidious portals opening downward into such chaotic worlds, arranging such painful descents, a furtive instant amid the north: grazed by illness; amid the south: a feverish meridian. It breathes through our pores; tides that carry us emboldened out to sea; the fragile plateau pitching; a threadlike tightrope that pulses with ebb and flow as placid expectation ceases. Riding across memory, as if at a gallop; headwind that blows me far from the water toward the treasured immensity of the desert: again expectancy: black stone, incandescent sand; another space in the foothills of mountains and passes stretching down to the river, the Nile overflowing its banks, spewing out the secrets of cities of both worlds, projecting images and splendors back and forth, joys and morbid sensations.

It was a time apart, shared out, bringing together disparate feelings, smiles and wrath, damnation and desire, bodies in search of an identity to upend: here, elsewhere.

Here-elsewhere: with deadly violence, a mixture of countries traveled, pieces of a life torn to shreds, a body scraped off the ground, appearance peculiar and untidy, blood stains; sweat, strife, toil: incursion of rebel assegais where the mountain rises up in fortification.

It takes events of some significance for the tribes to come together and threaten the fertile and subjugated plains; eagle's nests: impregnable regions that extend outward only to mingle with the rumblings of the desert; at first sight infinity, seat of the heathen: neither cities nor men: but beneath the lacy carpet of black scree, men, like underground insects, amass in silence the venom that serves as primordial sap to bellicose instinct, fire of female eye, mastery of the word, glittering jewel rekindled in the presence of blood.

Two worlds undivided into these dusky people and these others, white: always and everywhere half-breeds have contrived to whiten their hearts, seduced by a thirst for power, by the fascinating notion of unity, seeking to establish a center and impose authority wherever the peripheries harbor defiance and dissent.

Landscapes burned by the sun: fierceness and courage, temporary alliance that disconcerts and later offends; strife that lends the nomads their steady composure, fire that moves with the seasons: logic of such coagulated dust, intense odor, salts and resins that hold the skin in place: lands loved that stick to the body's cells like decomposed flesh, loose soil against arid ground.

RETURN PROSTITUTION

Here I am back again, spoken, city of mazes, moved to put aside thoughts of childhood, to recover bygone flavors through this Tunis of amorous pursuit. The doors in soft blue, black-nailed, landmarks encrusted with memory's teasing, slippery tricks. To fathom the secret of streets and alleys untraveled, if only as the former itineraries of a childhood still not make-believed into lost paradise.

Bab al 'Asal, sweet gateway to memory lane: as a child, I knew a certain carpenter there was a relative of sorts. He didn't recognize me. But I watched him in fascination and disdain as he worked, yardstick in hand, pencil behind ear: is he truly the only manual laborer in a family that boasts theologians, wealthy merchants, feudal lords, bureaucrats, doctors, notaries, lawyers, judges, and other notables?

Slight of build, he alone among us possesses the cunning certainty of accurate movement. I never before stopped to actually observe him at work. I knew him only as presence: a useful milestone along my route, a buffer against the danger looming over any ramble through the city, be it from one floor of our villa to the next, or from the fresh morning scent of spring flowers there all the way to the acrid stench of urine so ill-suited to the street's name—'asal meaning honey.

Primal breach. Like an obsession, the green-red-white door to the hammam, the steam baths where my mother would take me as a child: indelible spectacle of nude bodies, corpulent women, restrained violence giving way to bickering over buckets. And blood would flow.

Burden of books on the way to school.

This homecoming will not find me retracing familiar routes: I've followed the wall's meander, past crude furniture for sale, to watch the journeymen carpenters; that relative's workshop set apart, in the main thoroughfare that cuts through the neighborhood.

Meanwhile, adjacent streets scattered with recognition: friends of my father once lived in a house whose entrance is covered in enameled mosaic: Andalusian tints, familiar patterns. To recover a few faces, often time-worn—pastry chefs, butchers, greengrocers, meat grillers; pungent odor of spices, marinated peppers, capers, pickled vegetables, preserves. Cumin.

Façade of the Halfawīne School, once so impressive; now it looks like some ludicrous stage set. The restored mosque, lovely and spare in marble and ocher, warm stone, Italianesque residue buried in floral motifs, Ionic or composite capitals atop columns.

Children still playing that same game: marbles, a sinkhole for one's scarce pennies, prizes varying with the seasons; only the tinny clink of the basest coins, engraving worn illegible, remains the same all year round.

Countless hammams: especially the ones that weren't my haunts. Clamor to discover anew. Yellow purring of hookahs.

Women's secret sweat: that oozing intimacy, effluvium of love beneath veils often draped carelessly, alluring.

Body jostled, nudged more than shoved. Fertile scent, pinches and winks revive desire, always there, almost childlike.

Blind alleys unexplored, or merely disregarded back when. A thrill to retrace footsteps, unrushed, promising. Bath towels in geometric colors hung out to dry on the terrace roof of the Qa'addīn hammam, home to my induction into the company of men, into the brotherhood of the circumcised.

Reticence. Vivid scenes of bachelor intrigue. Deep down, far and wide, overwhelming oppression. The sun's out. Past Bab Swīqa, the street leads up to the school for girls and my early passions, their slow burn. Mysterious house where a limping uncle resides with his faithful retainers, home to the tabernacle—O shades of yesteryear! O wondrous treasure!—depository of the celebrated family tree that certifies Bedouin ascendency, bloodline of the Prophet, Saharan origins, Sāqyat al-Hamrā, all the peregrinations of our forebears. Oddly pleasant sensation to be bound forever to blood that's congealed into a falsely sedentary existence, while an urge still propels you back to this nomadic ancestry, back to the mythic.

Faces that never left home, those Sunday-only streets you came to know, and Friday's prayer-day lull, all these conspire to produce a series of nagging questions, for you know one false step is enough to set you off course for good.

My senses spatter the coherence of my itinerary. One street calls out for another. But I'm loath not to forge ahead, something magnetic about the very place names: Pasha, Qasba, Saadūn, Tawfīq. Hard to cover all the streets without turning in circles, reliving the wool dyers' palette.

To be body afoot, shaping the distances as they scatter over all the paths that lead from home to the far-off school: the limits of my boyhood audacity.

Soon to come, with the nationalization of repression, the maze of basement torture chambers, dirty work handled by the scum of the city, thugs the puppets of fools: crimes designed to preserve the tribe of privilege.

Grazing walls and watchtowers as I go: the civil prison bloodies the eye. Shouldering my burden, always attracted to petty disobediences, always in favor of the inconsequential revolt.

Sediment of meaning: overlooking the prison is the institute that treats trachoma. To the gangrene that saps the body's energy is added the plague that gnaws the eye bloody.

But eagles are impervious to incarceration, to tiny cells. Screeching eagles aren't in the habit of letting themselves be plucked. The eye sees all, omnipresent, intractable, wall-piercing, ravaging those narrow windows, startling the wardens, immobile but ever-present, present in every detail, supremely lucid, never seeing things broken into fragments to be looked at and discarded in turn before moving on to another time or place, but watching with equal acuity and presence all the floating, shifting cells, projects, memories: politics of possession, an artless exuberance, climbing the steps, vigilant, free to thrust out ample wings at the moment of enlightened nocturnal ascension, in search of possible prey; the solo voyage is a necessary, a powerful motif, while claws stab at the ground in accidental bloodlust, hungry for flesh.

But in the cell, in tribute! Ahmad's eye remains, piercing approach that preserves reality undivided in its unfocused pulverized dust:

this seed, scene of a child's sex erect, that flower fragment tattooed on Āïcha's vagina, this second love, secret madness, that particle on the brink of breath, this gust of sand and arid temperament, this atom, lunatic brother of torture, that obsession, nothing but the maternal nucleus itself dislocated by hate and denial, that star, source of life, transmuting weariness into a pleasure that cooks the silent, patient labor of thought, accumulating, honing.

Where the eye proves all-knowing, then wings encumber, unable to spread to their full span, to beat, to help at least simulate the loss of self, endless flight, open skies. Imprisoned eagle that nothing can subject to the eye's victorious escape.

Along ground level, still vying with the traces of the ancient city walls, in concert with other extramural institutions, the Charles Nicolle Hospital has expanded: seen beside its towering chimneys with their air-poisoning discharge, the disparity of the nearby buildings and the incarcerating monotony of the walled enclosure is astonishing.

Bodies crammed several to a cell, no breathing room in a space eroded by despair, dirge of groans and paralysis, rations of suffering that constrain the body's every move.

Fear of invisible evil threatens to pluck the flower of youth. So many bodies I've known have met that fate: swollen, yellowed; eyes: wounded, bulging, bursting from within: split-open display of green disease like the memory of some contorted Bacchus in his death throes: it was an affair of the heart, of clogged veins: Safia, whom I loved, the passion that led us both astray, that contained a pulse swelling with shrieks and the tearing of matrons' hair.

Safia is dead, apparently unwed, an unexpectedly long funeral. Rising from oblivion, the first suitor, turned away by her arrogant clan, made a show of his weeping to the assembled crowd, channeling Majnūn, pride eternally bruised but living on in knotted or well-chewed remarks: expansive joy of men who tried in vain to conceal their faith.

Dead, and the corpse washer's middle finger penetrated the wet chill, coagulated dampness, of her defunct sex: the young lady was deflowered, they whispered. For she loved riding those winds, scandal and fascination in her wake.

How did she endure being confined in the hospital, how did she overcome the helplessness that bound her to the bed, carefree as she was, an insatiable lover? Unfettering members, lightening the belly's comely softness, tightening the breasts' jewel-like florets, damning languor of almond eyes.

The corpse washer decided to stitch up her vagina to simulate virginity in the afterlife, triumph of law and order: emergency surgery to transform the cadaver so that the clan might save face before the law broken by the intimate infraction of bodies in cramped corridors reeking of confinement and overuse.

Everything is back in its place: if, out of a desire for violence, you'd like to disorder them again, you'd best veil your intentions; enemies of the law are appointed only in the shadows.

Disregard of nature's spirit arouses us, causes bodies to clash or reconcile: archaism fears no burns, its tents lower no curtain over our secrets: starkness drives us to bend toes back to heels and to bite right into the horse's mane.

Or that other practice, common among Nubians, whereby a palm branch is stuck into a dead vagina. Beneath her shroud, the woman seems to be in possession of a phallus far larger than a man's: is it not relic of the Pharaohs, inspired by Isis's creating a mock phallus to graft onto Osiris, relieved of his own by the voracious jaws of the Nile? A phallic woman, hence castration. And this transfer of the remnant of a male god onto a woman's body rearranges custom to extend phallic law to both genders. But this acquisition of an absent part affirms death. And Osiris's arborescent vegetable shoot—buds sprouting everywhere along the branch except where grafted to the body—designates the female sex, a corpse for burying, soil for watering.

And there you have the Nubian vaginal operation that, rather than reestablishing the law, as does the Tunisian stitching job, makes absence the rule, sentences desire to death in the service of a standard laid down by the example of statuary, making a show of reparation.

And what of the analogy between sex and tree, the palm whose fermented nectar, a mere drop on the tongue, transports us to the bed of Eros, ardor impatient to flee the Saharan heat by immersion in the sweat and wax of this henna-tinted, finely tattooed body—a minbar on a hip, the Ka'aba on a thigh, winglets on her shaved pubis—bodies swelling together until the eye of the needle is opened and threaded, freeing you, putting you beyond limits: musk, floral essence, mingling of honeys?

The palm proves a fragile monument, erect, sun-baked, like a tombstone in place of the vagina, woman taking to her death the instrument of pleasure, detached from the man's body, exorcising the desire to mutilate, sign enthroned on an obscure clod of earth, turned over, tender, as it fuses with first desert sands, sign of womanhood where desire spans life and death: water of the Nile, edible plants in the shade of acacia or sycamore; earth, a shelter or sleeping place; beneath sand, finally buried.

In this palm exhibited to us at the moment of female death, they seek not only to expose an absence, or to reinterpret the death of the body by mending a supposed defect: rather, they are celebrating our primordial alliance with the daily, serial intensity of desire: source of bodily vigor and localized damage both: bodily fulfillment is total once beyond the everyday growth rings that cause teeth to fall out or feet to swell or legs to wither.

Woman, this swaying wave, this steady head balancing a necessary burden, made lighter by subtle cranial positioning.

Fresh foray into core of new Tunis, venturing among the edifices of power, barely hinting at the East: along the boulevard, only one thought emerges, made up of fear and hatred at once, get beyond it, by way of an uncanny attraction, a spell working its magic: the aggravation, the annoyance I experience seeing those steely blue cop eyes flash from under helmet and visor, armed protection for the courthouse at a time when the disorderly maze underground was spattered with the blood of ordinary people, while the bourgeois remained sequestered, torn between their interests and the moral high ground, storing up their courage for a possible struggle to come, one can never tell, profiting from the cycle of history. While liberal-minded, petit-bourgeois intellectuals were daydreaming in their cells of a State modeled on the image of the very powers that had prevailed over them: choice was not the issue: their narrow, lawyerly turn of mind led them to give preference to the notion of the nation-state, to the detriment of so many other fertile alternatives: *Arabité* becoming institutionalized, a common front used to exorcise our symbolic fear that any diversities might survive on their own.

Such relentlessness has produced a gap: these policies bartered the country away, grain by grain: might this be one of the first non-European places to bring about, slowly but surely, the anthropological death of a people? Picture it as the unhappy Belgium of the southern Mediterranean! And what will you see? The age-old brazenness of the common people—the so-called second power, beneath the rich and the mighty—refuge of the latent, bawdy, serf-like boisterousness of village fairs, their Dionysian energy, their extravagant intrigue, now turned into dreary, uniform crowds, pathetic, sheeplike, in silent procession, seaside holidays on the black beaches, bad-breath Blankenberge, slot machines, the sun ashamed, so stingy at their funerals, such pedestrian twilight itself in league with the grimness of their bodies.

Centuries of history show us that the people's voice has always managed to jam up the strong-armed apparatus of central power: the tribes have steadfastly resisted conquest and the armed imposition of respect for the State; temporarily joining forces to oppose foreigners or even those among their own ranks who start showing evidence of Punic, Numidian, Latin, Arab, or European culture: the old ways boldly advocate the notion of oneness, yet relentlessly reject it whenever events outside cease to impinge. This same archaic urge allows each sort of specificity to organize into the greater whole according to the depth of its desire, giving way to standards that will ensure the protection and fruitfulness of the exchanges among the mosaic shards that still recognize one another in the dazzling plenitude of their oneness.

That is how these people won their battles: though by all appearances, and as we're told by our chronicles, they lost more than they won, and at each qualitative step of historical development, their unity collapsed due to this persistent defect: the inability to think in terms of the State. But they managed until recent times to endure as they were, roaming mountain and steppe, humans who have interiorized, by ecological increments, glints of institution, a divvying up of their power. They are forever reborn of their own ashes. And have founded their experience on an economy of pleasure, precarious or extravagant indulgence, depending on cycles of famine, precious plunder, the weight of their spoils.

And what has become of the country now? Its body trampled by the world's twittering flocks, bulldozers and bleach, varying degrees of resourcefulness: its rough bits pruned away by master schemers, company physicians, the tottering Hotel Africa, that derivative, clumsy alma mater that somehow came together—to the joy of those who sold it for a song—as a compassionate substitute for Frankish Europe.

The steely blue eye guarding the courthouse in 1953, the days of maximum resistance, triumphing only after the euphoria of independence: seeking a national consensus to become the free province of a former metropolitan protector. Strange story: twenty years of national statehood has done more harm to the country than a century of colonization. So what? In trading their backwardness for decadence, the people were forced to submit to a policy of standardization, body and mind, starting in the schoolhouse: brides shall wear white, and black shall be the color of mourning.

Blue eye causing me to shudder: in spite of myself, I was feeling a vague desire to compromise with him; but recovering my wits, and like the child I was, I spat. Experience the temptation of permissiveness in the body itself: cowardly, raining down moral prescription, it seized power and contaminated the land while all transgression remained contained. A tinge of the desire to flee, and then the urge dissolves into dream. Desire a flash in the pan that might not have set the prairie ablaze, desire to assimilate with the humiliating colonizer, a belated negativity which is not, however, a new, exhausting renewal of life—so long as the seven heads of the hydra aren't hacked off in one blow.

Down stairs leading to the sloped street that ends in the school's cul-de-sac, I find I'm feeling fully medina-minded, medinating: shaded passages zigzag, footsteps oddly resonant. Vaulted portions of alleyways ringing with cymbal and echo.

Slight trembling, ostrich eggs, clocks and mirrors, portraits and prints: *Adam and Eve, Yusuf and Zulaikha, Ali and Sons, Sulaymān and his Army*, a shudder before the home of the epileptic saint, stripped bare, the stuff of fable among the adamantly beseeching female believers.

Spirited swallows whistle at the morning. Door ajar, through the embrasure to discover a stray lemon tree in a courtyard, brother to fig and carob. Spiderwebs obstruct the tiny windows of a rundown storehouse whose door hangs half-ruined and lets out the persistent autonomy of dark, damp-smelling air. Nothing of that odor of dung and horse breath, of steaming donkey that one would have liked to conjure up with a stroke of the pen.

Hand on pleasingly round hip, flesh trembling beneath raw silk veil, sugarcane stripes on summer white. Townswoman of that ancient and dying breed, vaguely degenerate, ethnic entanglement blending the glory days of the Barbary corsairs and Turkish aristocracy with dash of the Venetian, Albanian, Greek: the result ample, buxom, womanly, a kind of Venus in the manner of Boucher, body meant for touching, rediscovery of our borderlines with regard to a past un-reenacted, but where I become a untroubled flame consuming everything in view.

I smile at the lady. She beckons me to follow. I'm soon hot on her heels. Where is she leading me?

Only follow, maze of discovery, of recognition, attentive to losing all convergence, predella without door figures, retable to meditate prayer, among doors that entice, those of a house belonging to a gentleman married to a lady at a time when, *cousin-cousine*, protective endogamy reigned triumphant. His refined patriarchal lordship, happily debauched: an impressive man; he had foppish air in his younger years: an occasional philanderer; worshiped by the gentle sex; the sort of womanizer who takes a real interest in his female peasants during the summer harvest season: mongrel offspring would then result, illegitimate, passing for adopted daughters, raised by the grandmother: distinctive Bedouin features, dark country looks mingling with the ruddy whiteness of the city.

Then the house of that sheikh who flouted the gambling taboo, who kept European mistresses, who drank. Ah, such rumors! With all that in mind, I laughed to myself as I headed toward the Grand Mosque, the Zitūna, where I found the same sheikh now heading prayers, imām to throngs of believers; bowing in mock piety, I wasn't fooled by this latest addition to the general nonsense of religion and the gullibility of the faithful. This helped resituate my godly hierarchy far beyond the tediously intransigent constraints wherein my father had sought with such urgency to place it: that tawdry, see-no-evil morality—we feeble creatures, let us prosper, scrupulous, mechanical, fastidious in submitting to the law.

A heap of garbage and a colony of flies. The sons of this venerable house each inherit a share of the paternal legacy: the one a mollusk—grumpy, a whiner, conservative, unappealingly fragile, a kind of unmentionable degenerate in therapy, self-indulgent bureaucrat still proud of his now hollow-sounding name; the other, scandalously appealing, a hulk with a heart of gold, unmatched in strength and generosity, raised on the street, held to a wholly different standard: the ethics of teamster and longshoreman, a matter of honor and respect, gather friends and hold them close, basic need to save what can be saved: to be is to give. Boundlessly dissident smugglers' pacts made in bars, alcohol and hash: so grand, so simple a man, beyond words.

I shuffled along, and the woman, seeing me linger, slowed down. Something like heavy silence, cool morning. No sunlight can reach such narrow meanders. The trellis of streets, the tight weft of houses allow only patches of cloudless sky to appear, irrevocably blue.

Where lane meets alley, turn of the wrist, door half open, she beckons; follow the white veil erased by shadow as it moves through the sqifa, vestibule linking city to home via sun-soaked interior patio. Through creaking door and courtyard, discover ruins overrun with weeds, scrub, faded poppies here and there, stunted daisies. Sections of collapsed wall opening onto other walls, windowless and erect. Caved-in vault: converted grotto. An aging black man greets the lady, nods to me and staggers away, reeling but sharp-eyed.

Horsehair mattress on brick-supported board. Posters and yellowing covers of Levantine magazines, thighs and Beirut's finest female vocalists. In a corner, ashes and smoke. Woman already undressed watches me drink her in, eyes moist, hands damp. White belly, sagging, creased. Fascinated by this flabby mass of flesh, my hand ventures: soft, hot skin, deftly kneading nerves, fondling to find the perfect touch. Her blue eyes rolling back lose color, whiten in emotion. She cannot wait: ardent. She spreads her legs, surprisingly supple, half sitting, half supine, fiercely erotic.

Such ancient loving, myth, Venus, the boudoir created anew: hedonistic, insane, transporting this bathhouse stoker's hovel to the black soil of some remote countryside, sheltered from the evil eye, egg-yolk yellow, unearthly cries, coming ecstasy, giving voice to even the willfully silent. Positively nirvana: her deep-drowning sex kept tight for the deserving. Voracious, burning desire: guileless, uncomplicated, an animal undiscerning and unrefined. Feeling for the slightest quivering of our deepest depths, she prepares on her own, restored, for a state of climax to occur: trigger to my own energy's release.

Glimpse of timelessness! Each time I address her, she says not a word but moans continually, crudely voluptuous, caresses teeth and palate with tongue. Sufficient unto herself, under pleasure's spell: speechless, she offers her gift; she accepts only slow-handed lovers, holding on tight to her desire, be he butcher, baker, beast, or prude. For the rest of the world, she plays prim and proper while arousing delight in velvety flesh. Screamed incantations to the god of small things are the only words uttered throughout her cavalcade of moans, gusts and sighs, bites, breasts heaving, she is expiring, collapsing into deep diaphragmatic breaths, nasally expressed gratitude, rib cage a shield to the heart.

Stretched out, fast asleep, satisfied, lids lowered, state of bliss, weighing heavier now, young lady asleep in her lover's arms, unembellished, a figure from Courbet, midday nap, immense plaything, inflated then deflated, sweat congealed, surprising hints of spice unsticking the air, hand plucks out straw, pricking skin, moves to scratch nether regions, restful tint of time and morning as it progresses, ceaselessly beating back the mist. Lying languidly, hardly noticing the door's creak, she raises her head and lowers it once more onto the thin, filthy mattress when she sees it's only the master of this flea-ridden squat, wearing his rough, homespun garment against bare skin.

In an unsteady waddle, he approaches us wordlessly and rummages about until he finds the pipe he's looking for, an ancestral sebsi, bone and metal stem with clay bowl, to be filled with kif, drawn breathlessly on a flickering candle flame then holding in the stored smoke long enough to enjoy the warmth as it plunges deep into all his organs. Descent into the self with the hungry hollowing of smoke.

Smiling, bowl refilled, he offers a toke. Drawing to point of exhaustion, throat scorched, I wait, relax, borne away on the trembling wings of instantaneous images racing by. Marvelous animals, O colors, O mirages: an infant with enormous woven gray membranes between arm and torso, like a bat. And the sun's diaphanous brightness now accessible and enticing casts me mercifully into the role of imaginary beggar.

The goddess awakens, rises, half covers herself in a bathrobe before wrapping up in a body-hugging veil, ready to go, leaving no name or address in her wake.

Silence and words, hand in hand with myself along this circum-ambulatory pilgrimage that takes me out to see vast spaces, fitting me into them, immobile and irrefutable product of various imaginings, such as those the old man revealed to me as if by telepathy: those that add to the winged mount the face of an ebony-haired woman, teats as numerous as a she-goat's, fed on spring flowers: fruit-bearing, flavorful juice, taste of bitter honey.

Hair rubbed in juniper tar, the old man, sparse graying beard, eyes emerging from the receding flood, jaw thrust forward as he blows on ashes, reviving embers, adding little twigs to the dying flame, warming hands, fingers spread. Top and bottom, the little snuff box is decorated with fancy, exaggeratedly cursive calligraphy, volute resembling the scrolls of an Ottoman seal.

He brews me some black tea, potent beverage, sickeningly sweet and boiled down to a glue-like resin, that I drink in tiny sips to savor the density and diminish the burn.

Not once does he break the silence. Calm, he occasionally lashes out with jerky, threatening gestures, as if attempting, with the sharp edge of his hand, to slice into some foreign body, some source of constant harassment. Then, satisfied with his victory, he exults broad-grinned, seeking neither to charm nor repel me, disconcerted as I am by his own dubious behavior. With filthy fingernails, he scratches his head, leaving behind deep furrows made by the ill-timed passage of digits over its greasy, glistening surface, giving off a full-bodied, comforting stink.

Does this mean I should be leaving? Yes, since I've about had my fill of the old coot, so wordless yet miles from the enlightening clarity of silence. I would have been long gone in a moment had his arms and legs not started to wriggle around nervously, controlled by who knows what occult presence, what art transforming the mechanics of movement into disjointed rhetoric, helpless in the apparent confusion.

Skin tingling, this frisson signing our encounter. Maker of talismans and other writings, carpet of sand, foaming at the mouth, plotting out astrological tables, reading into the microcosmic lines of my hand all the components of my being, watching me with a kind of detached pride, yet communicating none of his findings, as if certain that I remain somehow sheltered from life's perils, as if the pitfalls and quagmires awaiting me are not worth revealing.

Loss of self, loss of reason: approach of seagull in flight no doubt straying from some cesspool of a lake or what remains of the port.

Birdcall signaling the sob of departure or melancholy of a piazza in the *ghetto vecchio*, stunted trees, scattered leaves crunch underfoot in an empty Venetian square besieged by their manic movement, famous place of the enthusiastically insane, caricature of the smell in an asylum.

Or that squawking seagull become siren at Fondamenta Nuove, I was shamelessly barefoot crossing over to San Michele, autumn gold and All-Saints foulness of the air, wafting humidity misting the surrounding haze, picnicking on Ezra Pound's grave, repeating his Italianate verse, mauve fire, incandescence, recovering for dessert on Stravinsky's tomb nearby, swept away by the memory of the annoying soprano, believing herself actress enough to revive the grand maestro's ghost, consistent with Berio's experiments, cemetery as echo of the living, poet's and composer's tombs located in an enclosure reserved for non-Catholic Christians, the only place not overrun by flower-laden throngs bent upon celebrating their dead, pallor of daylight bearer of dread. Unoccupied space, empty, a wilderness, invitation to the solitary wanderer: nothing circulates but the buzzing of invisible insects, mosquitoes lying in wait for nightfall to assail the human breath that by daytime permeates the cypress trees and assorted conifers. An unease that made it increasingly difficult to continue my meal of bread, *provolo affumicato*, and shaved prosciutto, washed down with glasses of *vino negro*.

Venice, all glittering gold! How to capture the strained, sporadic, tentative, painstaking flight of your seagulls? And the Giudecca extends before eyes ravished by contemplation of lightly rippling watery space, undulating surface caressed by the wind. The cityscape extends to the outer shore beyond the church of the Salute: time won't allow me to venture into that uniform horizon that culminates in near ruin, factory yards, proposing yet another abandoned architecture that finally emerges as monumental, thanks to all the timid imitations: so what could that white Palladian façade be, so Redentore-like while making majestic use of a double-order façade not unlike that of San Giorgio Maggiore where one spends countless hours of contemplation and dissolution without ever quite exhausting the seething strands of light that pulsate within its irrevocable limits, blurring thought and reducing capacity for analysis to a steady nothingness.

Trail of meaning, rich signal of this white patch of a bird, trajectory between two blues: it speaks water, and the city is white with salt, wet with guano.

What more could there be but the unexpected and joyous arrival of the swallows exalting the paternal home: astonishing return to the same nest built this time last year, bird-memory of dwellings. For years the swallows would come back to their nest perched high on a wall, swooping through wrought iron grillwork between kitchen and living room, in the vestibule with all the storage cabinets, doors open during the daytime. One of my brothers, the one whose eyes spark with secret irony, whose blue-black hair shines in sympathy with swallow plumage, would say that one could never be sure the same birds were returning each spring, perhaps they somehow transmitted to others the secret clues as to how to find the nest, a code we humans can't fathom. His theory remained unproven, for we were unable to tell one swallow from the next, even as we attempted to take stock of distinctive features; each time, however, our memories failed, and we could never agree on a recognizable profile of the previous season's birds, interiorized by each of us as quite different.

Springtime jittery, the swallows wouldn't drive out the colonies of other species of bird—sparrows, hoopoes, nightingales, pigeons, doves . . . —that shared the giant pine tree with them: voluble axis springing from the garden in a fusion of traveler's idioms.

To each city its birds: Tunis, apart from swallows that inhabit its plane trees at sundown, twilight chorus; apart from its punctual starlings, flash of metal, swarming in precision flight patterns; apart from the odd seagull wandering from the port or the excremental lake, flying over some medina terrace or courtyard, nothing signs the sky, lacuna of desire.

In Paris, aside from the sooty, ungainly pigeons, hobbled and sick, the keen, restless delight of blackbirds: wherever there's the tiniest patch of greenery, there you'll find them, Palais-Royal, neighborhood parks, public gardens, Montsouris, Jardin des Plantes, Luxembourg, flitting about the Japanese cherry trees in bloom, landing on the edge of ponds, with their goldfish and lily pads, the beak's splash of coral red setting off velvet black plumage.

Plastic toy pigeons in flat colors, illusion of flight over Piazza Navona, compete with the genuine articles startled to find such rivals not fighting over breadcrumbs or perches on ledges, along façade outcroppings, atop statues, nesting behind a stone sister dove carved into a coat of arms, trembling toys in flight, high noon August siesta time, silent scorcher of a day beating down on the wretched colony of piazza artists splashing their canvases with pigeons, swapping food or a fuck for the disappointing magic of a souvenir painting to illustrate a ritual voyage, a Roman wedding.

Atlantic gulls of Tangiers fly over dancing porpoises in the wake of the crossing ferryboat, singing the approaching shore, so slim a continental drift.

Cairo a tomb for the eye, small pigeons circling over the city's inhabited rooftops, alighting on the dusty pavement, finishing in a piled heap, plucked and ready for the grill; signs, stalls, or windows of restaurants offering nifa at best, tender young goat meat. Pigeons glinting silver and steel, dusty haze as nearby desert deposits its residue on their wings, glued in place by sticky Nile air.

Pigeons recall a tribe come up from the Comoros beneath the Magellanic Clouds one moonlit night to keep vigil over the Mesopotamian tomb of Hallaj, perpetuating his memory by endless rounds of prayer, ceaseless billing and cooing, discretely erotic affection: that phrase expressing oneness of being—*Anā al-Haqq*—that phrase which earned him insult, injury, execution.

Clearly these pigeons look like a sign coming from the south.

Beyond cruelty, the peaceful passage of carnivores over Cairene quarters turns nasty as birds and beggars fight over scraps. The hawk, straight-backed rider of the thermals, fragile head-gyrating surveyor of all that moves on the urban grid, serene prospector in search of prey, however small, to snatch from this city of scarce gifts.

Tombs feature in the world of the living, stench of decomposition sometimes sickening, the simplicity of funeral rites, coffins push their way through crowds, shrouds of green, white, or red, a popular desire to avoid waste of any kind, abiding by an ecological rule of energy conservation and transformation that encourages the otherwise lugubrious presence of vultures whose necessary role is only too obvious in these empty lots, occasional swamps, or the dumping ground that separates the Mosque of Amr from the ruins of Fustāt—heaps of ceramic, enamel, mangy dogs, shrouds floating up to heaven.

Fugitives from the highlands, on the prowl for easier plunder, these birds of prey, buzzards and falcons, skulk around the outskirts of Marrakesh near the pottery kilns, while the bolder among them size each other up in the shadow of the Kutubīya, or pass the city gates, leaving their droppings around the tanners' quarter.

I even saw a stray eagle owl late one night while climbing a dark and narrow street leading to the heights of Tetouan: eyes like two blinking lanterns, beak rebuffing the world, it flapped a wing that grazed the disarray of my hair, clawed by the curse of the night-blind.

The old man, determined to play the deaf-mute, seems to be deciphering my fantasies: Rare bird, I say to him. The words escape me, try as I might to enlarge upon the symbolic or analogical possibilities of the 'Attār fable, armed for the quest for some Simurgh.

Not that I deny the wisdom of such parables, peppered with edifying object lessons, sometimes erroneous, and often relying, in fact, on whatever details manage to escape the narrative's course through the valley of spiritual growth for all their forward momentum. And indeed, when I evoke the hoopoe, how could I ask the reader to ignore its capabilities as messenger, so universally recognized, apart from its part in *The Conference of the Birds*, remember its role as go-between in Sulaymān's seduction of Balqīs, a feature recited by a thousand oriental lips, and taken up after Goethe by northern voices too?

Is he not likewise a phoenix, life in death, blinding eyes, loosening tongues, fabricating wonders, having discovered its resurgent flight by reversing time?

Legs unsteady, senses adrift, I take leave of the volatile specter, wishing the dark-skinned man the opportunity to perfect his expertise in some other occupation beyond stoking the furnace at the Turkish baths. Then I was on my way, back to the urbane life, refreshed by my dose of weed.

The street is again perilously exposed to inescapable and ever more numerous noises. A dirge-like tune takes flight toward dazzlingly green cornices. Dilapidated mosque, home to an assortment of blind men waiting for an obituary, sitting under a mulberry tree spreading its foliage shiny green, tiny courtyard, whispering of barely cascading water. Single-strap wooden clogs worn by the faithful resound in the inner recesses, endless coming and going between the prayer room and the lavatory with its trickle of water for ritual ablutions.

Sewing machines stitch white circles overlaid with crescent and star, signifying bygone Turkish allegiance, set into scarlet red cotton cloth, pennants to deploy around monuments or to be waved by patriotic arms.

Greenish spittle resounds against a paving stone, slightly displacing the migrating layer of dust. Fragrance of sardine and harissa escape the grocer's shop, run by a Jerbi, stained gray smock, full-moon face, zebiba on his forehead, mark of the pious who bow in prayer, greed, and acquisition of wealth, honing their instinctive sense of deprivation.

Yellow door peppered in black motifs, kinetic studwork upsetting the false symmetry whose bulge causes vertigo to the eye. Cool anticipation, deep vestibule; in the half-light, squeaking soles.

Into the brightness, the patio at last; large disused well in the shade of a lone olive tree; children fidgeting; deafening clang of metal buckets, cymbals, and water; piercing rumble of rolling barrels whose metal belting leaves rusty trails on white marble.

Multicolor panes filter light through openwork screen playing with the austere geometric motifs of a kilim, echo of Gafsa tattoos. In the alcove, I recognize the bare behind of that auspicious ingénue busy washing herself; bath mitt barely dampened, sudsy water; she laughs as I approach, warns me that her parents are keeping watch. No, I reply, at the risk of causing a scene. Don't come any closer, she says; now look, the children think it's funny. Love drips from her plump eyes, double-lidded and dusky. Body's cavities freshly rinsed, she stands upright, towels her face, ears, armpits, sex, backside, hands, and sets about solving algebraic equations on a chalkboard, crunching numbers with pulverizing speed, a more than musical knack for handling letters and figures, degrees and unknowns to be elucidated. She is as flirtatious as she is mathematical: *vade retro*, she says, fearing she might yield to her brimming, aching desire, jump clear of her hidebound mother, cast off her clothing without differential coefficient to solve the equation that inhabits her body, to surrender to the sweet taste of wordlessness.

Another voyeur joins the party, a cleric's at-home attire, puffy Turkish trousers reaching just below the knees; a notable's spectacles: afraid of losing them, he incessantly lifts a hand to adjust, to replace on bridge of nose. Dazzled by the unquestionably amorous nakedness of our object of desire, the prudish voyeur pretends to speak, all the better to get an eyeful, serial opportunist, putting aside his obsessive fear of the seven proscribed bodily fluids in an act of decidedly modern betrayal. Such untrustworthy smiles, moustache like a rat's. Reconciled to the long blue-blooded line of descent that weighs him down; and by analogy, this impasse of reason splits world history into two comfortable zones: there is civilization, he says, and there is the rest, only backwardness and progress, as he repeats to his dutiful pupils.

As for the body, which our erudite voyeur pretends to ignore, it helps dig the ditch that will unearth the compromising roots of his clerical genealogy, the scholarly and social core of a family theology that realizes its golden age is now over, impervious to healthy criticism, manducation of the immutable precepts lying virtually undisturbed these past decades by those discreet stirrings that the surrounding vacuum causes to resonate until they finally swell into an event of sorts, a slender flame commensurate with our respectfully narrow national history.

Belated praise for that other portly sheikh, an underhanded snob, or so he appeared to me, a sense that still wells up long after his untimely passing, which distressed many people. His death crystallized the suppressed hysteria that prevailed in the family compound, that family whose numbers far outstripped the seemingly innumerable members of the tribe from which they'd come, converted now and sedentary and crazy as the city, mourning horizons lost.

Upon his death, body torn to pieces, collected as scattered remains, after a vehicle crashed into tamarind trees bordering the road, the whole family was in utter disarray. At first they decided to cut down the deadly trees; then they really got annoyed, though without triggering the standard delirium, or even the some fake or forced show of grief. No, even in this extreme situation, they had to appear dignified, to save face, refusing to allow one another to be themselves, whether dull-witted, absentminded, or reactionary, bound up or blunted, stifling all possible physical excess, redeeming themselves by suppressing any and all signs of mourning.

The same old refrain, advancing neither by perpetuating itself nor even its own omission, in no way partaking of that vast space opening beyond sight: those surprising countries that liberate from our bodies the opportunity to compose a fertile collapse or fragile desire.

The old refrain is no dream. And the death of the sheikh, despite strict orders, was still a trying experience for his family. One lady went mad. Another became paralyzed. A father found the unhoped-for opportunity to start seesawing between being a clown and a doddering fool: giddy or dejected depending on whether death was approaching or receding. He aged twenty years in the process, that masochistic mastication of an unformed conscience, that subaudible babble, a stutterer in thought and word, always, stopping short of a moronic giggle, arms outstretched, stricken by a constricting scowl. Given over to despair, a mere nothing would free him from his narrow discipline, allowing him into that yes radiating beyond law.

To live through the much-mourned death of the patriarchs, saddened because they preferred death to change, to connecting anew with the world? This means the loss of the final avatar of archaism—already rattled by history's way of forcing masks upon us, distortions; a city such as Tunis now taking full part in the monstrous Arab contemporary. Smiles turn solemn at such heterogeny.

Yet another patriarch falls, yet another grasping sheikh, reckless but endearing despite his pigheaded refusal to face the consequences of social and technological evolution as concerned his farming estate; a model of self-denial before his inevitable death or social mutation, the world so maddening in its newly acquired rationality: he remained a relentless curmudgeon with regard to his daughters and sons-in-law who sought to convert him to a more efficient means of managing his few properties, now practically fallen fallow. Hawkeyed, sarcastic, a wily fox of a man; bold night prowler, obfuscator of the steppe, illogical; incoherent and irascible nomad, impervious to hierarchy, taking orders from no one, of mediocre intelligence when it came to discussing some concept of Malaki doctrine, or to reserving the right to assert one's Shiite affiliation, Nasserian out of spite, flirting with the most vehement variety of Arab nationalism, at least in conversation; raving mad when choosing collaborators, precluding any effective contribution; a careless dresser, posture erect, rarely disturbed by the scorn and mockery of peers who, blistered and bruised, had all already more or less assimilated the disillusions involved in appropriating all the universal signs of modernity, speech and meaning like so many trinkets, everyone running after a career, after statistical evidence: factitious posturing intended to veil the void and keep at bay the body's bewilderment now that the edifice is quaking before the final collapse, before we turn the page on the principle of equality among peoples and classes.

I recall still another patriarch at the time when the world was first starting to tip toward uncertainty, toward a scrambling of habit and custom, when it was still possible to deny reality, when the propertied class could still afford to ignore the clarion of the common man's self-affirmation, the rise of the masses, their clear-eyed hatred of the occupiers.

Let's talk about the dead, shall we? He was one-legged, stuck in his wheelchair, a force to be reckoned with despite his funnel-shaped wooden appendage, silhouette of some wading bird. Prisoner of a gleaming architectural vastness, feasting his eyes on mosaic and faience, Venetian chandeliers, imitation Louis XV furniture, canopied beds, triumphant despite age and infirmity, authoritarian, sending for his wives according to whim: Tāja, whose serene Kurdish beauty is etched into concentric wrinkles; Sāra and her naïve tawdriness; Khīra, the Bedouin, whose every word was a rare pearl, exiled since she was fifteen, a study in tattoos and jangling silver jewelry.

Patriarch, tribal chief, arriving at the turn of the century from Libya to settle in a suburb favored by the Turkish Beys, a seaside resort and spa renowned in its time, protected by the double-peaked mountain, discreetly imbibing the marine salt and damp.

As far back as my childhood, it was already in a state of ruin: the house, divided up equally among the wives, was starting to fall apart, with no hint of restoration on the horizon. In an immense storage space adjacent to the laundry room, a shed, and some cubbies, looking out onto the long, wide entryway, open to the sky, there lay two horse-drawn carriages, minus their wheels, coaches worthy of a prince, covered in a thick layer of dust, delicately interlaced with spiderwebs.

The house was swarming with servants, with those young girls stolen away at a young age from their miserable peasant existence, ridding a sharecropper tenant of a female mouth to feed in exchange for certain advantages; girls to then be adopted, acquitting him of his duty as master, thereby strengthening the clan and its loyal clientele.

The villa was in the vise grip of repression: the son of the patriarch had entered into the political resistance, albeit through the wrong door, on the losing side, partisans of a leader who advocated pan-Arabism and nonalignment, more out of strategy than conviction. The general mood of menace was fostered and fed by the women in tense gatherings that teetered between tears and laughter, simulating grave contemplation and then seizing on the first outward sign of alarm to satisfy some caprice sparked by nothing and then extinguished just as easily, as though by a baby's breath. They fantasized themselves into being symbolic: puppets in copious layers of makeup, shouting, screaming, an embarrassment of intimidating chatter given how little they had to say: amorphous, lethargic, entrusting themselves to the perspicacity of their servants, organized by age, a gerontocracy of servitude, women adding layer upon layer of rouge, highlighting a cheek or chin with a beauty mark, sporting audaciously low-cut gowns to display their often proverbial bosoms.

But it would have taken real perseverance for someone to rise up proud out of this indolent milieu. Whether among the men or the women, it was perhaps possible that a body might have managed to find some specific strength, extraordinary and energetic asserting feverish selfhood, casting off forever the condescension that favored weakness as a means to ensure the questionable preservation of bloodline.

Or else, perhaps nothing more was needed than the bacchante smile of a girl who would put aside her virgin's bag of tricks to prospect the darker corners of the garden, abandoned behind locked gates that I clambered over in her wake to find ourselves alone together, emboldened, a different garden now, of desolation, of dream, of disorder, different among sand-choked pathways seemingly untouched by human passage, leaves mingling with damp soil, trees returned to that wild state only limited by the enclosure that kept them out of reach. Untamed even as we gazed at this forgotten foliage, in permanent contact with the sky, sun, stars, though deprived of any connection to sea, mountain, or town, receiving from them only the faintest emanations or sounds, like waves come to negotiate with the wildflowers, citrus trees, or the sterile bitter orange, all sorely in need of pruning.

The girl grabbed me by the arm and called me by my name, clearly emphasizing each syllable as distinct from the next: I felt agitated, disaggregated.

I was under the spell. In neutral tones, she told me the tale of her mother's death. She now lived alone with her father, absolute master, silent and enigmatic.

Once, she picked up a dead bird and between sobs began reciting over the trampled sparrow, then, regaining her composure, found a dry twig and poked out the bird's right eye. Having no desire to take part in this butchery, I went off on my own to piss against the thin trunk of a mandarin orange tree. Furious, she grabbed at bunches of nettle and scratched her hands bloody. What frightened me most about her laughter was its indiscretion. She took a tube of lipstick out of her pocket and smeared her face with it, one wounded hand adding blood red to the cosmetic's artifice. I licked her bleeding hands, mouth filled with the vaguely medicinal taste of lipstick blended with the burning acidity of nettle.

A cat hater, she would stone a feline on sight, yet had a soft spot for ants: she would never crush them; rather, she fed them crumbs and crusts kept deep in the pockets of her blue smock, which she removed and shook upside down, the better to dislodge the bits stuck in the pleats and seams, causing no small disturbance to the ant colony's disciplined workforce.

She didn't care for mothers and shunned men; but whenever she saw me playing his little lordship among a group of children, she would single me out of the throng with all manner of secretive, sidelong glances. She lived in a house next door to that of the patriarch: one day, just like that, she disappeared with her father, without a good-bye.

Backward in time, I discover myself walking in a daze, emptying out into the street as I leave the Pasha quarter, dragging my feet, drifting toward Hafsia where part of the Jewish ghetto was located, eclectic signage, architectural diminuendo: motifs parade by incoherent as if to lay bare the mixed alliances in this zone of intense conflict.

Noisy crowd, jostling, scruffy, the first I've come across since crossing over, smells and shadows, butchers and tripe at the Halfawīne market.

Raggedy throng in this devastated, vacant lot of a neighborhood: where the better-off flock to buy clothes. Frenzied hands grasping indiscriminately for handkerchiefs, socks, or shirts and sweaters from among piles of secondhand American surplus—puffs of cotton or streaks of shiny synthetics. Hands fly over the goods, picking up or dropping, whether silks or scraps.

Let's go, keep moving, take it or leave it, repeats a central voice, ever wary. And a pickpocket is caught in the act: a hand grabs the thief's: why rob me of all people, for God's sake? Son of Satan! Bystanders heap scorn on this petty crook. I wasn't meaning to pinch anything, really I wasn't; just playing around, that's all. Goddamn it! You're playing with fire now, little crook! Uh-oh, an informer! Look out, here come the cops! Oh no, let's not get them mixed up in this. Take off, clear out of here before we have to deal with those comedians who can't tell their uniforms from their pajamas—stained, crumpled, sticky with semen.

Crowdful of transactions, men bargaining, women scheming: people making merry, on a quest for that one-of-a-kind item. A middle-class matron in thrall to novelty finds an American-made blouse, something to really strut around in, but short of money, she kicks up a fuss: what an outrage, I've just been robbed, those monsters! all the money I had, what's to become of me? what shall I tell my guests? I haven't bought a thing yet! Oh woe is me, may they burn in hell, they who have undone me, she screams at the top of her lungs, bellowing at people with better things to do.

Taken off guard, passersby stare at her, some indifferent, others moved to compassion, still others ashamed, stunned: what misfortune! poor woman! how awful! Says another: I'm not going to groan over her bad luck, not me! She could buy us all twice over! Don't waste your tears, he says, spitting on the ground.

Come over here! she says, teary-eyed. Yes, you, addressing him. There's something you can help me with, strong and handsome as you are. Your gold tooth will light the way to finding the culprit. Oh saints in heaven, what shall I tell my family, my husband? I let myself be taken like some tourist—who doesn't know how risky it is to walk through this part of town? Come with me, young man, you handsome thing, help me track down the thief.

Yes, yes, shouts the crowd, go with her and Godspeed!

And so they go off together: the woman, charmed, clasps the man to her, and as they move away, slips an arm around his waist and draws him close, fondling his neck, applying little kisses, all the while weeping and moaning.

I am fixating on the notion of otherness. Secure obscenity hung over the entrance of houses, of hammams, of invisible courtyards where the air is fresh. Not even this crowd where I'm standing can unburden me of the obsessive, infernal hoop that's encircling my head, crushing meaning and suffocating reason; a mangled, hazy feverishness; a nervous state that unravels the sinews and merges time and feeling; thoughts and systems tossed all in a jumble at the protagonist whose presence cannot be steered toward the division of the story that would make the text effectively readable for anyone who chooses to receive it; the other's body losing what little it has to offer by putting a part of his life into fiction.

I won't say that what appears here are the words of a drunk. No, it's a dead man breathing life into his dulia, fragility that entangles the body and keeps it from any attempt to gather up all the inaccessible desire that blows away so jauntily on the breeze. Yet, at times, desire grows to be plucked flowerlike from the narrow valley of events.

Thus memories come and go, a plethora frozen into a static tableau that words seek to scramble once more, to guide toward the thaw of literature: it's all about knowing whether to render speech in its making and unmaking, or only to offer up its crystalline clarity. But don't go thinking the work you're reading was produced in a single ecstatic burst: on the contrary, it was sculpted, finished— but not in the unapproachable style of any particular convention.

Perhaps you would have liked to receive the product of my exertions and yet be spared the knowledge of all the accumulated labor here: the fruit of summer blooms after the deceptive sterility of winter. To repeat after Rūmi, accumulation, whether in the natural order or as social analogy, is invisible; expenditure alone is available to the senses, ostentatiously so, in fact. The leafless tree is not dead, nor does it concede to barrenness. No, the tree labors soundlessly through the winter so that, after spring blossoms, it offers its fruits, so that into their split skins the bee might deposit a multitude of nectars for honey gathering, so that this season spreads its golden bed to the pollen that fertilizes the earth and, with the help of the wind, scatters its secret seed.

There is a beating at the heart of the world: at the periphery, secondary activities yield to this tempo, gathering energy to produce, live, beget, give, and take. We need only be able to distinguish the spoils, our allotted share of opulent nature. Though when giving of myself, I shall be swallowed into nothingness.

Nature is to be conserved for its own sake, not to be made more tolerable for the foolish pretensions of Man, who fancies himself its uncontested master, though he be only a passing phenomenon, infinitesimal among so many forms of life, those self-sacrificial, trenchant trailblazers, a continuity containing the shoots sprouting every day, the signs to be sifted through the sieve of text.

For where does writing begin? The body, surrounded by events and books, spills back into the world words of another kind, as it keeps accumulating and expending, inscribing a mirror image of itself, testifying as to all the coincident details, raising a looking glass where the body's indescribable wealth and misery are displayed in all their glory.

Writing shows us the eye in the process of producing offspring, vomit, feces, children, fruit, puking, shitting. But through all this concomitant accumulation and expenditure, writing blurs its relationship to the law of nature whereby two phenomena must follow one another in time. Writing lives and dies simultaneously. As soon as a draft is definitive, nothing remains but a corpse to be served up to the undertaker—hence the technician's temptation to take scalpel in hand and perform surgery on the text.

Writing thus apprehended rarely lends certainty or accuracy to the explosion of events, for the event breaks free, self-propelled.

Autobiography, as a result, gets reduced to no more than edifying anecdote, a textual falsehood to help us get by, a cure in search of something always just out of reach, as you fall into the trap of writing as charitable act: between a simple knot that needs untying and a truly instrumental text, there remains but a hair's breadth, yet an unbridgeable abyss.

Writing mixes up the seasons, resolving the usual jumble of hot and cold, summer or winter: it reflects the messiness of the body more than any primordial law: it is chaos more than fiat, a battle of giants meant to obstruct the desire to invent oneself according to some divine order: it is with us, a descent, subterranean, underworld, regression, a groping toward totality: it is the gallery that cuts through the edifice end to end, the ambo breaking up the uniformity of narrative space.

Clarity will be asked of us anon: shall we impart it at the moment of our assumption into paradise, when the guardian of the gates asks the fateful question: How do you overcome the body? Better to start with confusion, dear Novalis, than with clarity. Through this gate, illumination and abundance will pave the way for the perseverant. No room for petty hedonists, hand-to-mouth rhapsodists, dying with each dawn, though failing to have perished still wise the previous evening, exhausted by pain.

Only when the body breaks through can it qualify as sacrifice to the avenging city. It is not because of some malicious pleasure that I find myself in thrall to these little streets bathed in damp adolescence, corrupting both straw and seed: a gang of us would dash over to Sidi Abd-Allah Guech and light lanterns for the long nights of the holy month, Ramadan, Saint Januarius, flinging ourselves, all mawkish entreaty, into the arms of fiftyish bottle-blonde whores, Gilberte or Germaine, assumed names, bawdily Gallic, smiles occasionally mean, more often obliging, nurturing mothers in a former life.

It wasn't difficult to tell the difference between those who were seeking to safeguard their social standing—civil servants, timid and tiny pawns—and those who burst cocksure into the little storefront rooms, puffed-up pigeons acquitting themselves of the body's timeless duty, bartenders and waiters, Jacquy, Eddy, Freddy, coming together here, in name and in the flesh, at an interstice of the races.

Black hookers with huge, porchlike backsides sitting sluggish on the threshold of their hovel, speaking loud and slow, never finishing their interminable sentences, teasing some skinny pretty boy who's all mascara, lipstick, and rouge, swaying hips like the drag-queen dancers of Tangiers, flamboyantly mimicking female movements, like some Amazonian butterfly, face painted, buttocks quivering, somewhat clumsily performing his own idea of a vagina in its back and forth, rhythm and caress, bump and grind, along with an unconvincing imitation of the diva's lyric: *come and get it if you can*, challenging the male member's arousal at the sight of its vaginal prey, the intended bait—though not at the lowly phallus nearby, impossible to conceal from the astonished, soaking client.

Drag queen color and light, shake that thing, dime-store exotic, sailors in a port of call, gobbling down leftover couscous chilled by the pathetic eyes of a fiddler playing with neither melancholy nor hysteria, sawing away at his kamanjah, held in upright position on one knee: Tangiers, rival of continents, from its perch obsessed by two seas, tumbling seasons scatter into color-splashed crowds, throngs, dense in places: waning lives or former glories ravaged, shouldering the insignificance of what had been their worldly past, walking Pekingese on a leash, silk kimono revealing wrinkled, once-legendary thighs.

Queens of Tunis, casual decor of the bordello—imitating the feminine, but not too concerned with accuracy. While relinquishing a certain maleness, they don't strain to achieve the womanly. They make do with themselves: artisans of a clumsiness now become its own code, intensively coquettish, unbridled joy the hallmark of difference, color and design, curls and rings. Still, as is said of clowns, this joy of theirs hides no small sadness. But the scenes they cause, falling in love or bursting into tears at the drop of a hat, sweep aside any reticence, eliminate the paralyzing culpa of neophytes, giving way to pleasure-seeking, amorous and tender.

Solicitous words all playing on the slit: prostitution, ritualized vulgarity, basis of all guilds' spirit of dissent, each with humor all its own: come over here and show me that tool of yours, ah no, not my type at all, hideous, who are you trying to kid, you call that a cock! You're welcome to come over to our side, I'll set you up with a surgeon, Marcel from Casablanca, I've got the address, you'll be gorgeous, sweet thing, I'll call you Aida, let's go see Salha, she'll do your makeup, she's adorable, you'll love her, she's so nice, very good at beauty marks with harqūs, or a little tattoo job on your forehead, I can already see your eyes shine, it's the green mascara. What? Can't make up your mind? Such a tease! Look at her show it off, what a cunt! Ah, you heartbreaker! Here, take it all, it's all yours, girl, my slave, my devil, my sorceress, don't play hard-to-get with me . . .

Pimps, terror: Habib, generally a pathetic type, finds power in his eloquence; but watch out for his well-aimed headbutts too, they do real damage. All present, queens and hookers alike, wait for clients on a slow night, silent, lying low. Stillness in abandoned alleyways revived by blue-tinted whitewash drizzled intermittently with arcs of fresh urine. Skinny young hooker already past her prime slams her door at the sight of Habib Fanfan, local lord, master of the alley, who then throws a fit, rants and raves, all for show, then settles back down, putting on an ear-to-ear grin: Vengeance will come in due time, he says, eyes smoldering, spiteful as a camel. Only this one drag queen, dwarf jester to the tyrant, dares turn Habib's uncontested authority on its head, bluntly, making openly disparaging gestures.

So let him say that a whorehouse has to have some self-respect, some laws, needs its lords and lackeys: it's neither ghetto nor citadel, but prison without walls, borderless fringe, alleys and dead ends, this boundary zone where meaning fails and all function is feigned: brothel that the city absorbs into the margins of the cosmopolitan outskirts of poverty: Arab, Maltese, Jewish, and Sicilian hands jerking off in unison in the shadows of roofs sweating damp.

By engaging the body outside of space and beyond the mere act of discharge, the brothel becomes a sort of boarding house where all the races residing therein find themselves reconciled: in Istanbul, on the right bank of the Golden Horn, not far from the port, the Zürafa Sokaǧi brothel is set apart from the modern quarter, in Karaköy: cool and tranquil, wide and unencumbered, the main street of the sex-for-sale zone, closed at one end by a gate, is not devoid of trees, fragrances, shade; café terraces add to card games the pleasure of the hookah. The display of practically naked bodies, hips wrapped in skimpy pareus, reproduces the rhetoric of the Tunis brothel. To see, to visit a ravishing but already ravaged whore, we first go down a long, narrow corridor, then climb a little wooden ladder set into the masonry to find ourselves at last, drenched in sweat, in a sordid little room where, with an aristocratic indifference, she is spread out on a sheepskin, undoing her negligible wrap and smearing her genitals with some kind of mucus-like lubricant; to penetrate in joy, yet unfulfilled, assessing the whore's workaday thrusting, indicative of a high art tarnished by this practice that, scandal of scandals, botches the whole question of pain and pleasure.

Same spillway again, a check on proletarian bodies, crossing the sea, continuing along the river to find themselves queuing up on Rue de Chartres, Rue de la Charbonnière, sex-starved immigrants, some of them impudent or irreverent, others shamefaced, stealing glances at the insistent enticement of the bodies crusted over, breasts sagging from the passage of time, wrinkles at bargain-basement prices, see-through fronds of black lace caressing her belly.

Different vision of bodies for sale, the Middle Atlas Mountains, desert's edge, mausim, harvest festival time, ritual prostitution at rural shrines, Moulay Ibrahim and elsewhere, outside the city, beyond the constraints of urbanity, theology, business, and all the various trades that organize the history of a city like Fez that extends its influence well beyond its borders, tending to centralize and cancel out all difference, incorporating the well-to-do of other towns and regions, Souss, Tafraout, Tetouan, Taroudant, even the intractable Marrakech, into a common and coherent project facilitating the exploitation of all bodies; ensuring, thanks to the new port inherited from the former colonizers, an open-door policy, and with the blessings of the royal Cherifian family, quashing any demonstration of local power unless this be tiny and fetishistic, confining its deviance to the mountainous backcountry.

Leaving Fez and heading into the mountains, encounters with unsubdued bodies, bursts of music, coolness of short nights. Love has burned me, fluttering with pleasure. Exiting the baths, she says: I am as clean as metal. Cleansed of what she had interiorized as an inevitable defilement, an odor that she preferred not to name, her periodic chastity; bad, black blood, she would say, yet not so bad for less delicate nostrils, curve of the waist embellished, complexion deep brown, eyes lined in kohl, thick hair, wavy, shining, black; teeth white pearls, gums like rubies or coral, rubbed with siwak, *Capparis sodata*, fragrance and sap of chewed bark.

Fez hammam, scrubbing and rubbing of bodies, two stones in succession: one porous and rough to remove the build-up, the other a clay stone, smoother, going for foamy softness, like another soap to grease the skin and refill the pores; power of cold shower, rinsed body, polished, ruddy in full light, glints and cascades highlight the body's relief, Donatello bronze, slender David mauling myth, victory and cunning as feminine attributes, more akin to Judith, slingshot or dagger, boundless smile of the androgynous angel.

Splendidly feminine, unpampered, she was in full bloom at the meeting point of the sexes, equidistant, conveying the most instinctive of desires.

Woman after hammam off to drink from the warm waters of fortune at the Sidi Harāzem spring, crowd jostling. Return to Fez and there she is on the road to Sefrou, her town, hitching a ride. I stop, open the door for her, she jumps in without invitation, throws her arms around me in a rush of passion, we embrace: just like that, I plucked the rose that leaned breathless over my breast; then she played at plucking at the sparse golden hairs on my arm, drowning her eyes in mine, conquering jet-black gaze, making me flustered at the wheel on a serpentine road: *bell occhio*, says Zaynab, as did the girl selling oranges in Venice, once.

Ask her: sing Berber: shrewd, mescaline voice, with an undercurrent of laughter, body warmth, sensations are shared in their abundance, are they not? Knowing, compassionate caresses, jerking me off, sex after a long period of abstinence, almost let go of the wheel, effervescent odor of pine and earth, rock and cedar, pulled over and laid down in the car, stroking between navel and pubis, lightly traced curves sketched by fingers and words, clever softness of the quivering place, tautening, releasing, lightening, annihilated by the game of love, lasting into hours forgotten, distances fled.

Fantasy lending flair to the feminine, child, on the verge of joking; haphazard shaping of the hilly landscape; just like that, she sold her body: perhaps forever, perhaps just to save up for her dowry, she didn't know: just like that, she was in the skin trade, neither fallen nor guilty. Yet it was more than a whim: enough to live on and then some, succulent mountain, umbilicus of the world.

This backcountry business is subjected daily to the passage of hegemonies that, nonetheless, do nothing to impair its ability to withdraw, when necessary, nor, on the other hand, simply yield to this plague of passengers. She looks after herself, makes time for life's pleasures, and all without hypocrisy: laws drawn up in the city with an ear to the ground of civilization encounter nothing here but deaf-muteness. Mountain country stands in refusal, effortlessly, in its tattoos and braids, giving and losing territory beyond officialdom.

Can't wait to arrive in Sefrou; come, you're my guest; you'll see, our girls are all very nice; there might be music, something to eat; we'll drink wine or tea, whatever you like; we'll smoke; the girls have surely thought of everything; give me the money now, it's better that way, then everything will be settled ahead of time, thirty dirhams, it's a bargain, I love you, she says nonstop, stringing approximate Arabic to her native Berber inaccessible to ears such as mine, coming as I do from a land overrun by Arab tribes, Hilāl, Sulaym, Ma'qil. While mountains, like desert, help preserve ways and idiom.

And we went in; house spacious and simple, entrance leading to patio, hardly any distance at all, immediately in courtyard, a couple of sickly toddlers playing, an elderly madam washing an impressive stack of dishes, running water into a large basin, rinsed plates and bowls set on the edge of the well. For the rest, three long, narrow rooms circle the patio.

Hellos all around, wait, I'll be right back, takes me by the hand, leads me into one of the rooms: five or six girls in full makeup are waiting, all a shade paler than Zaynab, chestnut eyes with come-hither looks for some, but cold for others: yet none had my companion's untamed look of naïve escape. A string of names, then laughter: they spoke in half sentences, vaporized Berber; but place names gave me a clue, cities and towns rattled off in succession, Fez, Sidi Harāzem . . . Zaynab gave a cursory account of her day.

Twilight, patio breeze, I wanted to be alone with Zaynab, shut into one of the side rooms, laughter and noise forgotten, water and dishes, disregard the children's crying, steal away from birdsong, their last outburst before nightfall. Slender candles lighting our bodies stretched out on a thick blanket, rubbing against one another, caressing, bathed in sweat, baby smell, she said, hers more changeable, though to describe it would make it into something else, like any color, any odor, Zaynab's fragrance, nothing can taint it, filling my lungs, for want of writing. Pungent odor: a strong flavor lodged in the back of the throat, a thick, fluid nourishment spreading over one's nerve endings. Bodily sap emitting from the tongue. Smell of salt and cinder smoldering on damp earth scattered with grains of cumin and pepper crackling on the fire.

Time no longer followed its course. Our emotions cast shadows: rare blue moonlight penetrated the little window's fine mesh.

Her long hip-length hair undone and oozing night: flow of murmuring sheen into which my head plunged, sudden creation of stars. More dense than a camelhair tent: a dive into deepest dark sea, losing sight of the sky, colder by degrees as you drop, breath held, eyes dissecting the submarine waters, chest tight, rapid descent, nose ejecting air, weakening gurgles, dense rumor of the sandy sea bottom: rays, starfish, diaphanous flora. Breathtaking, this hair, stifling even, an enigma unto itself, as I resurface, a seeker's lips lost in deciphering Zaynab. Gleaming hair reflected in a glistening eye, as hands invent caresses without end, beyond the prospect of pleasure, everlasting question, shades of an epic, extraordinary feat.

Eyes ever-changing with imperceptible shifts in light, alternating sweetness and bites, leaving bloody the flesh of a covering shoulder.

Our bodies hit the floor that was losing heat stored up from the relentless sun. Bodies united in filtering out independence, content with illusion, a paradise that even the floor's inconvenience could not erode. An expert hand pushed the door open and set down a steaming tray, mint tea, enveloping our bodies one in the other, moist.

And we drank, smoked crackling grass, late-night stillness broken by the occasional nearby ululation of some night bird. Mild grass, pollen and flower, wedding of seasons come directly from the secret fields of Ketama. Persistent taste of rebelliousness and insubordination despite the presence of Zaynab's breathing, expulsion of stray impulses of anxiety.

Oppressive sensation in the chest, tightening of the throat, piercing pain in the head. Then the body wraps in gossamer light. Silence broken, air within bodies is displaced. Union crosses a community of desires realized at fault's edge; egos collapse, ingenious tremors.

To be nothing more than ocean's wave upsetting you, stirring the sand. Hips unleashed to set an offbeat rhythm of well-rolled swells at equinox: one, two, three invasions in succession, carried away, immeasurable, breaking wave, sea flower exciting the body in free-fall, restless wavering, hollow tottering, allowing energy the time to rebuild additional barriers: one, two, three, four thrusts and she can no longer contain herself: fleshy vulva, sensitive clitoris, lair of my erect member after those pulses electrifying Zaynab.

Respite afloat, to recover movement and ready myself, second wind, to dissolve in the deep and monumental thrusting of hips . . . until I entered into her fully: You've had your pleasure in front, I told her; now I want damnation from behind; she laughs demurely, refuses, wavers; spit first and have at it, she says at last, womanly reserve, O depraved master, annihilated, undone, sailing on the wings of she who carries him, bird unfaltering, yielding: knowing its itinerary and destination. Depraved, I saw nothing more with my own eyes, nor did my ears hear anything more: crossing the heavens, nearing the star become vulvic eye, anal oculus, nose-phallus teasing the space in between, whitening with milk, coating with egg. No stranger to the moon, Zaynab lent me her eyes to help me drive into her excavations and grottos: all the features of lithic landscape, silver and cinder, precious stone incrusted with tentative shapes, intangible clouds transforming into portraits, the insubstantial assuming a face: haphazard sculpture containing furious fire-breathing dragons; burāq blending feminine grace and the journey's secret accommodation; fragile antelopes, instantaneous flight, nimble bounding; nubile angles, pubescent smile; grotesque figures engaged in some unspeakable practice, torment and torture, burnt genitals, pregnant women disemboweled, blood-soaked vaginas, wild boars inflated with a smithy's bellows inserted in their anus by little sniggering imps; forsaken hands dancing in the ethereal slowness of the upper stratosphere.

Images reproducing my fantasies of Zaynab fantasizing, insouciant, untiring, intractable when it came to giving herself fully conscious; to her, I gave myself up as an offering, relinquishing my obsessive fears; we came together, dissolved in oneness, admixing our "me," taking one for the other, expanding you, I.

Here I commence the digression of I, an initial I of the text, taking the measure of its wary intrusion, swapping sometimes with you, neutralizing infinitive, a core I, asserted or concealed, emphasis of this expression that deploys at the edges of language, of memory, an I an other amnesiac scribe in its repercussions upon work with language, freedom, infra-memory, indistinguishable from the surrounding dust! How to situate it within the economy of the self, with regard to the shadow of history, to this word body that comes so often back to sex?

Neither diary to rummage through, nor memories to justify, nor restitution or reconstitution of the past: the real imposes no borders on dream and fantasy; the space composed by these three wellsprings never grinds up the subject in the mill of analysis; dosage is controlled only by the energy of writing: yet the text should remain open to subconscious effects, insidious signs that find fault with a detail, first inflating it until guiltless, then abandoning it, no ulterior motive implied.

Observe the world if only as experimental token of the body by an unruly I; the only truths worth repeating are those marked on the body, it's up to I to admit them, otherwise be crushed by the weight, flowing into the real: judgments, analyses, descriptions delight in a truth that is neither in process nor subject to inquiry.

Beyond the merely playful, our core narcissism expresses through the I, seat of the speech act, sustained by maternal fabulation: you, son of the dawn, son of light: the beauty of your birth is without equal, you my son, child of moonlight to daybreak, you who hastened into life, born wrapped in the sheer membrane of grace, you who our saintly grandfather favored as the chosen one at first breath. Narcissism confirmed by the role of the father inciting you to acquire knowledge, take up the path to power. The mother elaborates upon the mad and loving representation of the body on offer; the father imposes knowledge to fertilize this body, with no regard for context; the I is fetishized for self-recognition elsewhere than within our historical conscience: to desire somehow, anyhow, to live according to that legacy, to conclude that reality can refuse to submit to machinations that seek to lend credibility to the representation of the self thus elaborated—and what should happen but Narcissus mingling with the I erecting itself as master, as protruding and paranoid master.

Next comes the wound, by which the body manipulates its reality, unloads its false representation, sharpens its potential to become dance, cycle of euphoria, a loss of self that is not a healing response, but a knife with which to deepen the gash: not to flee pain but move beyond it, gravely, to joy.

In this I, ideas that grow like weeds; whose negativity, I mean, has no improving effect: those ideas are to be banished; the talking cure does not call for your self-acceptance as such, but for your admission that you are an enigma irreducible to meaning, to law, to all standards; the I involves history in its story: those years that impregnated my birth, my origins, my childhood seep into the foundations of a class betraying itself to extinction; I the representative of a generation of Arabs caught struggling with a fractured image, marked as monstrous by Europe and France, experiencing exile, revising the self after side-by-siding with the other, correcting one's social body by inverting oneself, rectifying once and for all one's oriental consensus by eliminating from one's organism the unhealthy proclivity for spying, broadening one's vision endeavoring to revive the archaic: polished and restored, propagated in the indifferent mother country. Experience of forced entry that surrounds the I, symbolizing rebel history stuck in the seam that connects here and there: otherwise accepting oneself as a denunciatory rebus.

And this resonance, outline for future speech, this injection of parables, this blood clotting on the wound that torments the tilled earth or the chiseled tree, this infection of parables, these stinging nettles whose sap we drink, are yelled, howled, cried, or chanted, vomited, excreted, or ejaculated by the body, an eccentric invention among its fluids: an I revealed as speech circulating logic, history of a people and the grim unmasking of its shameful mimicry to then go forth in a trance to face the obvious, ongoing injury, Palestine, feeding its narcissistic need to seek consolation in a golden age, an elusive unity where desire means fragmentation.

Thus I speak the experience that sweeps the body away in order to pulverize the self-absorbed I and make of it the agent that crosses the minefield of history: to brave the political apparatus that polices more than it governs, a waste product that cannot conceive of itself as even remotely necessary without falling into self-parody.

So these are the waters the text is navigating, unobvious as that may seem. I wandered deliriously off topic onto I, while I was in the middle of describing my annihilation in Zaynab; and with reference to the specificity of body and culture, how could I fail to recall the Sūfi experience, in thought and practice, devoted to the glory of extinguishing the I, rendered wholly material and only very secondarily ascetic: Hallāj sobbed, lost in laughter: *Kill me, loyal friends, for in death I shall regain life*; cosmic offering of the body to shatter the screen that separates man from his nature, far from martyrdom's redemption in death. Suhrawardi goes a step further: *Nothing can defeat me. I triumph over darkness with my Light, and triumph over light with my Enlightenment. I repent for nothing I have done. I have not awakened as if from a dream. I am not of those who would change.* Maqtūl, slain, and not shahīd, martyr, blood spilled to water the earth, to spite political blindness and regenerate: archaic sacrifice to the pantheistic waves, liquid infiltrating into rock, expansion of being into something that escapes man, but is not god.

Sacrifice of physical energy: body in excess, victorious in death out of pleasure-driven defiance rather than a suicidal awareness; for martyrdom involves sacrifice for reward, a barter morality: I die to gain eternity in paradise! No, not that: I die by virtue of what I have seen, and I have seen all too much; I draw closer, too close, to the sun, body consumed, moth burned by the allure of the flame. My body has exhausted experience down to its very cells: may it cease in order to be reborn perhaps as someone other.

Final implicit consequence, marker of Sūfi rejection, expressed by Rūmi heralding heresies while taking care along the way to concede an apparent submission to law and orthodoxy.

Merging with the Eleusinian Mysteries, Sūfism prevails over politics, speaks of today's deadly hopelessness, the urgency to discover a historical model: O Burāq, so close at hand, soaring at the break of dawn, deference to the sword of Ali that struggles to preserve the demeaned word, loathsome of stratagem, eyes insane, ears severed, gonads dried by the sun; Burāq astride Iraq lost under the stars in search of water before venturing into the desolate Empty Quarter: take me to taste that honey, remains of the ages, soil rendered friable by its green ants, bitter milk, lips, and almonds.

But no one suspects our failings: did not Hayy, coming from his desert isle, acquiesce to the necessity of law, ridiculous in itself, but consistent with the erosion of the body dissipated by the burden of social exchange and urban standards of behavior? But we have no desire to return with Hayy to his island, to contemplate from afar the workings of the world, to discover his intelligence firsthand, to make sense of the days; we want to live nowhere but in this world, for we would be diminished in retreat; we were not born in a laboratory, a fetus artificially conceived, test-tube uteri. Our bodies emerged in blood from out of vaginas, we have mothers and fathers; we do not reproduce our bodies as one can reproduce theories or stories, accurate and flawless. Let us seek our inner flame while putting an end to the reign that so squanders the potential energy of the people, those embers that propel our bodies.

My body dissolves in Zaynab: nothing but matter, accident, boundaries, unbearable solitude; and the omphalos radiates: that source whose beats and pulses she swallows. Trances where we forget what we are made of; where, senseless, we quiver in unbridled violence; where the cult of Attis has lain in wait for us, until the cold season at last breaks through to spring, reviving the trees; transfixed and distraught, could I have cut off my sex and thrown it away, madly racing to bless the garden or the threshold, spattered by whitish water? Now eunuch of Attis, would I brood over my misfortune consummated in moments of delirious, incandescent self-denial, and of the emergence of spring, which will have caused me to lose my senses?

Supreme offering that would fertilize the earth and exile the I: it cuts and concludes. But the old refrain of regret is but a tombstone echo. I was ambushed, taken off guard, and circumcised at the age of seven: it's to make you a man, my son; I recall a celebration of blood flowing and clotting into wounded sex: bulging jaundiced eye, long hard nails of the spindly circumciser: and the loss of the foreskin was accompanied by a volley of crockery-smashing, boys and girls hurling cracked pots to the ground while women ululated furiously, pitch-perfect. Pain, then scar to bear henceforward, indelible trace of Abraham.

Zaynab and I didn't talk much; the night crept to an end and we dozed off, sated. I wasn't hungry, nor would I have any of her wine; I was left with an impression: inexpressive smile. Lights ascended washed-out eyes. A range of feelings settled into bone marrow. Slight nervous tension that the tiniest tremble would put to rest. Body discovers repose; and the intensely faded blue light, daybreak, seeping through the window. Eye half-open, birdsong dominated by the morning dove's coo, with incursions of gloomy crow caw.

Dry lips drank the sweat beading on sleeping Zaynab's broad forehead. Day was dawning. Dazed, legs unsteady, eyes making a mess of color, olfactory breakdown, skin gleaming, cold company of the light, I got up and staggered out: calm, the silent, dew-soaked streets of Sefrou; walking wild-eyed in pursuit of shadows and the discipline of self-detachment. Streets deserted, apart from the sluggish indolence of a black dog, the celestial swarming of birds, the perseverance of an old man, the nimble agility of a woman. The sun was already overwhelming, and I couldn't look it in the eye: head back to drink from the source, Zaynab's armpits:

body suddenly seized by a burning thirst, Zaynab's odor called out to me, sole reality of import on this feverish morning, shut in with the young miss; wake, take, and beseech her, find a cure in her again and again satisfied smiling, so quickly asleep, so early awake, what the hell, I'd forgotten the morning.

The region teems with feasts of flesh, women opportunistically hawking their wares, a fact of mountain life. What can I say of those wild violent nights at Aïn Louh, not far from a fossil field, at the edge of a cedar forest? Resourceful village where springs flow everywhere. All music perverted in the end by rhythms of irreversible invention; stoned sheikhs, sheikhat, sometimes whores, sometimes entertainers who overcome you with sheer pleasure of the eye: singing, dancing, body eloquent miming enthusiastic sex. The ladies' houses shaken up by their pimps returning from Meknes, from cities that recruit girls by force: jail is my only real home, one of them boasts to me; in Madrid, I got to know a few of your compatriots, good people; and look, I kind of like you too. Come on, let's have a drink: wine like vinegar lays me low, smoking does more damage, sick to my stomach, harassing the girls, exit woozy, middle of the night, body and soul rejoined at the party next door, exhausted by the inevitable scene, penal atmosphere pervading pathetic bachelor-party rituals, third-rate musicians, tipsy lute players arriving from al-Qbāb to Aghbalou n'Serdane; four or five sheikhat, girls hailing from al-Hājeb, some hundred construction workers exiled sans women on their work site, men who joke as they binge, raving drunkards that snort like beasts, verging on nervous collapse, shaking the pillars of the big concrete room in their haste, not even a coat of paint on the walls, it stinks of semen and cement, half-lit hiding faces that pale, evanescent flames barely reveal, furtive cigarette embers cutting through the gloom; earsplitting music, tone-deaf instruments, noxious voices: lute out of tune, drumskin flaccid, voices only fit to be cut out of their throats by force, ugly girls frightened off by blind solicitation: a mountain brothel in all its unearthly splendor.

Of course, nights of such strenuous folly were in no short supply: Khenifra, within stars' reach, atmosphere of twilight when pink-tinted houses were suffused with the dispersed fragrance of women or girls in search of lovers, each bearing some secret sign for ease of recognition by those wanting the loan of woman for a few hours, post-siesta stroll, relative cool of nightfall, bodies for sale, eyes meeting, conniving, cruciform tattoos so fine, shifting heel to heel while hips swayed: languid cypress beneath white of veil. Follow the phantom at a distance and there you are, after discreet passage through patio, master for a night of love, reborn, at least if you hadn't aborted the mission, bad choice, wrong body.

Such serene abductions are taking place all the time, surrounded by the secret, quiet connivance of the crowd. Though the body, in this region, which has neither revived nor quite abandoned its archaic ways, is not necessarily meant to be used up as an offering to Eros; it can find release in music too, subtlety of tone, strings that bruise the fingers, genuinely sorrowful voice undulating against the whispering flatness of water trickling out from under the earth to flow across the many green grasses sprouting scarce out of the rockiness, field planted at the foot of cedar-shaded slopes that tumble into a blue boldness whose far shore is mirrored in the muffled, metallic surface of Lake Aguelmane Azigza.

Brothel, then music on Radio Tunis, syrupy and superfluous, poured out after the roll call of dedications, a song for a Romeo, another for a Juliet: the voice of the Grand Lady sounds pathetic here, repeating her endless refrain of love and ecstasy. The same Umm Kalthūm refrain heard in Fez, late afternoon, jasmine and café terrace tucked up against the city walls, smoking kif and sipping tea in the company of refined, articulate elders, full immersion now to shape heart into arabesques, maze of the idle self, assuming all its spiraling potential. Incidentally, I have never been able to fathom what the song means, its very rhetoric an enigma: this refrain that goes on and on, changing, planting the dagger, arrogant wound, transcending the gloomier impulses of the orchestration, accordion, piano, electric guitar, all at quarter tones, accompaniment distorting the voice.

Footsteps give way to footsteps. Unvarying façades, bodiless buildings, pass in succession. Only doors leave a signature: color and design not only reveal the craftsman's whim, whether or not under a master's guidance, but the homeowner's social status, assuming monumental form enabling one and all to recognize, by virtue of the door's size and appearance, the original or now retroactive destiny of the house.

Each edifice remains enigma until the eye penetrates the sqifa, angled vestibule of connecting spaces, deep and dark, where the door's salient features are either confirmed or disproven by both size and odor, limiting one's mobility, the transition between patio and street.

Patio: inner sanctum, navel, breathing space, the virtual center of the city broken up into countless openings to the sky, disseminating convergence: each patio in itself a center, the city a hierarchy of navels: those of the public body, open to scrutiny, lawful access, a mosque, for instance; then, navel of the hidden body, woman for sale, heart to cloister. Navels are banned from the street, where those near occasions of sin, though within reach, are deemed inaccessible, where the body is abstraction: perceived as such, the body is returned to the real by the idea of private captivity, within the confines of the patio, via a dim passageway that cuts off home from city, vestibule of enchanted reincarnation where abstract body rediscovers imminent desire.

To open the whore's chamber right onto the street reifies the body's representation: what takes place there gets relegated to a negating banality, overly charged with passion in order to arouse desire. As an institution, the brothel claims to deal in matter: flesh by weight, occasion of discharge to domesticate destructive/creative energies. Prevention as means of averting the ravages of rape, following the northern examples of Hamburg and the display windows of Amsterdam.

Each navel-like breach onto a patch of sky discloses the secret of rooftops, like a staircase to be climbed with ease, where upon day or night are etched the itineraries of women in search of affirmation, of overflow. There, silence is deceptive: banned from street cafés, the unruly women swarm on the rooftop terraces, all unbridled gesticulation, having their disruptive say. Consensus as to a plot has reached its peak. On the face of it, from a panoramic viewpoint, the eye observes nothing but empty flatness, with the occasional sparkle of a skylight.

And when I stroll through the narrow confines of the street, through sounds muffled or resonant, footfall and wheel, desire turns me voyeur: I fly to a bird's-eye view, I find anecdotal evidence of the repeated separation of space, territory of my body. So many games revived by this interiorizing of space, its divvying up that parked us children safely in the shadows, in places of unfathomable purpose, indeterminate alcoves, up ladders onto the rooftop terraces, thighs powdered by fresh whitewash, unsupervised games, attraction, touch, caress: sexual reckonings, boys and girls absconding from the overwhelming oversight of their elders.

IDOL GHETTO

The deafening din of the metalwork souk: apart from the sharp and sure pounding by finishers of vats, pots, and other utensils, a series of codes circulates parallel to the signs that overwhelm the senses: auctioneer selling clocks, manuscripts, spare parts to the highest bidder: elusive, quick-witted, he singles out a buyer among jostling passersby: bidding takes place in secret, precluding one's knowing which bid belongs to which face mouthing its rising offer: the bidders merge into virtual points, occult subjects, figures combined as though by magic, a waltz of numbers in succession, marionettes whose puppeteers delight in concealment, illusory absence.

The street rises; paving stones washed down in struggle against dust, slick underfoot; vision smoky, ephemeral. Old man rages against these modern times that keep changing and changing: warns of imminent catastrophe, and his eschatological message proves banal: the end is near, the cataclysm is fast upon us, O good people, lend an ear, believers or nonbelievers, prepare and be cleansed: the earth shall cough up its bowels; moon and sun clash, the stars scorch our humble plains, the mountains crumble to dust, the seas swallow us: the age of calamity is upon us, the fifteenth Muslim century: before the end of time, strange tribes, not unlike yourselves, accursed manlike creatures, despised homunculi, shall invade the lands, and for forty years shall convert men and women, boys and girls, to lives of the wildest hedonism and lechery.

Shouting and gesticulating in expressive excess, he tears at his flowing beard and howls words, some hammered out clearly, others spewed forth, naïve and nonsectarian. Merchants and shopkeepers let the old man preach into the wind; a couple of cowering children cling to their sister's or mother's veil. Yet there are a few passersby who fall under the speech's spell; some gaping, still others weeping. A crowd gathers: prophet of doom failing to mark their presence or notice the effects, the agitation his pronouncements are provoking, as if borne aloft by some unknowable double lending spark to his eloquence and intensity to the changes in his voice: his body floats in some elusive neverland.

Rarely have millenarian preachers enjoyed such a willing audience. The city swarms with such prophets, and this particular example is but another in the endless repetition of same. How, then, has he cast such a spell as to subjugate the most skeptical merchants, usually so indifferent?

Bands of little brats, local delinquents always ready and willing to throw stones at these truth-peddlers, have suddenly disbanded, paralyzed. The narrow street is completely obstructed by an enthralled multitude, men and women alike, sobbing as they repeat the preacher's sermon chapter and verse. Chanting in plaintive voice, his evangelizing message stripped of any provocative description or useless polemic. Rocking head and upper body to the breathless beat of rhyming prose, the old man weeps and the gullible crowd belts out the refrain in chorus: O Eminence, our bodies burn for remission of our sins.

Three women in the first row reprise his brutal, half-circular swinging motions of the arms, like machines spun out of control, first right, then left, a compensatory contagion of symmetry: the crowd, like a sea whipped up suddenly by storm, unleashes wave upon wave, rolling, crashing, blossoming foam: arms move to and fro as though detached from the body's volition: however, each individual preserves their autonomy of movement: arms and torsos each sway to their own rhythms, abruptness giving way to elegance, contortions to howls; but the bodies taken together, though their limbs and shouts each act independently, unite into a single pulse, a systematic set of movements: an unraveling circle of unity surrounding each body, preserving in each a precarious respiration. Several nearby metalworkers pound their wares in time with these seething bodies and voices, bright clang adding fire to the scarce sunbeams that filter through holes in tenting or openings in the barrel vault that covers part of the narrow street, damp, rolling, trampled by a crowd now on the verge of insanity, gradually descending into a trance that coincides with the assonance and iteration of the old man, unflappable cross-legged yogi, hoarse voice rising from deep in his center: futility in attempting to name Him when a thousand names have failed; I am body scattered, you will inhale me like dust! Immobile, I have journeyed through lands and encountered saints, archive of the world, from Tafilalet to Senoussi country, their white domes dazzling hilltop and desert; sacred lentisks, holy ash tree, blessed waters, healing springs, benediction and grace upon your relentless desire to be.

As far as the eye can see, the people have become physically disengaged from their usual routines, and delirium is in the air. Merchants scramble to close up shop, alarmed by what the preacher's sermon implies, its outrageous logic; only two or three stalls, seemingly abandoned, still give off their neon glow. The mob is churning, rough sea growing stormier still. Children take part in this tragic delight, clearing the heart of the underbrush penning them inside such narrow destinies: cherubs floating about the heads of madmen; sure-handed messenger boys, masters of the moment.

The crowd punctuates its dance: voices rough as though coughing up blood as their movements grow more refined. Not everyone follows the same swift upward motion. Some remain earthbound, playing at a loss. Others take flight, fabulously plumed travelers. But these bodies sense their common destiny: those who can neither soar above the world nor, with eyes rolling back, break free from themselves that they might delight in this effortless glide, the jewels and thrones of a thousand gems, emerald and tourmaline, peridot and jade, olivine and serpentine, those other ones mimic the movements of a raging ocean to better help those predisposed to visions to lose their footing and drown: vertigo submerges everything within range.

There are those who sweat, petty and ungainly; those who cry out in despair; those who hang on, exhausted; those seeking renewal in the cinders that cling to the body; those who gaze at themselves in ecstasy; those wreathed in light, so close to the prize; those who, by unveiling, weep at having reached the pinnacle but are unable to withstand the intense heat of intimacy: these dig nails into their cheeks and mount the burning pedestal once again to revive the spirit that overcomes incandescence tamed by breathing that annihilates awareness of pain. Some keep an eye on the real, others lose all sense of proportion.

And the old man, eyes now very wet, has ceased to speak, an ancient, wheezing old ram, lungs shriveled and congested, bleating as he breathes. The rumbling of the dance intensifies as more women fall into a trance. Spent bodies lie in repose right on the paving stones or lean up against the shuttered shops. The old man, taken by a higher form of lucidity, strokes his beard and draws from his throat a baritone laugh that breaks against the splendid shield of dance, wrought alloy of man and woman unburdened of their opposing fates.

Laughter that disturbs the dance, breaks its momentum, divides its effects, offers the respite of dispersion. Faces bear the marks of rapture. The guarantee of impunity channels all energies; bodies freed in their posture of the model haunting memory—wild-eyed master of my wandering self, at first intent on rediscovering the monotony of a city so passive as to seem no more than a puzzle to be solved, to be made plausible at last, lid on my hollow body that flight into exile has yet to exhaust, basis for a journey alternating between insidious anxiety and the temptation of tiptoed return to a landscape that celebrates sedimentary events.

Diaphanous bodies, unspeakable light at this moment of repose: the unpretentious city folk circulate among themselves, speaking plainly about their behavior: we must do something now that we are all here together, says one. Women's veils are used to wipe the sweat from damp breasts and burning faces, buckets of water freshened with lemon and orange rind are passed from mouth to thirsty mouth. Water shared undisputed, sign of an implicit pact sealed among bodies all in expectation. We need orders, says another. We're not here for the fun of it. Shall we start dancing again, one woman proposes. No, what would that accomplish? You'll see by other ways and means the seas of fire that stir the sun, replies the preacher. Then, a voice trembling with unerring desire speaks up and says, I want to be consumed in His Countenance. Old-fashioned nonsense, snaps an adolescent with winglike bangs grazing his eyes, eating into his face. Hear me, O brothers and sisters, says a black-robed, flat-chested, smoky-voiced, dark-skinned girl: cast nothing onto the ground of infamy! Let us hasten forth and lay waste to the city now that we know. Yes, she's right, adds the wobbly-legged voice, our passion will soon be defeated if we dance instead of descending upon all that which is not ours in this city.

What is this plan of yours, O carefree children born yesterday?— calm down, lest you share in the flames of hell, warns a slave to the dhikr, sanctimoniously reciting the names of Allah and turning in circles since the dawn of the century.

Stand back, all you followers of sects and speakers of stale words. My hands tremble, my fingers itch for action, my toes are set to spring, a fire of passion devours the bush within. Let us hurl ourselves into the race, into the carnage, get on our feet again; our city needs blood to nourish the soil eager for its startling, sickening smell. I call for intoxicating deliverance—no second thoughts: brother bodies, beloved ones all, need I say that the song of glory is within reach of your voice? Repeating the words of Hadda, the curly haired ogress, impressively corpulent yet possessed of that fragile, quavering voice, urging on stronger women than she to answer the unexpected call to battle.

Let us await neither judgment nor counsel, least of all from our fathers, before swooping down on our prey, for it's not every day that we celebrate ourselves as being something other than sheep waiting for the slaughter. Our empty stomachs will be filled with hatred, and we shall break our fingers on the rocky ground that no longer carries the marks of our plaintive sowing—we shall bruise and bludgeon it, as did those traitors from among us who helped the foreigners colonize the land.

The joy of disorder spreads again through the crowd. The old man, the rabble-rousing preacher, appears in control. It is up to you, he says and repeats: your wishes shall not be in vain, but you must act upon them, even though the bridges you build may well collapse. Do not blame me, for I can only provide you with the watchword; you must use it as you will: Justice upon the earth!

Then, the people rise in concert and proceed to molest their city: pulling up paving stones, buttressing ramparts, gutting shops to distribute food and drink, sealing up the breaches in their barricades, courtyards overtaken and occupied, to the misfortune of those few remaining dowagers who had not yet absconded to the residential suburbs—cries of brotherhood, voracious ululation, women on the prowl.

Provisions grow scarce in the city. Available stocks of dried fruits and nuts—almonds, raisins, walnuts, hazelnuts, pine nuts, figs—all are divided up among those present, who stuff themselves on the dizzying abundance. They then decide to organize commandos to go out and fetch foodstuffs from the source, from the farms and market gardens surrounding the city: Mornāg, Slimān, and as far away as Testūr, vestige of Andalusia.

The terrified dignitaries find no safety even when locked into their fortress houses, those not already abandoned and squatted in by legions of the rural poor who break in and settle by force in those now degraded monuments to another time, former palaces become oukalas, palatial slums.

From Bab al-Khadra, Bab Sa'dūn, Bab Swīqa, Bab Jdīd, the folk of the *faubourgs* rush in and pillage. At nightfall, they decide to halt the devastation and start organizing their resistance, to close the city gates, ration food and water, better to withstand the siege that has already encircled the insurgent city.

Whom do they distrust? All those who once reigned supreme over the city: the Spanish under Charles V, the Turks under Khayr ad-Din, the French of Jules Ferry, the henchmen of the Party become State, the secret police of our national independence, torturers and mercenary militias.

Threats are issued to the reticent, while imprisonment is reserved only for the enemy within: defeatists and bureaucrats. Disarm the police to arm the people. Issue gag orders on the landed gentry, such as the squire sheikh who failed to nationalize his lands at the time of the reformist wazir: the imām, leading prayer throughout the long Ramadan nights when the Book is to be recited in its entirety, a few verses and suras at a time, this hysterical sheikh collapsed at the news of his assets being co-opted, falling to the ground and hitting his head against the faux marble of the mihrab, compass point that orients the unanimous rows toward the qibla, the mythic east of sunrise.

The city focuses its efforts neighborhood by neighborhood, street by street: meeting in alleyways to talk and plan, idly chatting in courtyards where vigils last until dawn. Everyone has his say, gives her word: all their secret bad habits corrected, trash cans to be collected by the people, by turn. No longer any question of carting the foul load to the far-off dump beyond the city walls, but rather of incinerating each day's refuse among the ruins left by recent demolitions: half the space for burning, the other for clucking hens to peck.

Minor experiments in trade between one neighborhood and the next: chatter and laughter, analysis and thought beyond the old self-imposed restraints during these gatherings open to all at every hour in the Great Mosque, the Zitūna, no place now for long-winded theological harangue, in the vast arcaded courtyard and white portico where thugs had always tried to pretend to speak for the people. Heft of the walls, dichromatic façades, blue-veined marble, porous yellow stone, all trembling at the sound of these words heretofore unheard, words shunned and cast out by officially sanctioned wisdom for fear of its casting a coarse shadow upon the city. Living words of experience, officialdom laid bare, toothless mouths accustomed to chewing furtive speech in rage at a ghetto of words with its rules and laws, at the foundation of a cenacle in need of a Judas. At session's close, selection is made from among the pillars of the local cabaret: pimps, queens, criminals, lechers, and opium eaters, a privileged few to watch the performance of the flying tattooed vagina, that bird in the form of Bedouin dancer who spends her nights dazzling the eye with hip thrusts, jabs, or quivering shimmies.

The text resists, the word spreads wild, rarely vindictive, into dark recesses, over gleaming white flagstones, mirrorlike, footprints on the vast slab pavement of the courtyard, ashamed of speech so alien to such a place, so provocative, words more likely to be heard in the dives of Halfawīne, in unlit bicycle shops or shoe-repair stalls, Zāwiya Būkria, elbows on the bar, shoe-shiners, drug dealers and gangsters jostle, butting their ram horns at the al Hafīr fountain.

Alias Būraçīn, "daddy two-heads," eye twinkling, a froth of words: me, I'm not the political type but I get you, I'm on your side, no respect for those jokers and traitors. But patching up differences in the neighborhoods, that'll take some doing. Let's move ahead anyway, and we'll just see. No pulling punches if it comes to that, we'll be busting balls all around if that's what it takes, and don't think we're going to leave the knives at home. But how are we to know the enemy, to leave yesterday's enemy behind, to invent one if we can't find him? And anyway, I've got some rich friends that you'd better leave alone, or you'll have me to answer to. Būraçīn, thick head on a smallish body, none too bright, name worn like an emblem, verbose but rapid-fire, famously adroit at handling a knife, superb aim: if only he would teach us that lightning draw, gash to the cheek, scarface for life, e.g., the deferential street tough Chwirrib, caustic braggart with slow, nasal delivery, dragging worn-out espadrilles, soles agape, hanging by a thread, verge of disintegration. There he is, brandishing his street-smart snicker, self-important, giving us his piecemeal spiel indicating complicity with our revolt but unconcerned with conveying its principles: no way around it, a joker's got two roots, one's the mother, the other's the street. As for her, the less said the better—seriously. They say the big man's got no manners, but when she's around, it's like I'm a schoolboy. Like I said, there's the street and there's the mother. But every once in a while, out she comes out into the street and mixes things up: mother in the street, that's hard to handle. When she's out there, I keep a low profile, me, the giant killer! To see her on the loose, terrorizing everyone, I lose my usual catlike grace and stumble roof-hopping. And anyway, when some old fox eyes me the wrong way, he'd best go dig a hole somewhere, friend or foe, or else there'll be blood. Scars on chest, belly, back, and shoulders, shirt open, flapping in the wind, stigmata of the night prowler. Cop hater. Not to confuse those who secretly fantasize about being cops with the card carriers who actually torture by profession.

Among other signs of youthful indiscretion and ingenuousness: piss wherever you please, where you've got to go when it can't wait. That's how it is, like a baby in diapers, a turmoil of piss against a Roman column topped by a Byzantine capital, floral arrangement with nesting birds face to face. Copper-colored piss, stinking of excreted beer. You could have answered nature's call minutes later at the latrine, spacious and beautiful, right around the corner, there for just such emergencies. And anyway, your trickle of piss bound for the rivulet: where does it go? Into the reservoir by way of the well with its deep-grooved edges, timeless trace of ropes hauled up. Don't like what you're insinuating, no need to gripe, I didn't piss to piss everybody off. Then a disgusted Chwirrib spits on the ground, a viscous wad of phlegm splat on the stone pavement, jiggling gelatin.

Power vacuum, allowing bodies unbridled display in support of raucous, fast-moving card games at every turn: you, jack of hearts; me, ace of spades; I take all. The winner's peasant origins show through undisguised, unscorned: man of the backcountry, accent of the high plateaus crisscrossed by the Numidians, Algerian borderlands where all revolts begin, Kēf and Makthar, men and women upright, demonstrating refusal. Some come settle in the capital in search of adventure, rumors of El Dorado, putting some scrap of food on every table; following on the heels of some nephew or neighbor come to study law right here in the Zitūna, and who got himself a rich town lady and a civil service job; judge with tattooed forehead eaten away by some ineffectual attempt by a charlatan to erase the degrading traces of tattoo, leaving only diminished outlines and noticeable scars sometimes taken for a zebiba, mark of piety imprinted by one hundred thousand rak'at, compulsory and superfluous prostration causing the forehead to scrape the ground, carpet, flagstone, prayer mat, dust, or sand. And such notables as are unable through their own efforts to develop this distinguishing sign are free to call upon the services of surgeons specializing in zebiba enhancements: a reverse circumcision of the forehead, as it were.

Everyone's at it, playing and parleying, circles within circles, sacred arcaded courtyard revived, hypostyle hall left to the more resourceful among them to revitalize prayer and ritual, the ten-arched loggia open to the street, where over here shkubba players keep an eye on cheaters, over there aces take all, somewhere the sound of dice and dominos, elsewhere a game of chess between two refined elderly gentlemen, pederasts surrounded by handsome boys making faces and gesticulating, sticking out tongues at any eye that lingers too long. One a perfume merchant, rosy hands quavering, pastel jebba; another, pastry chef of princes, won over to this break with convention, observe him loquacious, bombastic; and a third, along for the ride, maker of leather slippers graced with redundant reproductions of desert imagery, pathetic icons, camels, swaying palms, cupola of marabout, the calm of oasis, face unadorned, unthreatened by the agrarian urge, the surly timelessness of cliché.

A spindly cat, each step a slackening of the body, winds through the circle of men and women chatting as they cut fresh pasta between thumb and index, hlālim, noodles to be dried in the sun before preparing the communal dish involving a sauce spiced with thyme, oregano, and guiddid, meat dried and salted, leftover from sacrificial lamb, blood flowing into courtyard drain, peace be upon Abraham, blood permeating lunar date that moves along the course of seasons, blood that waters anemones and roses, buttercups and small gardens, ripe pomegranates, bursting, autumnal wound.

Contentment in this broad and beautiful space. Today's words no longer explode on impact with arguments, decisions to be made, justified, deliberated. The city remains surrounded on all sides, yet no one panics, each experiencing an inner peace, power vacuum leaving those determined to resist—without eluding the violence of quarrels or hand-to-hand combat, the pact with death—neither repentant nor loyal. Each is prepared to fill the hollowed-out body with the redemption of defending the city with a multitude of energies bent upon resistance.

The sundial over by the well announces midday, zero shadow crouching beneath the line. Raids allow the insurgent city to survive. A returning party is greeted with applause after breaking through the barriers and making away with tons of fruit and vegetables, midnight spoils from the gardens of Sukra. The folks in Ariana helped us out, they say; they're ready to back us. Ariana: settlement of Jews and Andalusian refugees cohabiting, light of white and blue, tidy streets, town squares like little stage sets, harlequin or Punch and Judy, graveyard poignantly earthbound, salt plain culminating in a shott, then sand and sea.

Some other group, led by Saïda, sorceress rallied to the cause, woman of grand proportions, hurriedly giant-striding the streets, urgent tasks await, group disguised to pass for Europeans by accent, by dress, to cross into the modern city bristling with enemies rigged for battle, tanks and armor, sons of ordinary people in the pay of foreigners and compradors. Heading through the city, via the main avenue, past the cathedral across from the embassy, then by the theater and art gallery, turning at Avenue de Carthage, passing in front of the café terraces swarming with arrogant youth, casually joking, wasn't this merely the path of the sewer system, the most basic invention of an ersatz Paris, Left Bank in arrested development, mockery of outward signs, enveloped in a living farce, freed of feeling, full-time display that allows no one to deviate from the technocrat ritual, punch in punch out, surviving splendidly within the limited landscape.

The group marched onward, skirting the mayor's office, on their way to Jallāz, cemetery, truncated by a new highway, profanation acceptable only when perpetrated by the national government, eager as it is to ratify all the remaining decisions and infringements left unrealized by the colonial power, which had backed down in the face of popular protest. Civilization has its reasons, and the cemetery is but a seat of barbarism, memento mori to be hacked away with impunity.

Onward pushed the group to the slaughterhouse, where, in league with the watchman, they awaited dusk to begin their work. Some couldn't bear the sight of bovine blood running in rivers, prelude to the insatiable cannibalism that slumbers in all mankind. The sorceress gave the signal at nightfall. She was first to return to the cemetery, where she prospected, noting names and remains, among the freshly dug graves and indicated to her accomplices what they were to take: open up that grave and remove the heart; from this one, the liver; the choice based on the corpse's name and particular crime; from that one, the left eye; from this one, the spleen; here a set of false teeth in solid gold; there a left limb; and so on, until a strict selection of organs and dissected remains reconstituted the totemic fetish, restored to view and now reproduced all over the city, simulacrum of worship.

Those taking part in the expedition seem both fascinated and baffled by the disgusting, frightening spectacle being inflicted upon them: phantom passengers, dark night of necrophilia, slaughter of the deceased.

Now that she's ready, we don't know where to exhibit our puppet idol, nor how to stage her presentation, nor even how to come up with the words and gestures most apt to enchant us as we sing her praises.

Body stitched by the skillful hands of the sorceress, tall, slim Saïda of the superhuman voice, insistent laugh, lean arms lined with protruding blue veins: one prick of a needle and out spurts black blood against olive skin.

The organs sutured thus send the odd odor of symbolism wafting through the air: head of a woman; long, weightless hair stirred by the bubbles that appear in the formaldehyde wherein it bathes; the body shifting in its transparent cylinder with each move. Three-eyed: one sea green, the other blue, and the one in the middle of the forehead dusky and plaintive as a gazelle's. Large ears, wrinkled and hairy. A mouthful of gold teeth gleaming behind lips stiff and fleshy. Round-tipped nose, but with hints of the freed African slave. The neck long, slit once in a passion that's now anyone's guess, deadly quarrel now on public display. Narrow shoulders, long limbs, elegant bearing. The chest: four mothering breasts, Artemis of Ephesus or some unlikely incarnation of Ceres. Navel, fountain amid taut skin over slightly rounded belly, culminating in narrow hips. Overpowering rawness of a vagina now enlarged into flower or wound, scattering of hairs between two legs: thin, disjointed stems, knees missing, fine ankles, bony toes, inordinately long.

Here is the idol: now what? Fascinated townspeople rush from all quarters hoping to rule supreme over her fate. Storytellers are already prepared to make up a story, to celebrate her retrospective legend. The sorceress is promoted to high priestess, upon whom it is incumbent to step down at the first sign of incompetence. The musicians, players of rebab, utar, and ney, endeavor to hammer out tunes in her praise. The poets, demented vagrants that they are, manage to infuse otherwise blood-soaked lyrics with seasons of shadow and light to devise for her the most brilliant of eulogies.

Now what? What else, I said, well, out of a deep conviction: you need to mummify her. Yes, yes, embalm her. But who knows the mummification technique? Let's go see Ya'qūb, the Jewish goldsmith, an alchemist proficient in ancient sciences. He surely knows a thing or two about mummies. That's right, he's been to Egypt, and his father was member of the rival sect of archeologists, grave robbers who'd memorized the locations of mysterious ancient tombs now known only to them.

We leave the idol, this anthropomorphic reconstitution of myth, right on the flagstones in her cylinder. We exit via the door that opens onto the wool souk, in search of Ya'qūb. Most of the shops are closed, the covered souks mostly deserted. No sign of people shopping for carpets, hours and days of labor, sweat, desiccated lungs, twisted fingers, offering cheap exoticism to some, decryption of Providence to others, via this plush pilgrimage, return of the master pilgrim enthroned in his shop, gum arabic to sweeten the mouth, cleansing waters from the sacred well, zemzem, rebirth and purification to resume life's blank page, reunion with his fitra, his innate temperament, blank slate that awaits only the reed qalam and ink of days for the feverish birthing of an inaugural calligraphy, ivory bartered in the Sudan, ancient electric amber, coral from ear-splitting depths, rare pearl and wondrous shell, flora and fauna deep within sand, chest exploded, lungs burst, nostrils destroyed.

Picking up the pace, we skirt the garments market, items auctioned, today obsolete, for whoever wants to dress up simply helps himself to the bounty: no shortage of pass keys. But apart from the ferocious delight in reckless transgression in the early hours, no one complains of an urge to plunder. An afternoon of ransacking was enough to overcome age-old fears of bullying and resentment.

Along the way, the street grows steeper and the crowd more intense in the saddler's quarter, the area now diverted from its original vocation to become an arms manufactory, mystery of fire and blacksmith smells replacing the fragrance of leather and saddles that once permeated this street that widens to accommodate the green-white-red catafalque of the martyr, beheaded, or so says legend.

The massive gate to the goldsmith's souk is shut. Hard knock, admission obtained, only a chosen few among us granted passage through this most closely guarded street that shelters recipes for explosive devices used to great effect against those enemies seeking to breach the ramparts, impregnable until now. Goldsmiths transmuted into pyrotechnists, gunsmiths, making grenades, shells, and sundry incendiary devices.

Where is Ya'qūb? He's not here; like a good many of our ghetto-bound Jewish fellows, he doesn't dare leave the hāra. We have to find him, you know where he lives, take us to his home. One goldsmith refuses, pleading busyness. But Master Mahmūd . . . a laugher, white-haired, himself a goldsmith in service of the revolution, probably lone member of his family to have unwaveringly supported the movement and just for fun, to go with the flow of the people's will, involving no act of faith or show of bravado, no abuse, no monstration, no penchant for scandal. Adept at rhyme, at a ripe old age, toothless, ever smiling, impressed by rats, possessing detailed knowledge of their ways, their tribal hierarchies and disciplines, the only species capable of ruining man and his cities. Politically shrewd, pleasure-seeking, a great friend to the hāra, he speaks the language of all-night revelry, respects Jewish customs and holidays, learned their poetry, recites Genesis in Aramaic, has uncovered the secrets of cabalistic interpretation, settles disputes regarding peripateticism of the Toledano and Hispanically Judeo-Arab sort, contests Avicenna's theory of emanation, combines discursive reason with the solemnity of the vagina, delights in elliptical and allusive language, lover of several Arab and Jewish entertainers, old-fasioned in taste and dress, a word lover, heartbreaker, keeper of the night, nocturnal wing, lunar matrix of riddles, noria cascading water: creaking waterwheel, wood imbibed, whispering trickle, jasmine and sweet summer, hatred of the occupier and what came before, neither is of us by body, by will: mockery of the cops and other prospective betrayers who, once they've agreed to kill, nonetheless seek to save face.

Master Mahmūd, dodging any further discussion, decides to take us to his friend Ya'qūb's house: yes, he surely knows how to mummify; what doesn't he know how to do, for that matter? On many a late night, he has disclosed to me a secret alloy unknown to the enemy, employed to manufacture indestructible devices. Spry as a hopping bird, glassy eyed, unshaven, speech hindered by inability to pronounce dental consonants.

A rowdy, wildly gesticulating crowd moves through Souk al-'Attarīne: magic and remembrance of the dead turn the everyday into feast and exhilaration, consumes all sorrow. Some purchase long, twisted tapers adorned in bright, candy-colored satin ribbons; others are kneading henna, recorder of marriage and mourning. Here's one bargaining for a rare takchi, device useful in orienting a search for buried treasure. This other one ducks into the back of a shop where a famed creator of talismans reads the stars via dusty translations of extracts from the *Enneads* of Plotinus, from whom he most often borrows insipid analogies between various bodies, microcosms as eternal reflection of macrocosm.

Master Mahmūd greets an old friend with open arms, invitation to dance, tossing out sardonically expressive onomatopoetic jibes at random passersby, genuine colloquy of ferocious beasts troubling a club-footed, hoarse-voiced beggar who cannot be persuaded that his mendicant days are over, as he persists in calling upon gods, prophets, and saints, let me have something to eat. Then, giving a Turkish salute, Master Mahmūd is off in a rush. I warn him that he'd best not get caught up again in an apologia for Kemal Ataturk, an obsession that landed him in prison during that era of bland, harmless agitation against the French Protectorate among the city's notables. Such adulation today is liable to clash with the current political atmosphere, since this same Turkish hero, unyielding re-builder of the State, is the role model of a certain person who fancies himself a shrewd manipulator, a real political wizard: he whom our revolt in progress is aimed at unseating: decidedly unnamable, not so much out of caprice or coyness, but because we hope our reticence will make us seem especially gracious to those who have figured it out, initiated or not.

Into the leather-crafts souk, fragrance of hides tanned with su-mac and nutgall, shadow striated with light, green the dominant color, metonymy of the city. The women, chilled barefoot, consider nabbing some wool-lined babouche slippers, hesitating between a smile and surrender to the serpent's wiles: body heat radiates be-neath the veil.

Hand slapping water, waves escaping bucket, dust-maintenance man sprinkles the uneven cobblestones. Other man in green turban arranges his moustache caressingly. There. Description of detail de-livering neither substance nor excitement; rather, a wandering eye rummaging about, sometimes distractedly, transcribing the street, thus allowing its nuances the opportunity to escape from any official surveillance, any archive, any spy, any bureaucracy, any orientalist outrage, by the skin of their newly acquired, distorting abstraction.

The parade continues, at its head a spry, jaunty, yet temperamental Master Mahmūd, mood darkening without warning, switching to melancholy murkiness all at once, pursuing the echo of distant laughter; catching his face, in a moment of repose, in the act of sadness; or else seeing through the slit of an open door as it slams shut on some inner turmoil.

Go on, keep moving, the others are waiting; this is no time to be reveling in drink and pipe in the backroom of some artisan's shop, some wasp-faced engraver with an agile burin, admiring the brass platters where he unfurls his arabesques. No, says one of the guildsmen, we have to make it over to Ya'qūb's and fast, and get him to help us. The people won't wait indefinitely. But no amount of prodding or entreaty can prevail over Master Mahmūd's dreamy desire for a little toke, just enough to feel weightless, to overcome his nervous clumsiness, heart tempest tossed, here's a rib-cracking, chest-shattering cough.

Just a short stop at the smoke shop: the proprietor wants to close up and come along. No, don't bother. Master Mahmūd picks up the pace, bellowing in surprise like a madman on the loose, carried away by the high stakes of uncertainty; we follow behind, along an insidiously plotted itinerary, lanes and alleyways, unexpected detours, hairpin bends and knots, goodness, so many dead ends.

On our way again: detecting the wrong-turn inference of a cul-de-sac, we figure that Master Mahmūd is trying to get us off track, only to pick up the broken thread on a main thoroughfare packed with swarming masses, sunken eyes glistening with sleeplessness. Shop counters become forum, endless talk and high spirits. Others hollow-cheeked and weeping all over the countertops, acting out their inconsolable passions in front of cloth merchants, mottled colors, jasper variegation, gaudily floral, caftans, taffeta, percale, brushed cotton, velvet from Homs, satins in dusk or dawn tones, bougainvillea: the Grana, the Livorno quarter, with its endless gesticulation, no purchases but much counsel as to which shade or tint goes with which complexion or eye color; people are preparing to dress up to fete the idol; despite fatigue from the previous night's excesses, the passersby don't seem the least bit tired, slowed down, or inconvenienced by this wasted energy. Apparent inaction not to be construed as vegetative but indeed a serene availability. At the end of the street, before getting to the empty lot, the crowd disperses, apart from clusters still hanging on every word of whispered talk in the back of a shop emptied of its displays and merchandise.

The nested ghetto of the hāra is set apart from the city by its state of desertion: sole remaining inhabitants are Jews though self-acknowledged as being Arab in body, in celebration, in sex, in food, in song, in dance, in their secret lore and eloquence, in their feelings and their reason. Most Jews have Europeanized, sworn enemies of their own past, rallying to the call of upward mobility or new cultural identities, confined now to the suburbs, when they haven't decamped entirely, agents of comprador capitalism, animating the city imposed upon us by Europe, phantoms of the metropolis, vine-covered villas greeting the dawn against retreating cypress, seminal infusion of pollen, filling the musty vacuum of springtime, sun and dust devil. They insinuate themselves in harmony with the body that corrupts the Arab world, Israel, display window through which they entice consenting rulers, giddily fascinated by the prodigious success of the occidental machine beneath the torrid Oriental sun, taking it as a model by which to reinforce their own increasingly dilapidated caricature through assimilation and transposition.

The ghetto, muffled and self-enclosed, affecting in its awkward silence. Will daylight ease our admission? With each period of change, upheaval, the moment a crisis appears on the verge of major event, the ghetto, prison of the self, shuts its doors. And nothing could prompt its surrender, not even the crushing fury of riot turned pogrom, forcing the gates.

Master Mahmūd gives the secret whistle. No response save concealed wariness of this breach of their usual schedule. History of oppression, source of temporary respite: why won't they open up? Fear of scapegoating? Sacrifice sheds light. And such hysterical cities certainly did produce their share of atrocities: condemning the Jewish community that, in periods of pestilence, knew best how to defend itself behind its walls, barrier against any infection; the hate-mongering necrophiliacs bringing the seeds of plague to the thirsting mouths of that vigilant minority, cloistered that they might be spared: how often did the ghetto experience the deadly surprise of succumbing to devastating attacks of typhus or cholera after a tributary aqueduct brought them drinking water infected by the stinking runoff from where the majority washed its dead!

Think of that lone Jewish shoemaker, left behind by the great exodus, accumulation of ambiguities and pacts with the invaders. There was once the Soleil Levant, favorite bar to puffy-eyed shrews, ghosts of their former selves, fish tank for a lazy afternoon, post-menopausal celibacy, little horde of the defunct, creaky music hall, limp circus, fortune stunted by braids trussing buttocks to the softness of seats, ladies and widows deep in gossip: say, that one over there, he's married now; I hear Jacky can't get it up anymore; look how made-up she is; let me borrow your lipstick, won't you? smells nice; I could use a drink, too; lend me a couple dūros, and I'll get us some nuts. Big breasts, bigger bottoms, cheeks smeared red, swollen, mouths with heart-shaped clusters of wrinkles in each corner: this spectacle, this migrating zoo, decamped north to Paris, to the *Vielleuse* in Belleville, thereby depriving Tunis's chic *passage* quarter of its opulent clientele, leaving the Jewish shoemaker alone, melancholy, longwinded, a she-wolf offering her teat in a foul-smelling alcove, giving friendship only to lash out in self-pity as soon as your back is turned.

Master Mahmūd calls yet again but the ghetto remains a sealed tomb. Are they fearless, those Jews I saw aiding the cause by helping to manufacture arms; that is, by ascertaining the correct ratio between melting metal and consuming fire? All Jewish cities have been emptied of flavor, both culinary and sexual; what a horrible fate is that of resentment and submission! Does anyone know a medina Jew without a story about some youthful face-to-face encounter with death, a cunning kids' game, malicious torture of bird or ant, delectable show of force, a refinement of pleasure, of libido—if only to crush any mute admission of powerlessness?

Like in Marrakesh, where one just barely got away after being cornered by a determined band of street kids, between vision of blood and imprint of a hand coated in henna upon the turquoise wall in the dead-end alley: with survival in the balance and torment imminent, courage parted his lips whence issued the prophy-lactic Koranic verses that forced his young attackers to take to their heels: *Say: he is God, the one and only.*

Again, in Marrakesh, coming up out of the folds of memory via a sequence of signs, led by the above anecdote: I saw the mellāh practically deserted by its Jews. And I saw, along the lively itinerary of my licentious strolling, between the mellāh and Jāmaa al-Fnā, by way of the souk selling buckets and rubber items meant to be im-mersed in water, a technique for recycling truck tires to be carved into items other than sandal soles, between ghetto and heart of city: music, serpents, flies, and storytelling; magic, charms, herbs, and medicines; sex; madness and audience; I spotted and followed the apparently serene stroll of a few Jews, an isolated group, skullcaps loaded with that inextricable binary composed of the oppression of a minority and the incurable wound of Zionism. Brings to mind the idealized image in a document showing the Jews of Marrakesh applauding the arrival of the French invaders, that day of mourn-ing for the defeated city.

An equally irreconcilable hope urges Master Mahmūd to keep knocking, in expectation that someone might open. Could it be they've all left, slyly under cover of night, one of those mass de-partures encouraged by Zionist propaganda, emptying Tiznit or so many other Berber Ksours, such as Ifran in the Lesser Atlas Mountains, scree and tattoo on the rock face, heat like a furnace as we pass through scattered argan trees, relatively dense prelude to the desert.

No, not this time: assumptions prove false and the heavy door creaks open a crack, while negotiations nonchalantly commence:

stand by us now, share our anger, our forward motion, join our movement and free speech will be yours: our actions will put all discontent to rest, whether it issues from common sense or just wanton selfishness; we shall decide whether the vanquished will live out their days in chaos or fulfillment until at last they reach their points of no return; and notwithstanding the massacre required by the intractable degradation of all bodies, we shall never sign warrants for your exclusion or death: thus did we speak all at once to the emissary. Furtively, Ya'qūb comes out, recognizes Master Mahmūd in surprise, and invites us to go in; and in we go.

Chickpeas, cumin, fava beans, artichokes, fennel, boukha: have something to eat, here's a drink, you're all welcome. One for all and all for pleasure, I say. Ya'qūb, bandy-legged, eagle-eyed, a cheerful voice. Have some bottarga, it's good for you, makes you strong. Master Mahmūd peremptorily announces the reason for our visit: do it, in the name of our friendship, don't let the boys down. From a window looking onto the patio, we hear children squabbling. Women leaning on a balustrade opposite watch us with amusement; certain ones, young and lovely, pale-skinned and silent, as if crazy with desire, awaiting the nuptial call. Stairway zigzags up to the rooftop terrace divided by a column striped red and green in a downward spiral.

Ya'qūb answers promptly: yes, I do know the art of mummification; yes, I'll come help. But what a mistake to have assembled limbs from fresh corpses to marinate in formaldehyde; you should have let them all macerate in a natron solution. I'm certain the error can be corrected, though you ought not have grafted the viscera together, and the abdomen needs to be filled with linen soaked in resin. Take your time, let me take mine, I need to focus, to find the necessary instruments and ingredients in that mess in my attic.

Master Mahmūd beckons one of the young beauties, pale eyes, peach skin, a vaguely debauched air about her: Hassiba sings us songs of the trembling night, of the moon and its mad pranks, of love and what unites and divides us. Accompanying herself on the lute, timeless delight, the day culminates in music, voice carried away by passion: indescribable nostalgia for the night that is in fact the splendor of the body, stifling mingled breaths, the sky a riot of stars drawing nearer, raising a toast to what the eye beholds. Caressing the strings, fingers slide along the neck, agile lips reach for and circle around the high notes, sending a shiver down each listener, freed of all ideas and reason: castles carried on the hint of breeze that rises stuttering after sundown.

Hassiba vibrates to the words, adjusting tune to text, drawing from the songs of eastern Algeria, Constantine, from the repertoire of Raymond, the one they called Sheikh Raymūn, celebrating in melancholic memory the valiant struggle of the city against the Christian, the Nazarene, the killer colonizer, Stalingrad of Numidia: Arabs and tribes of wild wandering, to you we say glory.

Like a tree gone dormant in the cold season, Hassiba recovers her secret resistance: why don't you come along and sing with us at the Zitūna? There's a procession tomorrow, freshly minted words; why shut yourself in with rats and tedium, O tulip of the lofty lover's lair? Hear my plea and join us. But she beseeches me to cast aside eloquence and argument, for nothing could persuade her to leave: come see me whenever you like, she says; here is the signal that will allow you passage at all hours, but do not ask that I accompany you into town: neither mosque, nor maqsūra, nor secret alcove could contain my demands. A tad cheeky, a touch brazen, she alone has the knack of thwarting my overtures.

She lifts lyrics from Raymūn, shot dead by the FLN, bon vivant victim of the Organization's battle against debauchery: it was forbidden to run a brothel, to frequent taverns, to smoke kif, to partake of alcohol; one had to be devoted heart and soul to the revolution, to set an example, be unforgiving of unchecked hearts and voices: people were helpless to counter the harmful effects of these blood resolutions handed down by the state of total war: judgments struck terror into hearts while bodies moved about as if in a trance.

I'm familiar with the most Jewish among Arab cities: battered by the ocean, rough swells on one side—rocked by the icy brine—and on the other, stagnant sea. Between beach and scala, the ocean is domesticated into port, ideal set for an operetta, clowns and pirates: Essaouira, formerly Mogador, spotless rooftop terraces, all outward signs proclaiming harmony, stars of Islam, of David, reconciled to each other, Kufic square of prophetic fortune, baraka, Solomon's seal, the green of conquest splashed onto doors; the same components basic to each ideology, so few they can be counted on one hand: outline of cypresses, five- and six-pointed stars, angular arabesques animating polygons, cursive ones braided about circles. But above each door, lintels bear these figures mingled, each example utterly unique. The colors are green, blue, and white, rarely a red.

Such serenity is disturbed perhaps by the departure of the city's Jews: there remains a community, once a majority, of only ninety-three; the city of a hundred synagogues, now turned into attics, warehouses, wretched dusty dampness. Visit some, curious and eclectic, rococo furnishings, clocks and mirrors, lamps and chandeliers, textiles and Torahs, lecterns and candelabra, plain tiling adorning the floors and thresholds, heavy keys reluctant to turn in their locks.

City of asserted Jewishness, walls permeated by a Hebraic atmosphere despite desertion and dispersion. There remain only the elders, women married to Muslim notables, a few sea-salt tinted teenage girls, a woman in her seventies who runs a guest house and restaurant, the Atlantique, best food in the city, though not the most sanitary.

Terrace glows in the moonlight, blinding silver dust, head severed by pain, body riddled with Artemis's arrows, devoured by the hounds that tore Actaeon to shreds; somewhere the ocean feels, sounds furious, roaring nearby yet invisible, infusing the nocturnal air, lingering: this place plagued by headaches, visions, phantoms, and specters swooping down before the eyes, monsters in flight, swift steeds cleaving the star-studded midnight blue, the sharpness of the vision more disconcerting than frightening. Back down at ground level, through street after street, excited at the sound of the bell announcing the evening show at the movie theater, karate and cowboys, carpenters and marquetry shops close for the night, chests and tables that might have been beautiful, but the slapdash work reveals more a lack of basic craft than the sort of arrogant mistake, caused by whatever symmetry-ruining creative quiver, that marks the inspired craftsman. Rush toward the main street, breathe in its desertedness, straight ahead but lasciviously slow along the barely noticeable curves. Weep below the arch of the starkly monumental gate, yellow hewn stone, mix of too many styles, a form that calls to mind—by the vertical superposition of two rightly articulated architectural structures—the Porta Pia, where I sobbed one night, deranged, out of my mind, empty of reason or feeling, abrupt end to a lingering sadness, Trevi Fountain, Quirinal Palace where I reprimanded an impolite guard, dousing my face in fire, arms at the crossroads of the four fountains, breaking into the church of Santa Maria della Vittoria, banging forehead and fists against the glittering marble of Saint Theresa in ecstasy, supreme orgasm that tears through the dead of night, that lasts and lasts. Bruised hands on lace, wild eyes, suppressed moans, aging voice that dazed me all the more: you come to exhibit yourself before the supposed pleasure of the mother at the moment of your conception, avert your gaze and cease to taint yourself with this silence that gnaws at you from within.

Nothing more to say, save the overwhelming intensity of weeping, plunging me into the sickly waters of the Fountain of Moses. Caked in filth and slime, I staggered over to the Porta Pia, fell before the portico and, recovering my composure, I was struck—in a kind of revelation—by the subtle intelligence of its rediscovered structure, randomness of monuments, benediction of sources, culmination of multiple schools; and now in Essaouira, riveted to its nightmare of typhoons, of immersion, of flood: groaning waters, a permeating dampness, a milestone perhaps, an obvious sign, for all to see, make-believe menace, experienced now as a daily torment: is this why Essaouira was chosen to celebrate a minority experience, to push back the boundaries of the ghetto so that Jews might become masters of a city by sheltering behind lofty ramparts, warding off with mingled curses and prayers the incessant fury of the ocean, testing the uses of vigilance?

I embrace Hassiba, promising to visit again soon, and exit on the heels of Master Mahmūd and Ya'qūb with his satchel in hand; and all the others, simple folk fascinated by the universal, muted fragility of this hermetically sealed daily existence wherein the Jews' minority space is organized, and they make no fuss—dipping their bread into honey and olive oil, unctuous sweetness—over the danger that threatens to disrupt their cohesion by further scatterings.

The news of the soon-to-be embalmed idol has spread throughout the city and beyond. Converging by the hundreds and thousands on the Zitūna, streets are drained of their normal pedestrian traffic, making it easier for us to pick up the pace. Ya'qūb: alert, tight little steps, but quick, despite his age. Public fountains, usually swarming with buckets, seem desolate, apart from the murmur of water. I attempt to drink from a spigot, flow unpredictable: frustratingly slow trickle or powerful, choking gush.

Shops shuttered, lending our steps the echo of abandonment. Every so often, a nimbly determined silhouette rushes past, adding a touch of enigma to this air of desolation, olfactory memory now coming nose to nose with the smells of the city, odor of perfume and sweat: rival sorceresses to ours, the learned surgeon who stitched together the idol, are gathering at the Zāwiya Sidi Mahrez, with green ostrich eggs and other relics of the celebrated saint, and will decide on their collective course of action: either join forces with their triumphant co-sorceress, or mobilize against her, possibly to their peril.

Addressing these shrewish dissidents, Master Mahmūd shouts obscenities that fail to reach their ears, though these are hardly unused to vulgarity. Go and report back what they decide at their meeting! No, replies the designated spy: we should either go en masse and present our case to them, or abstain from any underhanded tactics. Let them work out their own disagreements; they'll come over to our side in the end.

The city prepares to celebrate the re-membering of the idol: from afar, certain streets reverberate with the rumblings besieging the Zitūna; closer by, certain alleys, whether sheltered or swept by violent winds, offer nothing to the ear but the sparse habitation of silence. A few late arrivals rush to melt into the grand gathering. The closer one gets, the more impatient the stragglers appear. In time, the opacity of the crowd seems to be obeying some physical law demanding that all gaps caused by diffusion must in time be filled—solids and voids, clouds and fissures—rendering them solid, a skin of invisible pores, cells woven so tightly together as to require a complete unraveling for anyone to slip through without breaking our chain with sharp-edged shoving.

People in clusters around the ramified omphalos of the city, occupying every level that affords a view, an earshot. Let us pass, break through the ranks: we infiltrate the mob, in the wake of Mahmūd, the master unraveler. Streets, rooftop terraces, shops, inner courtyards, all swarming with people. Some are resigned to the inconvenient spot they've landed in, others anxiously seek a more favorable vantage. The nimblest among them manage for no particular reason to keep a low profile, Zen-eyed, cleaving the crowd as they progress, fish in water.

The anxiety of expectation is expressed in their eyes. Festivity, prelude to the offering, is latent in every body. All colors harmonize; who gives a damn whether what we wear is quality or fake: our clothing pink, red, black; our women in faux gold and silver lace; ankle bracelets jingle; pendants, drop earrings, and amulets, gilded brass, swinging, tinkling against bushy blackness of hair; jewelry worn as belts or in cords that highlight the deceptive splendor of quivering breasts. Heavenly ersatz silk dress torn when caught on the satchel of Ya'qūb wearing a celadon tunic with gold fringe. Perfumed water, red costumes, cowry shell and pearl necklaces, metallic bangles crinkling the air, tintinnabulation with every raising of an arm, every shuddering of a breast. Combs, scarves, hair darkened jet black with mardūma, trinkets transmuted by proud bearing and attitude into incomparable jewels. Good luck, fish and hands, baubles made for a heave of breasts. Planted in the lobe, earrings, openwork crescent with dove in midflight: gold and silver tossed into city foundries in open resistance are no longer material for show. No highlight is lacking for she whose finery glimmers most brightly.

Almost anything is dress-up: we are liberated, mellowed by our fete's gravitas, we megalomaniac Arabs love to dazzle, even with junk jewelry, love to rub shoulders with anything that glitters, make frills from any fabric that titillates. Glad rags on parade, a display of sensuality! Enormous broaches and fibulae, trees or windows, heft of Eros, measure of what the costume conceals, hold bodices in place: gleaming new women's tunics whose colors rub off and into the body's, drowning, sinking to the bottom of a bath of violet and mauve, blood red and vermillion, plum and saffron.

Despite the intrepid forward march of Mahmūd, there is no avoiding the jostling exhaustion of hacking a path through the indivisible mob. We arrive at the old Janissary barracks, converted into a library; on the heels of the master, we enter: courtyard garden, serene, hospitable edifice. Catching our breath and taking turns drinking cool water from deepest well: the heavy sweetness of water!

Ya'qūb stretches out on the ground, cool flagstone beneath narrow portico, cabled columns in repeating tricolor green, white, red. He issues a dreadful cry: apostasy is calling, forces gathered, a flying dragon, flaming from its ears and pendulous jaws, face mired in the dung of the apostate, renouncing the one God: join our ranks, each a renegade from his religion, illusion itself. Master Mahmūd silently conducts the ceremony that engages our expectations, deflecting all calls for the divine presence; we drink of this tonic that readies us for quick action; to clear the ground of myth, of the rags and tatters of rite. Ya'qūb's cries fade; standing now, and as if inebriated, he fills a bucket with water, slowly washes his face, scrubs his arms and armpits: a redirection of the ablution rite, no longer an act of purification but one of readiness, he says: let us prepare for what awaits us; everyone shall attend to what he must; the operation to be carried out is a tricky one; I enjoin you to breathe deeply, to soak your bodies for a more focused and precise meditation.

We burn Ya'qūb's celadon tunic, swapping it for the same in citrine, conserving the crucial green hue. We exit through the other door, making our way down the former Rue de l'Eglise, hoping to cover this short distance before falling back into the unavoidable snare of the mob. A darker street, though no less congested than the one running parallel that we'd just now come through. But Ya'qūb's new and somehow heroic determination supplants the caution that Mahmūd was counseling—a hindrance to our opening up a secret passage through the crowd. Force like a staff parting the Red Sea, we snake through dense dunes of humanity blocking the magnetic space of the Zitūna. The stairs to the main door greet our swift egress out from under the vaulted street. A handful of companions on the lookout recognize us and strive to clear a path through the final corridor.

The courtyard, diligently renovated by ingenious invention, is discovered transformed into a vast stage where so many bodies, sects, and guilds prepare the fundamental spectacle to better garner future allegiance. Saïda is keeping vigil over the idol, now sheltered in the central prayer room, where we finally make our entrance beneath the glare of the pompously vulgar Venetian crystal chandeliers, in the shadow of oil lamps and candles, buds of flame that swell and contract, light's breath that bolsters the steps of our band of the faithful: cautious treading upon rough mats and soft rugs. Here and there, circles of men and women in silent meditation, in persistent search of a flawless ritual: gestures invented as simulacrum of self, enchantment of blood, channeling the mirage of identity via this studious odor of sweaty feet.

In the part of the room ordinarily reserved for women, nubile splendor, male and female, dressed in ample silks, transparent to the body, are conversing in groups of two, three, four, fondling one another, repeating words of love consumed with desire upon the litter bed, Ya'qūb and Saïda transporting the idol into the alcove, the maqsūra, where in normal times the sheikh imām would wait in repose, mystery of entry, aura of hierarchy, before passing before the mihrab and on to the minbar, staircase and scepter of the commander of the faithful, in order to preach, on the appropriate day, speaking in veiled references, understood by all but the uninitiated, the intransigence of morality, built upon the fault line of universal vulnerability.

The skilled twosome of Ya'qūb and Saïda, assisted by Master Mahmūd and three others in our company, undo the linen wrappings and soak them in a mixture of natron and pitch. We then empty the formaldehyde into a marble basin, to let the idol dry out before tarring it. The stench emitting from this drainage process is stomach-turning, vertigo-inducing, the ground spins beneath my feet. The reek triggers the organ of nausea and the stomach cannot help but purge, a hollow that engulfs, that dims vision, opens a yawing hole in my resoluteness, breach in body's flotilla prior to collision, final gaze through a window that bespeaks imminent abyss.

The preparation of the mysterious, foul-smelling mixture— a single draught would render bearable the too human presence moving around the idol—proves too much for me: I collect what remains of my wherewithal and bound out of the theater of operation, contrary to instinct, ejecting myself from the maqsūra, a ray piercing solid matter. And by some miracle of speed, there opens, then shuts, in one movement, the Ottoman-style emblazoned double doors enclosing an alcove.

Moaning, I steady myself against one of the varnished Ottoman armoires loaded with books, crackling with insects at work. Shattered images, a divided world, woozy visions. And the smell of the idol, like that of the potion, still clings to my stinging nostrils. Arms crossed over panting chest, eyes open, vibrations and veils, multicolored bursts of light drape the world and streak across the incandescent diadem arc of the firmament, blinding trail of kinetic stipple swirling in my head, diverting the ear from the ambient din toward deciphering discrete sounds from street and sahn, the courtyard given over to strident music, mix of noise and instruments: the solemn call of Tibetan horns, inaugural incursion of vibrant little cymbals striking extra-aural sensory regions: infrasonic music, chaos of tuning, each instrumentalist off on his own without ever meeting up with another to play a joint melody; sidereal hum accompanying the breakdown of the body brought about by a heightening of the olfactory faculties.

My eyes now focused, veils lifted, calm restored, I discover a black man dressed in white standing at the rostrum before a large lectern, reciting the text of the future, rejuvenated revelation, a new craving for reiteration of the word, no longer immutable but transformed into a call for an uncommon spirit ceasing to respect official law, the signature that standardizes behavior. But the swaying of the upper body remains at root Koranic. To the cadence of these whispered phrases, needle perforating the face, I rediscover the world once relieved of my discomfort.

The same circles confer, the same adolescents cuddle. Still unable to attain a standing position, queasiness returns. Lying there on waves of silence, I engage in dialogue with the numerous slender beams supporting the vaults that span the room; my eye races at the speed of perspective over the shifting columns, and I recall dancing barefoot on the powdery flagstones of Ibn Tūlūn, a day of defiance triggered by the desolate solitude of the place. The divided space obeys the mechanics of a dream; the shadow of this Cairene mosque is remembered as vaster, more varied, more musical, more sufficient to the task, more systematic: perhaps it reigns so supreme thanks to its lack of clutter or furniture, these armoires, thrones, carpets, colors, chandeliers, restorations, adornments, paintings, diversions, civilization's invasion of inhabited space, beliefs so diverse, each celebrating its landscape—desert, steppe, mountain, sea, she-camel, or ship—the urge to relate to one's birthplace, nostalgia for the south or mercantile fascination for the ascendency of the north.

There is a kind of dreamlike unity about ruins, and I am unable to celebrate the singular significance of this ceremony that moves through the body to free it from the obsessive fear of its own reflection. Uncanny recovery of self in this chance encounter with vertigo. The body is rekindled as a fragile other. And the square of blue that hovers over the sprawling courtyard of Ibn Tūlūn is too vast, it's enough sky to stretch over a city, skirting the monumental cupola, fountain and pristine water. I have so often simulated a love for old stones, rehearsed the memory of so many cities that my vision is now a blur.

See the towering height of the Sultan Hassan mosque: there, the walls soar higher than cathedrals, shrinking the view of sky captured by the confines of its courtyard, as defined by its four iwān: patch of blue so moving, unleashing the sobs so avidly yearned for, liberating the body.

The parade of images sends me beyond the hall, courtyard more than ever dominated by games, jousts, feverish rehearsal of our procession. The fragrance of incense wafts over the hall, a reminder that my jostled body is suspended somewhere between alcove and mid-morning sunshine.

The reader rocks and sways, kneeling at his lectern, a bobbing turban. The circles pursue deliberation, a posture reviving the grand and uniform theological tradition, endless consensual commentary upon immutable law.

Al-Azhar, its two halls clumsily open one to the other, two epochs separated by levels of unequal height, functionally similar and complimentary. Mercenary penchant among those who teach, centuries-old submission to the Word, perfection of reading methods, backed by a plethora of powers: Fātimid, Ayyūbid, Circassian, Bahri, Mamlūks on parade, Khedives; a people surveyed and mapped by the benediction of doctors of the faith, totalitarian sheikhs, sects paralyzing the true fire, man's faith perpetually consumed in a hearth that quells any ardor or rebellious flame, bellows at hand to check disruptive urges, to contain faith's harshness, to eradicate its chaos, quicksilver and gold.

Wine alone, whether real or imagined, makes for an unbridled outlet, allows access to the three sexual states in each perfect mourner, each madman secluded between heaven and blasphemy upon the steep and eroded slopes of Cairo's Moqattam Hills: Ibn Fāridh, your wine alters experience, inducing pleasurable withdrawal into the self, yet the very confines of such soul-searching open the mind onto a vastness that sparks an intuition of what will become history.

Al-Qarawīn, pedantic gem, archaic presence, gangrene of the just, omphalos among the thousand other openings more visible to the sky, nothing but void among so many other wells that decide how water and sky are to be apportioned. Here education is subjected to ritual, designed to garner protection from the powerful, keeping them at bay through imitation; a corpus of fetwas is deposited there, all questioning in vain. But things seem more severe here, the hierarchy more deep-rooted, science less successful, punishment more capricious. The tradition of call for justice has students, vindictive tolbas, pouring through the back streets in search of some opinion to start a fight over, striving unsuccessfully to endorse the triumph of the city over the countryside that forever escapes its grasp.

For never has Fez been able to subjugate the tribes, north and south, whenever the mountainfolk would rise up in deadly reprisal. The law encourages them to support a pseudo-unitary course. The legal expert, self-satisfied rhetorician, will tend ad hoc to his business; doctrinally, he will perpetuate the all-absorbing gaze fascinated by the promise of the East.

The Zitūna, by way of closure to this erudite triad in the death throes, is here and now being recast by an emboldened people that have had their fill of returning to their roots. If only to redress the ancient ritual, to uproot the ancestral tree, become a gallows for anyone who calls it an outrage. Thoughts of grafting must be banished, for the branch thus attached shall never mature into soothing shade for a wandering musician. Reap seed and sow underfoot, to test what is considered barren soil.

A certain boy's father taught him in this eminent mosque: hear the words of a consummate scholar of the hadīth, the law reverberating among the polytheistic columns and capitals, Satan be cursed, reclaimed for the sake of the true faith. A father honest and bookish, so unassuming in the way he way he transmitted the precision of his knowledge, whose various compartmented subjects could be blurred together only at great risk to life and limb, out of obstinate respect for the letter, the hard-and-fast formulation of law, to be handed down exactly as it was received.

But how can such mathematical accuracy be imposed where fable might have better expressed the subject at hand, which defies all measure? My first quarrel with this father broke out over my scrambling the words of a recitation: rebellious, I couldn't stand having to regurgitate verses of the Koran from memory. I would pout and go speechless, or mix up words or phrases; sometimes, either as bid for personal appropriation or a symptom of encroaching madness, a normal word would sound disturbingly odd to me, so I would gleefully change it, distort its meaning by syllabic inversion. Semantic breakdown, tears, angry father. "The Bride of the Book," a sūra that used to intrigue me because of its mysterious double sonority, its indefinitely repeated doubling, all in the name of the twofold, sun, star, moon, Orient, Occident, tree, seed, scale, weight: two of each kind, two seas divided by that which separates, barzakh, isthmus, two lands, twice Eden and two others beyond, two springs, ruby and pearl: and to coral I wanted to add carnelian. And the refrain, repeated, in the spirit of doubt, which questions God and untruth: is man capable of uncovering the mystery of creation?

Imagining something brilliant and perpetually all-consuming, I was quite undaunted by the penance of eternal flame. I enjoyed looking at anything that burned before my eyes: flames, sparks, glowing embers, incandescent matter that evoked hellfire and restored me to an unyielding and otherwise inaccessible state of serenity. My hand is burning, my blood racing. A balcony onto this grandiose spectacle of magnetic force, mineral transformed by the heat of hell, Gehenna inhaling fire, abyss facing Eden, below the furnace, above the shaded garden: the choice a troubling one. How to celebrate myself between these two worlds, sinister left or dexterous right, low or lofty? Tempted to yield to what is known concretely of the two alternatives. The hūris, fantasized intensely, after all, more than just a cliché or milky disgrace, taste of honey, the hūris, feminine perfection, flesh reflecting the eye's gaze, short-limbed and attracting the energy of inalterable desire, driving bodies out of their minds; not marble statues, but carnally chaste: prior to us, no man or jinn, no creature of fire or clay, has touched them with hands or gaze.

This father did not grapple with the meaning of the text, didn't try to defend the indecipherable image, would never wield as a threat the punishments and tortures scattered throughout the pages of the Book. And I was less impervious to its meaning than to dutiful submission. I encountered the father through the practice of the text. I endured the rigors of adapting to his rough mnemonic.

And all the rest was lost to petty nastiness, in search of trifles, sweets, opaline candy box, silver tea sets concealing praline-coated almonds, coveted multicolored treat, reward for approaching literal and indisputable knowledge of the text. Learn the analogy of meaning, for the ornate sugarplum stalactite woodwork of the armoires would snap on contact with the supple switch, the whittled olive branch, body whipped, a performance tempering the attraction of feigned anger, a case of nerves more than intensive exertion, grandfather pleading for mercy; with puberty, I grew into a tyrant myself, imitating the violence inflicted by the father upon my frailer younger brothers.

The father trembles, but death is only resurgence of symbol. The image of terror cannot stifle the laughter in the mouths of the innocent when circumstances bring comedy back into the scene. No one can escape an act that leaves the law in tatters. The father returned one day, victim of wrongdoing, wearing wooden clogs instead of the fancy patent-leather loafers that someone had stolen while his students' knowledge was being put to the test. The thieving someone was to remain faceless and nameless, though motives were in no short supply, from vengeance to hatred, jealousy to simply crankiness.

It is for you to grasp the meaning of these anecdotes presented in safe doses. It is for you to assess the evil whose origin eludes us. It is for you to let yourself be swept along by text's poison, to surrender surprised by the movements of my body waltzing before your eyes. Provided you not filter out even the briefest of terrors that has neither color of sorrow nor light of revelation: something about to scare the body into a struggle that must not be absolute, for this would break the flow of the fiction, momentarily suspended, and would speed the flow of raw energy, accosting all the potential orphans who didn't have the time to go through with the death of the father and the subsequent embrace of the mother, who instead swallow and suppress their feelings in endless succession, caught unawares by weeping and jubilation.

Blood circulates, revealing the chaos of the body: arm paralyzed by coursing electric current; feet as if cut from their legs; sex swollen for no reason or truth or even image; cock on call, raised by who knows what capricious rotation of stagnant and flowing blood turning in a severed body.

Return of the father, message delivered, says Master Mahmūd, after exiting the maqsūra in my pursuit: how am I feeling, he asks. Better, fuzzy-headedness no longer hampering my movements. The idol's mummification is nearly complete; we've accomplished in one night what the ancients spread out over sixty, adds Mahmūd. There remain only the finishing touches. Ya'qūb demonstrated unrivaled skill and inventiveness; we worked, enlightened and obsessive, to the tune of the impatience that's been gnawing away at the expectant population. Nearly noon now, and though still serene, we worked through the night without respite. At dawn, tenuous daylight seeping through the slit in the secret door onto the narrow alley, we got an hour's sleep. Upon awakening, we worked with all the more accuracy.

A few adolescent bodies are stretched out in slumber: angelic pose, head against head, lips parted, each face wearing its serenity differently, the closed eye its signature. A few limbs jerk, frenzy of dispossession, persistent memory of being grazed by vipers and scorpions. Have you seen the relentless panic of the snake when, grabbed at just the right place, you taunt him with a piece of raw meat that you snatch away just as it bites down? Disastrous consequences for the animal, which is dispossessed of its fangs. It celebrates this loss, this tearing away of its venom, with dances, death throes, expiration, which the hand can nevertheless contain, despite the brutal frenzy of movement: tomb of instinct, future now stagnant.

The adolescents are still asleep, while the reader, descended from his lectern and now sitting on the floor against a column, is meditating. Certain circles from the previous night have broken up; others reconstitute in whispers and deliberations. Gradually, the murmur of music has once again grown invasive. In preparation for the imminent exit of the idol, the instrumentalists and psalmists stick together, rehearsing, polishing and perfecting bits and pieces of repertoire: entire works for reeds, fife, ghaïta, Mauritanian flute, Tibetan trumpet, rebab, 'utar, buzuk, sitar, lute, balafon, tabla, taarija, daff of Khorassan, darbūka, bendīr, bagpipes, kaminja, snake rattles, gumbri, drum, tambourine, Rhenish horns, ram calls, blaring dirge of desert, river, and mountain, strings, winds, percussion, skins and metal, resounding and overlapping, intersecting entities that bear aloft the throng's raw desire.

Commotion among the teenage ephebes busy primping. Here's a doe-eyed, long-lashed one applying kohl to his girlfriend's eyes—turned-up nose, fair-skinned, an unassailable beauty; here's another smoothing a brow, nocturnal benevolence, parting from an embrace, she is satisfied and confident, sweet abandon, smiling, mirrored in the face of her lover, chaste stallion, yes, sure of himself, he traces the brow's arch, protective sentinel of the eye; with silken kerchief dampened with a bit of saliva, he wipes away the tracks of uncontrollable morning tears passing over beauty mark, unexceptional happiness now dripping, temporary blemish on reddening cheek.

The circles close in tighter upon themselves, and the representatives of the guilds pronounce and repeat the words signaling allegiance to the idol, a simulacrum that shall rid us forever of the archaic resonance, and celebrate our outmaneuvering of the powerful. In order that power might pass irreconcilably into our hands, we must destroy said power with violent eloquence, besieging the city with cathartic spectacle. The idol produced in such a way is nothing in itself, does not feed a new fiction to furbish faith and belief; rather, it puts an end to a kind of power, a cult of submission. It exorcises not a reputedly tyrannical, often bloody past, but the bewildering instincts that bristle atavistic with each new spilling of blood.

We have no idea where this road will lead, which new world, miracle or disappointment, though we pursue it head-on, straightforwardly, touching the road's raw nerves. We say life where our enemies think extermination. But in our adventurous, headlong pursuit of new ways, by flushing out the old—storms, thirsts, tears, deserts, groundswells, drowning—we shall know how to choose our watering places: not the fresh, cool water liable to provide respite or extract a treacherous confession, abandonment of the march in order to participate in pretense and be won over by indulgence.

The circles are stirring now in greater numbers, more agitatedly than the day before. Each guild has gathered around its symbol. The master craftsmen are no longer to display the marks of their mastery. The new convention, out of concern for truth, has called for suppression of the Name. I stand up, once leaden, now golden, cramped legs now recovering their ease of movement.

I am moving toward the calligraphers now. On the tight weft of the red fabric, they have written these words from Hallāj, purged of their theocentrism: *The point is the principle of any line, and the line is but an assemblage of points. And all lines, straight or curved, spring from this same point. And anything that falls under our gaze is a point between two others. Here is evidence that* [the void] *is apparent through each act of contemplation. This is why I declare: there is nothing in which I do not see nothingness* [the void]!

Replacing the Name with the void prompted this guild to unlearn calligraphy's central representational theme: *In the name of God . . .* At this point, we must inevitably state that calligraphic styles and evolutions differ; the bismillah, the "In the Name of God," is the focus of collective imagination that materializes the pact of faith and channels representation, as does, in Christianity, the image of the Virgin and Child. In Western painting, the theme remains, while the style is renewed more through color, line, and the question of space than by the rejuvenation of the sign itself: Christ, Virgin, Apostles, or sacred cycles are reproduced from one style to the next, one school to the next, while the loose, vertiginous flow of the calligrapher's line gives to each new style an immutable quality. Inventiveness, a desirable thing, is not as ephemeral as in painting: it neither fades nor does it alter over time.

Those who adopted Islam practiced more calligraphy than they did painting; or rather, they dissolved the meaning of the written word in the calligrapher's sweeping, jubilant gesture, whereas Christians, especially during their Palatine Catholic phase, wasted no time in soaking their plaster in the colors of a fresco or patiently effacing one color with a new one laid on top of it: oil on canvas or wood panel; Islam practices calligraphy while others paint.

And writing becomes monumental loss of meaning, perceptible signature, carved, lead set in marble, hammered relief pattern. The moving hand transcribes on skin or stone, with brush or hammer, qalam or chisel, focusing the gaze, dissolving the eye, describing the itinerary of the line, plunge into the abyss that unhinges the senses.

We do not write with the intention of giving idea a body, of generating a theory, of formulating a truth, of preparing minds to receive a message, but rather we write to make real the possibility of an act whereby, in the One, we might endure. The repetition of the word as standard form, and therefore a perceivable meaning, does not summon up the same references as an image repeated as credo, vector of its own echo, expanding by degrees beyond parable to into the esoteric, or live on as shadow, projection of the Platonic idea.

For if writing, abstract alphabet, overruns the bare space of representation to flourish and ferret about, arabesque-like, to the detriment of the image—that dissimulating, illustrative accompaniment to the handwritten word—is it not simply to help the word break free of its reduction, of its exile outside these illusory forms that empty the world, in order to rouse the word into an implicit alliance with the loss of its hieroglyphic or ideogrammatic origins, to set it aglow with color, to procure it the dignity of transmutation and transformation, to unleash it from its mode of signifying and draw it toward a process of designation that would unify word and image, that would posit a similar kind of signifier derived one from the other, graphic or iconic—that would propose a similar strategy for naming things, widening the distance that separates them from the thing signified, and would finally liberate both representations through transmutation of the letter!

Painting encourages the compartmentalization of expression; it is not an art that leads us to a deeper sense of inscription: it serves as rival to the two-dimensional medium of writing. It does not embody the gesture or restore the scope of the word, as does architecture, nor does it defy volume, or by its very fixedness tear at and provoke the air, as does sculpture. Painting is potentially the core of monotheism, unseemly proclamation of the One. Why does it triumph only as mute wall in the Jewish painter Rothko's work, or as miniature in that of the Muslim Wāsiti? Why is it that painting is so invasive in Christianity as to inspire Christians with an illusion of superiority? Europe conquered the world with its sovereign, invasive art—despite those few exceptions to the rule that the territory of their expression betrayed: Simone Martini, Piero di Cosimo, Andrea del Sarto, Parmigianino, Goya, Van Gogh, Brueghel, Klee, and others so movingly self-destructive by virtue of their alliance with the breaking of boundaries.

Let us be clear about this irremediable difference; let us call for an abstention from the act of painting. Extreme monotheism, curiously enough, results in Christianity—not that our conjecture as to the purported genesis of painting is the substantiating argument confirming our position—yet this religion was able to impose on lived experience the rule of One while at the same time advocating symbolic division: the trinity divides up representation, reducing lived experience to the One without taking into account the transshipment of bodies.

Islam is governed by a reverse dynamic: the One is affirmed by the violence of the word. But its life's breath is only an exhaling of dust, dispersed and drifting, dizzying exhilaration of meaning; in short, calligraphy is at once the key that holds the universe within reach of measurement, and a threshold of peak experience with respect to concision: below, the fringes that outdo one another in ornamentation. And Christianity, rescued from its illusions, leads us only to the domain of the sovereign ego. Is there any pretension more vain, more hegemonic, than the art of the painted portrait? While Islam, east, sun, dawn, desert, affirms the One that we might annihilate ourselves in it, to disappear as an I and become a self drowning in selfhood, pliable abstraction, ship or serpent, dragon or meteor: calligraphy.

Christianity gains its strength by recovering the scenography of pantheism and polytheism, is more robust for being closer to the instinctual, to the fabled, the fictive and all too human origins of myth. Yet Christianity amputates man's urge to laugh, to dance, to celebrate springtime; chalice of blood, refuge from instinct setting a scene where painting unravels the materialization of dreams, becomes a way to accustom the eye to exertion, all the better to keep it at bay through the accumulation of symbols. Painting masters the key word of Christianity: it says *sacrifice*.

The alphabet separates writing from image. Rather than acknowledge this split, and crash into the unmovable walls that seal off those regions of expression, instead of displaying one's diminishment, abstruse music, word or figure, we might as well reinstate the orphaned authority and continue to laugh at this divisive, alphabetic reign.

Alphabet, are you not a seed to flower in the monotheistic desert? Calligraphy, might you then be the orphan of meaning, profanation of the tomb containing the hieroglyphic remains and finery of the gods? The Chinese, who have conserved their ancient system of writing, who have allowed it to evolve, demonstrate the extent to which it is possible to avoid this division. Their words are other deserts; they repudiate the memory of voices to better preserve the alliance with the objects they mean to designate.

To test our conjectures, one need only single out the behavior of an atheist in the following places: here he is in China, where we find he is a calligrapher, Taoist, in harmony with the world, untouched by crisis; in Europe, we discover he is a painter, Christian, feeding on pity and resentment, misfortune and mortification, pornography and nihilism, individualism and pathology of an institutionalized sense of self, disease to be spat out of the social body—rare among this fauna are those who can hope to transform into blacks, Chinamen, dervishes, barbarians; and finally, he can be found in the Islamic, either Christianly contaminated, or regressively pantheistic, brainless, lost, Sūfi, vernacular, all complaint and compassion, imitating jubilance, crushingly archaic, revivifying the reliquary of the ancient—always preaching, able to remain ante-Islamic, pagan by body.

But our East surely knows that China remains to be heard. Must we, by necessity, single out the disturbing beauty, bending and dancing, of the sinicized Arabic calligraphy that reiterates the Name above the mihrāb of the Canton mosque? Eastern winds, sister Asia, we need only seek inspiration there in our impatient preparation to take part in the procession, even while eliminating the Name and supplanting it with the void, hearts' delight, gift of Hallāj, which controls the corrosive art of calligraphy.

How then can someone write, when at first he practiced calligraphy and only later honed the language that, from the very beginning, fascinates thanks to its mastery of what seems to be a chimerical sort of power?—only to be found irreconcilable with the psychological facility for blasphemy, thrilling fear of the void, boundless experience of textual adventure, in pursuit of bodies and sex; soon revealed as a pseudo-atheist, deceived by the morbidity of religion, cut off from his hierological being.

I write calligraphy that dances; the hand first seductive, then trembling; I divert this too logical language through openings where it can breathe; like this, coming and going, digressing, true to the body, forgetting to do away with the father, sailing, poisoning, flashing of spears, silent night shimmering, silver coats of armor and depersonalizing helmets: irony has it that this writing of mine should import the image of the *Battle of San Romano*, by Uccello, Paul of the Birds, and his *Story of Noah*, badly damaged by the flooding Arno: words, spears that score out the homogenous spectacle from behind the text and destroy more than they reveal: spears that move through the foundries of Shanghai to acquire their springy pliability, shock absorbers for comfortable carriages: the museum image that emerges in this here-and-now where I write turns into something manufactured, so that memory loss and physical frailness have taken me back to the Zitūna besieged by a ritual becoming more and more focused as the unexpected but considered density of the text develops, locus where so many wayfaring energies cross paths—where time, more amorphous than space, furls and unfurls: unfamiliar labyrinth where I've lost my memory and bearings: anxiety of one who discovers himself to be writing while escaping from the world, delighted, sailing on the clouds beyond, dancing away.

Uncovered, half naked, the adolescent girls shiver as they yield to persistent caresses. Hand travels freely, dusky gaze, dark thighs, copper cleaned with lemon and sand, the panting young lovely stares back and says: come with me, that you might be sure of my love!

Meanwhile, the various circles assemble pennants to be waved and lyrics to be sung. Light has outdistanced shadow, and the room is turning toward the courtyard, dazzling daylight renders the feeble lanterns all but superfluous.

Diurnal embraces continue uninterrupted, those generative forces that already shook the night in every quarter; serene yet abundant call of the stars: come to the rescue of unending pleasure. Come, says the lovely miss. Your name is not unfamiliar, and I don't want to wait for the close of festivities or to find some hideaway to make my love for you known to the world!

I love her as much as she intrigues me, and we duck behind the curtain that conceals our unbridled bodies swiftly met, entwined, an almost secret space, niche veiled in a pale pistachio-colored drape that rustles and ripples, a consecration of our breathing. Her gift is poised, open, passively active. Surroundings melt away, our lovemaking tilts back into memory, Ramadan and its pious nights of long, backbreaking prayer, both alluring and exhausting, in this same place where never was I able to concentrate enough to think about God.

Adoring the belle, pleasure of silence, recollecting my only two moments of searing fright and religious doom, both governed by dream: first the garden transformed into barnyard and the prophets—pigeons, turkeys, pheasants, peacocks, guinea fowl, and roosters—all pecking away, feeding on my body, tearing at my infant flesh, child fallen by some inexplicable miracle behind fencing. The pecking was painful, I started awake, seized by an obsessive fear of the mosque where I'd finally fallen asleep.

And then the tribe assembled to celebrate some good fortune with couscous and the grilled meat of a female cousin of mine whose flesh was heartily enjoyed by all save myself, upset by the thought. I refused to chew, and began getting threats from all sides: you have to eat it, or next time you'll be the one we'll roast and feast on, rosy and tender morsel that you are! I woke up covered in vomit, hunched over the indelible image of the Zitūna courtyard that had countenanced this scene of cannibalism, blood-lust of family and friends.

I cannot muffle my breathing, timing respiration to postpone climax, then exploding to be constantly reborn as the one ready to embrace this belle who presses, skillful, available, independent, those little flowers, the body's favors, begetting torch and flame. Yet the fire of passion does not char the vegetable part of my nature; rather, it heats, coursing through me like sap, at unheard-of speeds, with no trace of wound, nor any need to prune me back to a stump.

Others of the adolescent tribe have paired off into their own trysts. Their moans form call and response, indistinct heat in shadow, in the glow of the body's hospitality, monuments to boundless desire and other such precious opiates. This cleaving, hymn to our bodies, bears us up and away from the shards and stuttered preparations of the great procession to come. Unless, in all their talk of harmony and concord, they fail to unite behind their fabled manifesto of separateness, fixed firmly at the heart of the tumultuous assembly.

Make of yourself the unwavering master of this burning flame that devours your heart, voracious instant, at each glance. Seek neither to rouse nor sequester me, for I am enchanted by the secrets of this adolescent girl, revealed as one Fātima, so that, though manly, I approach her as a woman, while the various circles all still fancy themselves masters of their domain, warriors all, quick to conceal the sounds and wounds of love.

At first I would have thought that penetration would cause an inaugural gush of blood, thick and dark, on the mat tattooing its weave onto our bodies. But, surprise, Fātima is a seasoned habituée of delight, she bears the mark of experience, singular body already attuned to the intensity of her tears and laughter. The alcoves we lovers occupy might appear as if they enclose nothing more than some chaste expectancy; but at closer range, the searing, spiced scent of terra nostra is thick in the air, flesh to be breathed in, consumed, offered up, sacrificed, questioned, spelled out and magnified, sealed and wrung and molested, scrolls of fervent grace.

And so it wasn't for naught that I deferred my death. And so the peeled-back acanthus leaves that grace the column capitals that I squint at upside down give off vibrations feverishly registered by our bodies, providing provisional translations of their meshwork. Adjacent to our mingling, token of our solitudes, the noise is starting to swell, and the rhythm of choral repetition takes hold of us against our will. Our violent impacts end in fierce caresses electrifying our striated, dented skulls beneath our scalps.

Hammering noises gravitate around our heads, pushing back the ruins that sanctify the bodies in mosques where zealous squatters appropriate a dilapidated Cairo fallen from glory, still clinging to those splendors that persist in echoing a righteous vehemence dulled since somnolence infected the speech lurking around the monumental complex of Qalā'ūn, still to be witnessed at the dawn of these times of change, such Romantic truth—Nerval, dead by his own hand, grasping the necessary prism, through age-old vision, through worsening hallucinations, a greater incineration than the sun's.

Who knows what coincidence sets the body on its journey, projecting itself onto some experience or figure, incoherent energy, nothing but dust and sweepings to collect, whore to deliver for an alcohol-soaked night of damnation in Bēja, grain market and honey-coated fritters, a place suspended in its longing for the sea that lies further north, beyond ravines and valleys, near the high flatness, color mingling with sky.

Could it be the resonant voice of the bard that consumes within me, atom or seed to be lost, the ravaged face of the eerie whore with gold incisors who leads me toward an obscure garden belonging to one of the town's notables, an important landowner whose daughter's curious request I was later to decline, a question concerning carnal exchange, in her case inaugural, to sneak an exchange of pleasure when I was wandering in my tenth month of exile, too clever for my own good, one day in early May, ground down by betrayal and sorrow, in search of an inaccessible oblivion, in an empty Grenoble, Sunday and a holiday, streets cordoned off by mountains, aimless ambling, perspectives severed, relief sculpted in the heart of the city, cold wind.

As in Azrou, where I encountered, beneath the metonymic rock, a soldier on sentry duty, an Alouite, bearing traces of torture, a man of proverbial subtlety and decency, recounting not the least bit boastfully his resistance to ill-treatment following his second-hand participation in an assassination attempt, ending just short of regicide—he regrets nothing, cast out of the barracks now, and out of his military vocation, selling kitchen appliances from his tiny shop, a way to wile away the hours and scrape together a living; I'm out in search of fresh mint this morning, he tells me there isn't any; I say I have to have it. He disappears, then returns with arms full of mint, making fun, punning: *voici la menthe, ne te lamente pas!* (Here's the mint, quit your lament!)

Teasing, lively words. White teeth, massive but decalcified, protruding jaw, hazel eyes swarming with life, pug-nosed; someone whistles us over later to share in that late afternoon the season's first dates, the only kind that grow in the Tafilalet region, taste still sticking to teeth during my morning walk through the dust floating on the already autumnal breeze, dulling the colors of the weekly market.

And the lilting voice of the bard leads us to separate after our union / *fedele d'amore* / without our lingering over the complicated concocting of the elixir. Curtains are lifted, Fātima takes me by the hand, and we prepare to find a place in what will become the cortege. Doors are flung open and the room fills, part sunlight, part fresh shadow.

Outside, musicians, placard carriers, and guildsmen are jostling, intense crowd of a thousand hues, discrete voices intoning improvisations, each flowing autonomous, an effortless tarab, barely contained joy. A hedgerow of men carrying white parasols line the path that cuts through the crowd, leading from the axial nave all the way to the western gate, passing through the courtyard.

The head psalmist, the black man, shouts the words, alternating high and low, presto and andante, high-contrast tempo, with his guild members each repeating the words that will soon earn the title of refrain, as they sway and bob, break off and catch breath.

Final rehearsal where the idol is about to emerge from the crowd. The psalmist adds further emphasis to his already full-throated voice: the bird at least has shown us the secret path; the sky's blue is not real; I have found it far away at the ends of the earth, meeting my gaze; the screech of the owl contains all that we know: it swoops down upon the mouse, beak seizing it by the tail before dropping it onto the usurped throne; what is said here is true; I speak to you as reformer of the message, but do you know I can shout it without understanding? there are no words for the wisdom of our hinterlands; we have been waiting, in the hope of restoring the world; let us hold fast to our kumiya daggers and turn their sharp edges into whistling bullets. Never will the enemy have power over us. See how the sea has lost its vitality; yet, the wave still carries its voice. My eyes are infected with tears, weeping deepens my thirst; on the rock many of us have meditated upon, royal blue, crimson, lacquer red; we have felt rekindled, poppy red, whole flowers whose stems provide weft to the warp of the text, O my faithful, my veil-faced followers, come: we shall partake of the food of union and sail unhindered by deafening machines toward the heavens where the almost incandescent colors of twilight endure. As long as the journey lasts, we shall die and be reborn. Ours is to echo: as long as the journey lasts . . .

While the bard slashes the air with indecipherable threnody—caravans, perhaps, hearts, tears, lion, stallions, factories—certain of his words occasionally penetrate the ear more intensely than others and take on new meanings: mosquito, mosque, pure; and once again, meaning is suspended like an indefinite irritation. A curious absence of machines in this collective regression to the end of our dream, or perhaps back to a genesis different from the one peddled by this harrowing voice now crying out more distinctly: eulogist of the desert, lord of the arena, I gather you here that our city might defer the infiltration of contemporary history. We are prepared to throw down our weapons in despair as everything keeps changing, each time undeceiving we help one another approach then confront these objects in perpetual flux. Thus does he speak in unfathomable references, in the shadow of an unnamed poet who shouts out song, a Mayakovsky breathing new life into the substance of proverbs by use of precise words and a passionate call for a new, triumphant history.

But now the bard castigates all resistance to machines, to ovens, to the sullying smoke, to metalwork, shamelessly contradicting himself, provoking his shrewder listeners, searching within himself for an articulation worthy of each word, longing to take delight in their musicality: I know how the voice and accompanying rebab carry one away and become pure melody, cheerful companion.

Thus do we stroll together, Fātima and I, borne along by a volition as instinctive as forward motion. The bard's voice slows down and, after the unfathomable and contradictory flow of words, grows vindictive, blaming all the opposing currents that crisscross the hall, sound like light filtering through in equal measure, music of the heavens where each beam by its sound fools the ear or lulls it into sleep: various shafts of light play upon the exalted heads, upon the symbols of each guild in bright, primary colors, a dominant green, deep as inexpressible blue, a quiver running through the branches of a century-old cedar; red, of neither fire nor blood, the deep shade of habit, restful to the eye; white encircling waves, desert effluvia; black, to obscure the names on tombs by night at the unheralded hour of sanctification that weighs upon shoulders, burnūs of lemony wool with a fringe curiously embroidered with bister bees, with glitter-tipped emeralds.

What can be done that silence might fall upon these bands of outlaws gathered into guilds growing increasingly agitated, anxious to get moving in this space where their banished vehicles are nowhere to be seen; only unreasoning eloquence can appease them, the sight of these edifying persons in their midst restoring the primacy of the word.

The storytellers are going about their business: each weaves in his manner the same story thread in which violence and love clash: in the middle of their troupe is planted the scarlet banner, serrated wheel, dragon's head in its final throes, the two-pronged sword of the intrepid 'Alī, righter of wrongs, restorer of an advanced state of civility to the chaotic desert, seat of the terrifying beast, lawless kingdom, devoid of human presence.

Among the storytellers, a dwarf whispers his story seemingly out of sheer delight, tight-lipped, smile frozen into an inexpressive twitch, snatches of narrative that borrow nothing from the curves and meanders, the secret drawers and jewel boxes of Shahrazād as she filled the evening with story, delaying danger with her tale-teller's skill, until dawn when the drowsy listener had forgotten his power; he tells ancient tales to entice the greedy, hoping that, with the magic wand of words, they'll experience the marvels of Ghazna, Kabūl, Baghdād, the initiation into the clandestine world unknown to officials and royalty.

Meanwhile, a one-eyed ventriloquist blinks his good one and takes Fātima's hand, turns it over, scrutinizes it, changes expression convulsively, furiously scratches his cheek with his other hand, all the while telling his tale, voice cavernous, hideous, lips immobile, always using a confidential tone: and you might think that the saber slit his chest open, but with each blow, his heart shone like a treasure, brilliant colors gleaming, the death rattle gave off a strong scent of wounded thuja; the monster picked up and shook his seemingly lifeless corpse and the sound of cracking bones sent fleeing the brood of jinni that had rushed to the scene, attracted by the spectacle of combat.

And then another storyteller, club-footed, approaches and stands on the tiptoe of his fit foot to lean on my shoulder—menacing eyes, bland voice, dusky beard, white turban: but our saint triumphed over the monster by the sheer force of his words, annihilating the atrocious man-eating beast; the shepherds who witnessed the fight from afar could not believe their eyes; the caravan traders, exhausted and paralyzed by fright, had come to a halt, not daring to unload and camp, but now unpacked their things, set up their tents, slaughtered ten lambs, and spent the night feasting in celebration of the victory that had opened up the route to the Sudan; and ten campfires, sending up streams of grayish glow, aroused the appetites of the jackals and hyenas that pawed the rocky earth, breathing in dust and ash.

Bel canto tenor, well-chewed voice, chest the body's seismic soundboard, volcanically erupting, lava words, Hercules with cavernous nostrils, protruding forehead, jolting limbs beneath rose-colored tunic, dizzying fluency, barely awake a minute ago, now a human cave swept by bone-rattling winds in the glow of the first-risen stars, as bats bring twilight to a close: head aloft, stature soaring above the circle of other storytellers, whom he let babble on, abandoned by their audience, while repeatedly demanding silence of the dwarf and the clubfoot who, resigned and feeble, withdraw into speechlessness; now alone he celebrates his fascination with a story rendered familiar through sheer eloquence, hurly-burly of shields and dragons: metal resisting reprisals of fire.

The nerve-shattering voice of this gargantuan figure captivates entire portions of remote circles of the audience, in the far back of the hall where listeners are starting to shake: the air sweeping through the vaulted rooms is cool to the touch where it meets stationary shadow. Voice sonorous, tremulous, as though trying on its own to set in motion the thunderous events of the story, comet lighting the face of our lord, *Sidna*, the dragon slayer.

And the tenor, now grasping a gilded scepter, waving it about to punctuate his harangue, stirs up all ethical sediments, gaping earth, exploit, desperate refusal of solitude, inescapable state, fear of the mask that—whether it's a carnival mask or not—reveals as much as it conceals. As we hear him speak and candidly reiterate the standard phrases always used to describe an epic battle, the bendīr drumbeat goes wild, and suddenly we are absolute masters of our space as the crowd recedes, expanding the perimeter of our reclusion: and the saber struck on the right, and the severed claw of the monster continued to move a thousand times, far from the body now unable to recover it; blood flowed and the saber lit the way to the phantom paradise to our left, among the stumps, remains, severed limbs, strips, and tatters of so many victims.

Is it not writing that, after the rhetoric of the calligrapher, derives its laws by overlapping with the voice of the storyteller: all through the crowd, storytellers telling other storytellers a story already known by all? Pure creativity does not exist; the most original of texts is always repetition or at least a fresh inscription set into an already-there, a page previously written upon, where further inscription is added without erasing what preceded it, still issuing its raison d'être. Readers have to adopt the attitude of a captive audience, not awaiting with bated breath the next twist in the already familiar story, but all ears listening instead to pick out the originality of its delivery, the way the storyteller puts together his words, clothed in his own spirit, leaving the public likewise on the lookout—semblance of self-interest—making sure these apricot anecdotes don't contain any new interpretations that, insidiously, might disturb the immutable effect of their transmission, assert its own capricious preferences, giving birth to undoubtedly heterogeneous content.

Cunning storytellers make strategic use of passing the hat to suspend their stories: come now, what are you waiting for, open your purses, let it rain coins, manna, show your appreciation that this land shaken by our footsteps was showered with the good fortune of my birth; otherwise, I'll tell you nothing more and you'll never know the burial site of the dragon's severed head, carried off by the two sons of *Sidna*. On their way, they encountered terrible hardships, allies of the dragon, and again they were compelled to fight for possession of the head, their trophy to display, relic to inter, fleeing the far-off oases of Mesopotamia. Come now, why delay in giving me what I want? Penny-pinchers, are you?

Money is customarily disbursed only a coin at a time, in keeping with the untiring spirit of frugality. But our tenor manages to get around this closely regulated exchange thanks to his exaggerated gestures and howls, the sounds of the night forest, the ferocity lurking deep in the entrails of the desert; the sign as sound, gestating potential, narrative imagination: all this contributes to shattering the storyline while inviting into the very womb of this radical break a new beginning, leaving open the multiplicity of possible directions. The tale accumulates as a series of tiny dramatic samples, rarely played out.

These sounds and gestures, while reinforcing the solidity of the message, likewise extend the scope of the story. They entrance us more than straightforward language, for they comb through the territory of meaning in search of an ambiguity haunting the already familiar scenery, described over and over, though never worn thin. The dialogue of the dragon and *Sidna* is now nothing but cries and ululation. The wind furrowed by the saber's spark is revealed in the dryness of grass, and thus removed from language and its univocal resonance, its somehow native clarity.

It would not be forcing the analogy to sum myself up as writing in a similar vein, describing in a language not mine the insanity of a city. The reported dialogue is, of course, never intended to be faithful. Words are translated for the sheer pleasure of conspiring with the slide toward humor, of sharing a permissive connivance with readers familiar with Arabic. This language that lends me a body on which to affix the mark of appropriation, this language symbolizing metropolis and historical attraction to what so recently participated in world domination, language I would be unable to execute by simulation, sacristy of murder, of the tiny infamies of minor transgressions. Here I am, faced with the instrument that conveys my speech, adapting as writer in a place separated from its conventions, like the clever storyteller who halts his story in the middle even without the pretext of begging, temporarily swept aside by his own vocalizing embellishments, generated by some feral urge—stopping only so that the dramatic unfolding of events might then naturally begin anew.

Language does not settle for a flouting of words wounded or embalmed, free or hired: it gives of itself wholly and unremittingly when you track its course with authority, a sequence interrupted as infraction, as crack, so that the network of writing might emerge, sometimes compact, sometimes reduced to dust, sometimes stable, other times volatile, manly or womanly, sun or moon. And by virtue of all this wealth and deprivation, language casts its spell.

Apart from what my story might imply, writing allows me to migrate from the lazy habit of afterthought, soliciting languages all along the uneven road where text is most deadly. I breathe writing, without a doubt, and these words create the illusion of following a path of least resistance, royal road to the grave. Yet the era of storytellers unearths us serene, brimming, renewed. Our every utterance is a burning truth. We simply jeopardize the body to prove our disdain for the same old thing. Writing recovers its composure. By speaking pleasure, it assumes genealogy, a line of descent, sedimentation in favor of the word. It does not claim to bear witness.

Writing is comparable to the voice of the storyteller after its enervating betrothal to the calligrapher, before becoming perfect improvisation in the centuries-old context of established musical modes.

The point is not to tell stories about these bits of life in order to fabricate them anew or celebrate them as nothing but an indulgence, a self weighed on the scales of accuracy, drafted by the felt pen of beauty: reproducing a me that says something other than myself, in order to uncover the appropriate matter to write, to face the indescribable; and even the slightest hint of fantasy or the most trifling description are bound to speed my momentum. Not to go through life runny-nosed and decrepit, incarcerated by history, poisoned by its nightmare, but to rise up a thriving body. What remains is writing: a conclusion that crushes the subject; everything else is malleability matched to the thread of the text, the mastery of anecdote, the digressive hindsight, the rigor of demonstration, temptation to be moved by the story, thrice-sacred shadow of fiction: to debase the demeaning return of limits that cause words to seize up on the verge of insanity.

Fātima cuts through the circle of storytellers, dragging me along in her wake, nodding to some young male companions as she goes, and heads lightheartedly for the metalworkers guild. I tell her to wait and come with me to have a look at the company of mithridated charmers, settled between the mihrāb and the door to the maqsūra, while in the shadow of the minbar are piled all sorts of scepters, canes, batons, pennants, insignia, flags, bouquets of cattleya, and other parade regalia, mainstay of wisdom, support of eloquence summarized as sign.

There are several of them laughing, purple-faced from having been subjected to so many public and private snakebites as they exhibit the reptiles dancing to the throbbing, spellbinding, sleep-inducing beat of the ghaïta. Some are allowed to slither about their shoulders, steady-eyed cobras, flame-like tongue, glittering scales.

You recognize the old scorpion swallower, licking a tail without getting stung for the simple reason that he has gone over to the other side, to the side of the animal, beyond spectacle, intimidating sufferers of guilty conscience believing they are at the center of a cosmic plot where manifold natural phenomena conspire: earthquakes, volcanic eruptions, avalanches, crevasses, banana snakes, man-eating birds, ferocious beasts, tigers and sharks, ordeal by fire, castration, shivering in a darkened chamber, terror or torture unto to death awaiting whomsoever enters, staccato cries of fear resonating, three or four victims abandoned to the obscure and dubious justice of some Indian cobra as it circulates in a false silence whose slightest rustling weighs heavily on the shoulders, time's sudden accretion.

Never again to be stung out of sheer respect for the instincts of the tamed creature: but upset this decorum, even inadvertently, you'll see how ruthlessly it will delight in raising its sting to thrust it into rough tongue, appealing target. Spectacle of vengeance and loathing, I remember my youth and the hilqa tradition, circular gatherings at Rahbat al-Ghanam, the eating of a live scorpion, treacherously struggling between the swallower's teeth: I don't deserve the sting you've inflicted, he shouts! Secure in his rights and in his organism's immunity thanks to vast experience with venomous stings and bites, deadly to the uninitiated, he raged and bit down on the creature, hideous cracking, attenuated by the highly active theriac, an ancestral potion in use among those who fraternize with venom-dispensing reptiles: solidarity, philter of perils, syrup mixed with blood such that the body adapts unharmed to more lethal toxins.

Was it not in Cairo, I asked Fātima, that I dreamed of a valley strewn with reptiles of various hues, scorpions, arachnids, mucuslike matter on the ground littered with their narrow, elegant, nonchalant, pliable bodies? And I walked among them, steady gait, never a misplaced step, treading only where empty spaces would allow, so deft despite the invasive sepia, secret of cuttlefish, darkening my vision. Step followed step in this seabed where the waters had long since receded, feet never touching those shrunken bodies nor disturbing the serene multitude that scuttled and crawled nearby, oblivious.

Of course, this was a dream that followed a lengthy visit to the Pharaonic museum of Cairo where the cult of the serpent and mongoose stand next to the celebration of the hawk, transformed by dreams into the gentle and trusting approach of eagles, walking with wings spread wide, moistened by the chilly night damp rising from the Nile, cooled by the northerly winds, scattering in instinctive flight as soon as I irreverently reached out for it, drawn as if by some force.

Knots of serpents tie and untie as an eagle looked on, a less skittish one, unbothered by my presence.

I walked through this propitious, anxiety-soothing landscape, certain of my special dispensation. Light-footed, I felt I had reached the end of the rocky valley strewn with fresh traces of marine life, and discovered that the still and ancient space I was moving over lay upon the vertebrae of two monumental lionesses whose heads roared to the call of the infinite vacuum. Flying carpet, vessel bearing my serene presence among so many replete beasts, soothed by the journey, beyond the urge to hunt.

Didn't you notice, asks Fātima, how fine the metalworkers' emblems are? Their self-imposed discipline to design and create in a single night such substantial banners, all in graphic correspondence with each other: double spiral, double yin-yang vortex, Hermes' caduceus, soaring wings and entwined serpent, crescent, toad, *materia prima*: expansion, contraction, furling and unfurling, sulfur and mercury, solution or coagulate.

The proselytizing of a few clandestine alchemists got a number of workers to desert their factories out in Bourjil, to come in from their shantytowns in Saïda, Mallassine, Jbal Lahmar, aboard trucks, bicycles, motorbikes, cars, and tractors; they managed to elude the besieging armies and make a nighttime incursion into the medina, now mobilized around the great mosque in turmoil.

Handling metal, touching it amounts to patiently learning the first steps on the way to its enhanced transmutation, and by way of symbol to discover one's self, transformer of ore and stone, to pretend to have been schooled in the manufacture of arms, keeping it all a secret within our city walls.

Several of these workers keep wearing their blue overalls; others, heads shaven, with two or three days' growth of beard, sport the effigy of the bearded one, ruby and sun. And they discuss contemporary Asiatic thinkers and classically heretical oriental writings, checking their Ibn 'Arabī and their Ikhwān as-Safā' (Brothers of Purity): *The One is divided into two*; yes, but there is always a return to unity, itself the origin of number; these can be added, subtracted, multiplied, and divided; their combination is infinite, but their substance is crystallized in unity; eternal renewal, each number representing in itself an irreducible unity; the zero is not only the degree of neutrality; it favors combinatorial ends: it is the essential sign that perfectly expands all figures; its invention offered man, that settler of scores, sufficient sublimation of his megalomania; thanks to numbers, man travels from material absence into intelligible existence; nothing in the world is discernible, but man knows how to transpose the world on the limited surface of his intelligence: he invented numbers to organize the world, to cipher it, to deliver it from its orphaned secret, to abstract it, to finally name it, by the alphabet that proceeds from number, which is combination as well as abstraction; but if paradox can stir up language, child of the alphabet, rarely does contradiction disturb numbers: to each of their associations, responses multiply: *thus, realities mingle* and every question proves rationalizable by an analogy of number. What else is there to add to these storm-tossed wrecks than some advice once intended to enrich the corpus of adages: *If thinking is your desire, love numbers!*

Snatches of dialogue, scattered thoughts, blue collars fascinated by the novelty of their knowledge, approaching and associating the territory of esoteric thought with contemporary strategy. Blue-heads all fire up to speak the truth and arrange to participate in their way in composing a part of our anthem, out of the distinctions and fertile implications of name and number: the designation of metalworker refers, on the one hand, to the workers who partially joined forces with those rising up in the old town, and on the other, those among the elders who remain attached to, or even cling desperately to, the teachings of Jābir and company: *The Book of the Balances* and other recent translations of the works of Nicolas Flamel, including the famous *Book of Abraham the Mage*. The metalworker label extends over units that differ from one another, but by the action of those history thought it had anesthetized (the alchemists) over those located at the center of history's polished mirror (the proletariat), each unit seeks to justify the other. Basically, metal unifies them as a material and distinguishes them by method: one group makes the transformation of matter into a personal discipline meant to improve and perfect their behaviors, to feel the spark of euphoria; the others labor away mechanically on an assembly line to manufacture the instruments of their liberation, accumulating their exacerbated alienation in the process. The ones change at each stage of their research, making progress, moving through the ranks; the others remain immobile, conquering their independence from the very spatial constraint that encloses and exploits them. The former abandon the instruments of transmutation along the way; the others should learn to destroy the ties that bind them instead of insisting upon appropriating them.

Imagine the workforce at the Hilwān steelworks abandoning their blast furnaces, polluters of the misty river air and, like vagabonds of hopelessness, setting out on a quest to rediscover together the secrets of alchemy and the esoteric sciences that have accumulated on the shores and the riverbed of the Nile!

Found myself in Aswan, the day already heating up at barely noon. Got off the air-conditioned Magyar-made train out of Cairo. Not even able to make up my mind as to which hotel to choose along the nearby riverbank. Walked down to the Nile, cooled off as I drew near, dipped my hand into the cool water, beyond thirst, beyond blast of ovenlike heat.

Slept through the siesta in the shade of a sailboat, high-masted and rocking, the wind whipping up tiny waves. Listless, I heard the city slowing down from inside the boat's hollow. A passing Soviet-made taxi or bus broke the spell of slowness. Eyes opened furtively to discover a sky immensely blue. The boat's proprietor said nothing until surprising my half-opened eyes. Drowsiness vanquished, the sun on my side, I rose of my own volition, undressed, and dove in naked, suited to the surprise of cold water: a pervasive attraction was grabbing at my body, the unfathomable depths of the Nile: a sense of definitive rest was bearing me along the confident flow of the river, euphoric benediction, deadly alliance. Wits recovered, I sensed danger and found strength to swim to the safety of shore, cold body emerging torso first from water's magnet, experience of secret sensations in full sunlight, a gentle wellness, water beading on the skin.

Leave these shores of Eden after swimming, walk despite the scorching heat, gravelly streets of the town practically deserted, lament of bare feet that must choose between sharp stone and melting tar. Walk by the Prefect's residence, leave behind the school for girls, knock at the locked door of the Cultural Center, finally come upon the only street with any life at this hour, stalls open, siesta pursued at counters, dozing merchant drooling in slumber, flies swarm, scattered patrons dozing in coffee shops, scented souks of the city, colors bright even in shade, scarves, bolts of cloth, indifferent sides of beef. Enter a sleepily seedy café: here reigned lethargy, a couple of indolent elders secreting a lofty presence. Ask for a hookah, honey-soaked maasal tobacco, būrī, masri, the national brand distinct for its 'agami tombac, plant of Persia or Mesopotamia. Smoke headless in this scorched land of Egypt. Reassuring to be acephalous fauna. To edifying puffs were added sips of thick black tea, thirst suppressant.

Café proprietor, an old Nubian, octogenarian perhaps, white tunic, stooped shoulders, chest hair gray, eyes small and wet, sparse beard, coarse fingers, nails blackened and broken. Gets up, comes over, asks: where are you from? My reply: from the land where the Banī Hilāl emigrated. Lowers head, reverentially kisses my shoulder, exults, says: my ancestors are also from there; greetings and joy; welcome to you, countryman; ah! I bear centuries of nostalgia! I knew as soon as you walked in that you had been sent here, to me; some said: there's a foreigner, a khawanga, doesn't speak the language; and I say: no, I know, he wears the colors of the Maghreb!

Invites me to his table, offers me a better ventilated hookah, more tightly sealed, a finer brew of tea. Looks at me, jubilant, happy, toothless smile.

The heat in this town! No, today isn't such a scorcher; at least you can breathe without doing yourself damage. But then, there's a way of breathing that adapts to all conditions, hot or cold. Easy siesta today, didn't sweat as much as last week when the khamsīn, wind up from hell, suddenly came blowing through the city: even at night, and along the river, you couldn't go out for a walk! This street attracts dust, but I wouldn't trade it for the corniche road that makes the Nile unreal, flaming like some fake sunset. They built it a few years back: ever since Russians started arriving by the thousands to build the dam, the city has completely changed. They even built a mosque on the eastern hillside.

Now we're beginning to understand things in this country, in this city. Every change brings a new servitude! Important to know: yes, technology opens up a world. It was not so long ago that we lost everything, for we were easily fooled, but now we understand.

At the time of the Mahdi, downriver toward Umm Durmān, they would still talk about it when I was growing up, how it was so easy for the English to deceive us. We were unable to act, we had no foresight; we were second-rate, awkward in our thinking, unsubtle, charmless, never allusive. Once, a friend of mine happened upon a ring of inestimable value, a precious talisman, witness to centuries of wisdom buried in the bowels of the land. An Englishman knew it, sensed its worth; he asked to see it, gazed at it, polished it; for, he knew. He offered this wretched friend twenty pounds. Overjoyed, the fool accepted the deal: but what were twenty pounds, even in solid gold, compared to this treasure?

I'll say it again: at that time, we were like the peacock hidden under a barrel for ten years and who, accustomed to the unsightliness of its talons, all but forgot the splendor of its plumage that used to feed its vanity when it would still strut in full daylight! But today, our people are awakening.

What, pray tell, ever became of the Englishman, owner of the ring? If inadvertently a man does betray, water and earth pardon not. The Englishman wore the conspicuous jewel; it disturbed him, made him withdrawn. Never did he allow it near fire or water. He sensed the power. One day, wind in his sails on the Nile, idyllic twilight, lost in ecstasy somewhere between the Saint Simeon monastery and Elephantine Island, he allowed his hand to graze the river and the water made to devour the ring: in seconds, before the eyes of onlookers, he was swallowed up, followed by the boat and its captain!

Water engulfs: depository of secrets: just as power attracts power, treasure attracts treasure. All this we now know, we are no longer duped. But we lack experience, we know only half the story, for we have been amputated. Below its surface, this country shines with all the riches of the world. Yet nobody seeks to exploit its hidden potential.

He went on like this for hours, tireless voice, soft with an occasional guttural crackling. I would go see him whenever I could. Knowing that I was looking for some ambergris for a wedding night with a slender Berber exiled in Nubian desert, he was able to procure some rare lubān dhkar, precious commodity, burning thirst of love that contaminates the dance of the stars, borrowed from a Sudanese friend of his passing through.

Before I left the town, he asked me to write him a talisman, for protection, to relieve some tension or other, a spell, an eye to tease someone sleeping in his absence: for, you see, this café is inhabited by occult powers. I know that you're not empowered to design such preemptive devices, but I'm sure that in this specific case, you can be effective. Without such an intuition, I never would have asked you. You must understand that glasses break here for no visible reason, water begins to flow though no one touches the faucet, evil spirits suddenly materialize in this place and take advantage of the shadows to work mischief. It is my wish that this place should return to its previous state of tranquility. Incredulous, I didn't know how to respond to the old man.

Night of sleeplessness and ambling, of meditation upon the granite banks of the Nile while, on the opposite shore, a Nubian village was celebrating, deafening music, noisy chorus of voices, a wedding feast presided over, it seemed, by phantoms of debauchery, frenzied corporeal exhaustion. Neither in body or spirit could I move any closer, drained, insane, panting, a stag in rut. Forehead cold and damp, eyes a crazed stare, hand trembling uncontrollably. As I lay on the hard, hot stone, the sky beamed back an unmistakable clarity, the stars stunningly recognizable.

My rediscovery of the world was mellowed by starry inscription, revelation named, evanescent, remote: but I resisted.

This link to the archetype of revelation brought me back to earth, mind bubbling with unproductive ponderings that kept me from seeing clearly. Got up again, and then, with the force of prophecy, believe it or not, the talisman was revealed in its entirety, words, figures, and all, to fulfill the Nubian's request, though I myself did not fully understand its contents. And I set about repeating, calm but bruised: *The sword that severs / The crescent that shimmers / No sword like truth / No succor like sincerity.* Elsewhere, male circles and crescents doubled female, assembled, eye gazing upon floating sword, measure of history, qalam reed pen reassuring the will to write in emulation of the fiat, equivalence between the huwa, itself-ness of the Sūfi and the Tao ideogram.

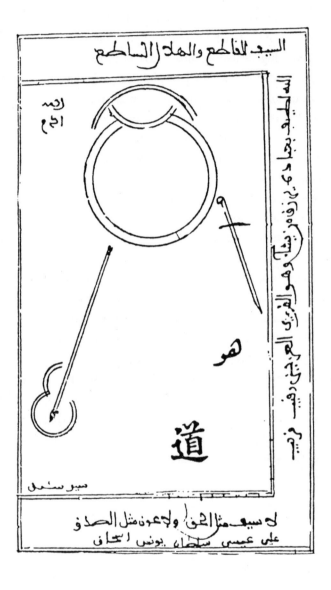

道

هو

لا سيف مثل الحق ولا عون مثل الصدق
علي عيسى سلطان يونس الخفان

OTHERWORLD PROCESSION

Fātima more limpid than in after-love stares and squeezes my hand. Increasingly lucid, I adapt to the greenish color of my eye that, though bulging and bloodshot, inspires not terror but intensely shared feelings in twin search of bodies: self-important conviction of impossible unification, rupture placed unhesitatingly before the eye to act according to knowledge drawn from past experience in the weaknesses and pretensions of the body.

The unrest was growing out of all proportion: gaping mosque at blinding high noon. The doors of the maqsūra open wide and finally there appears the mummy raised upon a four-posted wooden palanquin, the front two posts painted one red, the other green, and in back, one white and the other black; an azure veil bearing golden calligraphy wafts in the gentle breeze between the columns topped with brownish pediments. Palanquin borne aloft on robust shoulders, men and women, followed by Yaʻqūb, Saïda, Master Mahmūd, and the ancient ghostly preacher who had originated the seizing of power by its rightful claimants, the sons of hardscrabble quarters, neighborhoods home to so many crafts rooted in inaccessible layers of history.

Coup that in fact signifies a death blow to all power in its fertile allotment across the city, as many seeds as called for by wall of dust, erected as circumstances require, effective power quickly dissolved as soon as reason for action ceases to exist; by this process, we shall declare ourselves either real or fantastical, determine whether we are mere chimera or some other imaginary form. The demand of this ephemeral attribution of power imposes vigilance upon those entrepreneurs whose urge for new projects is a gnawing need, an ever-present reminder of the acquired taste for control. Insatiable usurpers that spring up under each step, and who make of each of their capacities a task to be turned profitable by dint of their own manipulations of power.

Palanquin bobbing along, allowing glimpses through the floating veil of three bright eyes, the sole shimmering points on the idol, focus of imploring gazes from all around, easily mistaken for mockery. Palanquin cutting a path full sail into the courtyard. Through a hedgerow of parasols, it is cheered on by a din of musicians and singers, mix of sound and idiom. Signs of allegiance have reached a climax and the crush comes close to dispatching quite a few revelers, saved only by the timely intervention of some moderating force to quell the tendency toward unruly behavior among the guildsmen and other sectarians from bygone eras breaking and entering into the present day.

From high up in the minaret, shower of fireworks fall exploding, pale bursts in full daylight, eclipsed by the sun's primacy. Meanwhile, on the terraces that protect the portico, the Zlassi, horsemen from the steppe come to stand sentry in support of the capital city in revolt, reenact a tight fantasia with yataghans and rifles held aloft, symbolic stand in honor of the idol, gunpowder shot into the sky like precarious bouquets, thick grisaille and scattered sparkle, spreading acrid odor, colors disappearing beneath smoke and fire, hazy incandescence redeeming its energetic presence by how instantaneously it vanishes, musical airs bordering on the chaotic, seriously perturbed by all the jostling.

The idol reaches the western gate, crosses through; and the cortege takes form, fleeting in color, sound, number, and letter. An uninterrupted throng greets the cortege at the perfume souk, in the opaque shade of the vaulted passageway. Hands are raised to touch veil or wood encasing the mummy, to attain black stone, grasp, mark, and interiorize, to be charged with that positive energy at work in the rock, place of desire, bodies resolved to let wash over them the contamination of this new approach beyond indecision and uncertainty. There are those who weave through the legs of giants, who climb bodies up to the height of the palanquin to perch on a nearby shoulder and boldly go so far as to dip their fingers in the wetness that continuously seeps out of the wrappings that embalm the idol.

Buoyed by so much admiring assent, the cortege moves slowly forward through ranks no deeper than four guildsmen. And for onlookers, the music settles in, varied and clear: the slow pace of the march allows the various orchestras to follow each other without clashing, instrumental and melodic variety, exotic Asian, sounding like nothing European, save that solitary tromba marina, sadly single-chorded and mewing low or high notes with slow or fast strokes of the bow. Likewise, songs are surprisingly distinct and decipherable: there is always a sense of what the text is conveying, in terms of passionate psalmody, both harmonious and well-deserved.

A stanbāli troupe: rattles click, steel and iron clang, bass-stringed gumbri played by several musicians at once, like some far-off vibrating continuo, seconded by round metallic petals jingling at the end of a stick where skillful and sensitive fingers adjust the tone eloquently. Boundless joy spoken in measured cadence.

And the voices of the black elders rise up, throbbing song, moving with the elegance of musical notation, eyes small and red with strain, alcohol, sleepless nights, sun, slavery, swing about in search of the liberating libation, powerfully addictive, bodies in flight, desert crossings, strips of fabric glowing madly, multicolored skirts scattered swelling to swaying of hips, cowry necklaces, drum beating out nostalgia for the steppe, freed wise men of their ancestry, wandering proud beggars earning a living by the sweat of their music, lucky-charm sensibility, clients when not serfs of wealthy families, eunuchs or masters of sex in the antechamber where the mother broods over growing old, enslaved to the hidden call of sexual indulgence, sons of lowly furnace tenders at the baths, some more traitor than errand boy but ruling like ministers, though inadmissible by official standards, aftereffect of racial disparagement, governable traitors eligible to marry some comely adopted girl bearing the grand family name of some aristocratic lineage; but skin sets apart, impromptu color excluded from the alloy that acknowledges the beauty of this fusion of Mediterranean races, Beys edifying the memory of the Christian mother, reclusive Venetian, by a church—sole Catholic remainder in the city, lending name to one of its important streets, channeling the energy of commerce collaborating to reconcile the colonial gateway with a receptacle for dying traditions.

Black race reduced to lovable comedy, accent a cause for mockery, corpulent women half veiled, dark women from al-Hama or Guebelli, barely blossoming oasis, with the scrawniest palm trees, come to pray to the bountiful saint, Sidi Sa'ad, to bring him offerings, women ending up as wet nurses for someone's illegitimate offspring, game for any experience, machine to unlearn awareness of the body by an abandoning of the self among beds vacated by adolescent males yearning for women, rising in dead of night, tiptoeing in fear of the slightest resonance of chattering bones, tomblike silence, barely disturbed by complicit barking, serving as go-between in lovers' intrigues.

Black race, expecting to assimilate, forerunners of heroism, solar or lunar, depending on circumstance, flash in the night, master and lord more capable of defending the city than the least prudent of the profiteers, factor in outsmarting the conqueror and ridding the city of his presence, hidalgos of misfortune, unbelieving blasphemers, imposing unexplained ill-treatment of the worst kind: black hero of this country where your black saint is respected only by virtue of his prophylactic sign, warding off the evil eye by a simple fish icon, by Lilla Fatma's hand, Lady who some—Louis Massignon and his disciples, for instance—fearlessly insist on associating with the Virgin, Fātima az-Zahra, declared mother to her father, source of wisdom, tabernacle where plays of light and oil and wax gravitate.

So the Stanbali band is playing, brothers of the gnawa, ana wa iyak, sidi Sa'ad ya baba; dancing to a strong rhythm the women come in from their uncultivated lands, barely supporting esparto grass.

Stanbali, guaranteeing spectacular effects, fantasy mixed with something impossible, archaic, but isolated, walled off, subjugated and dying a slow death. Perhaps these festivities at the core will spill over the city walls to break down this ghetto of history and revive other energies stagnant among those who see themselves as the precious elite destined to control power according to their training on the knees of their former masters, this elite proud to put forward to their leaders the model of universal amputation, to rally their circles of sycophants.

To divert such a ghetto from history, to set oneself up as an impertinent one-man diaspora, to produce for the well-to-do of Fez the long-awaited fart; recumbent after a succulent meal, first a pastilla, flakey crust stuffed with pigeon and almonds, then a mrūzia, lamb tagine with honey and raisins, and finally, gazelle horns in an almond milk sauce. The room an oblong iwan hung in gilt fabrics, heirlooms of the forefathers, set fluttering by the garrulousness of its overly refined occupants, tending toward the plump and puffy, too much postprandial collapsing into sofas. Intimidated guest, at first I could only laugh up my sleeve, but speech unperturbed, I spoke through my boredom, lighting up the domed room with the splendor of my enlightenment, false sign of my ability to recite the entire Book by heart, enticing florid decor, mingling circular and knotty stems, stressing the final Ns, those emphatic nūns that pulsate red, outshining so many other less conspicuous letters, subjected to the minority status of their color, murky black against grayish green, olive tree trunk coated in clay, ants creeping in single file in search of nutritious remains.

Beggar from Tunis, something chic about that, fording the stream of Wādi Bū Khārib that disseminates its turmoil throughout the ruined outskirts of the city. On the advice of a gnawa, I knocked at the door of a grand-looking home: I was let in, charming them with my accent, and was invited to take part in their marathon conversations. They were delighted by my logorrhea and declared me a worthy son of my city, a cut above the riffraff thanks to my boundless knowledge. After feasting on words, we moved over to the real feast, an all-male affair save one learned lady who was with us for both ceremonies. We ate, we belched until I was finally able to let loose the welcomed fart, sign of satiety and satisfaction.

The women strolled by, nonchalantly, pale-skinned, lingering in the light of the patio, dressed in those mauve or rose or periwinkle robes, transparent synthetic material held together with machine-made lace, a sure sign of private culture coming undone.

This ugliness is invading the cities, where in the past, the discriminating would hyphenate an aesthetic, however disjointed, only when it courted the kind of beauty that sifted through at dawn with a light that still knew how to play, infinite variety gradually coloring bodies with day. Those cities today no longer have any notion of daybreak: they collaborate with universal novelty, corrupted by a neophyte's perverse enthusiasm for the new.

And the child that I was witnessed the nuptial dawning that gleamed on the city and sparked a new arousal of the senses, a grasp of the universe, the lure of the impossible. Very early, music would sneak up on us, frightening us to tears; fascinated yet terrified by the Bū Saʾadiya minstrels who wandered drooling, foaming at the mouth, black, venerable elders wearing headgear decorated with raven feathers, open-necked scarlet shirts, sound of rattlesnakes scorching the ears of youth, all of ten years, perched splendid on the high wall that separated the garden from the street, through the drooping foliage of the mulberry tree that marauders would scramble up in late May.

Commotion of children that would run after the black musician as he begged for coins and scraps of food, often under a rain of stones, insulting the young intruders and singing in return, a dancing, musical, hermetic language, between shouts and lightly lisped words.

Followed soon after by the melancholy yet vicious face of the ragman, collector of old clothing to be thrown away, exchanged, sold, whistling between his teeth the vendor's cry, *robba vecchia* and again *robba vecchia*; or the empty-bottle man, who would trade for paddle balls, plywood rackets attached with elastic string.

Or enough vendors in summer to make you wary: fishmonger pushing crates of foul-smelling sardines or mackerel; fruit and vegetable merchant peddling putrid produce; milkman on a motor scooter, selling his diluted wares; baker on a tricycle; daily hustle, excuse for going outside, fleeing the overly protective household; waiting for the mailman in doorway shade, at the corner, facing the café, inaccessible lair of the idle, or farther away still hoping for a first look at incoming letters concealing perfumes and mysteries I yearned to access on my own, though never daring to break the seal that protected them from my ravishment.

Fortune-tellers reading palms, sand, coffee grounds, and tea leaves, bundled into the house by a portly neighbor woman, in mourning, in need of bad news, living with her brother: caged, merry-widow giddy laughter, thighs open as if inadvertently, letting herself go at the first hint of sun, of breeze, superstitious though a less skillful sorceress than one of her sisters whose evil learning lit up her face, transformed, a curious light adding a touch of saintliness to her evil fervor, accepting no in-laws, daughter or son, violent and spiteful toward anyone who dared undermine her authority, provocative in her measured and seductive use of lewd language, always seeking to focus the reticent gathering of women onto the unmentionable sphincter, constipated corpulence requiring, says she, that she plunges her hand deep into the recalcitrant intestine, wounding herself despite the coating of almond soap, until her fingernails extracted the excrement that had resisted all efforts and contractions, enough to empty a body of all its internal organs; and then, stories of cunts and copulations, pricks so pretty as to delight the numerous blushing prudes so ubiquitous in this milieu of discreet façades, not unlike that of Fez among those families, self-important and smug in their values, vast network of merchants far too entrenched to succeed in their bid for power, or even realizing what such power would involve, content to merely exude their lawyerly ideology, a far cry from the patronage granted by such castes as the Florentine Medici, feet barely grazing the ground as they hastened to render every corner of the city an ostentatious tool for consolidating power, for gaining wealth capable of transforming the world: libraries, palaces, tombs, statues, piazzas, gardens, oratories, chapels, hospitals, cloisters, cupolas, porticos, frescos, secret passageways, villas, and Careggi where so many fleurs-de-lis and finials at play, decorating this theater of life where minds felt free from the prison of the body to rehearse, interpret, act out these Platonic dialogues and banquets adapted to the Christian creed, making believe in pure beauty, seeking to stifle the moralist voices whose strengths bear upon the effects of rupture and desire for all things cataclysmic.

Not that Fez is any less prestigious. But the investment of its wealth is turned in upon itself, into dens of pleasure-seeking, a dynasty that could intervene in worldly matters, yet fails to arm itself with even a hint of the risk-taking spirit instead of dilapidating its fortune in the unending celebration of endogamous alliance, in the bitter secretions that lead to—but do not cross—the gateway to power.

In Fez, any reasonable attempt to claim power after having acquired a fortune, proves a modest but definitive failure. And he who does not command power in its totality cannot conspicuously, in every square and street, demonstrate his strength. His wealth goes dormant, then, as he moves to Casablanca to sell his soul in hopes of living the perfectly conventional synthesis between skill sets assimilated from the West and refinements preserved from the East. They then go about accumulating the proceeds of abundance, conforming to the standards of the petty bourgeois bitten by the free capitalist bug, trading away their daughters, modern in their pleasures, shedding a tear while taking a short break from their continual orgy over the dearth of production among our creative artists; and in some dark corner of a gold-plated drinking binge, they pledge the millions it would take so that pens would write, brushes spring into action, and cameras shoot.

Fez fancies itself the beating heart of Morocco, and it is not mistaken: geognostics have located beneath the city the physical center of gravity. Fez shines with a light unattainable elsewhere. Some of its gatherings are truly worthy of admiration; I'll say nothing of the sacred intensity of the patron saint's mausoleum where votive offerings pile up, Moulay Driss, fātiha of the perverse, nor will I go on about the ironwork, paintings, the delicacy of its architectures, medersas and mosques more so than its palaces; and its artisans, manual or mental, certainly do take one to a higher plane: that weaver who took you in and spoke in inflammatory terms, that other host who took up residence in Fez after unraveling many of the mysteries and ambiguities hidden in the landscape that it occupies: think of the Swiss convert who pursued the tradition of certain nineteenth-century English alchemists, and who came to live in Fez, peace and quiet for anyone who believes in the possibility of social noninterference and the marginality to revive, through the body and the city, a tradition that has elsewhere disappeared.

And what spoils Fez coexists with its strength. What is liable to destroy it stems not only from invasive modernism disrupting its traditions: Fez started misrepresenting its fragility as soon as it began to actively participate as the protective western boundary for a set of decadent ideas—namely, that of a hegemonic Islam, a reductive monotheism, bordering on Christendom, both masters of a civilization claiming to be unique and universal, believing in progress and taking comfort wherever natural instinct is suppressed.

Yet, more than the heavens over Tunis or Cairo, the Fez sky rumbles, like a seismic event to shake the dilapidated, half-abandoned palaces, last to resist the exodus of wealth beyond the walls.

Indeed, it was there I met the most liberal of old men. Modestly dressed in a white whiter than white, light as a bubble, ready any moment to dissolve into nothingness, levitating, not sitting as one might first assume, but leaning against a column at the far end of a bright room, smiling, meditating, eyes bright and mute, beaming light, burning, breathing, calming to behold, faraway yet present, a man of few words, responding to each query with the gentlest, humblest, most accurate, most concise of responses.

A reincarnation of my own grandfather on my father's side, I now recall, whom I so admired on the day of his death, which was a day of beauty, brightness, sunlight, and celestial joy, recapturing him so alive, so pure so precise and serene on meeting death, as he listened rejoicing at my teary-eyed father's full-throated recitation of the sūrat Yā Sīn, rising from his bed to correct him when he stumbled over a word, always a trace of a smile, he who just before dying heard the call to prayer and rose to perform the three rak'at, twilight prostrations, bowing over the softness of his bedding; he who at age twenty set out for Mecca on foot, accompanying his own father, who would die there; he buried him on site, wept over him, exhausted ten times the Book from memory, meditated upon its teachings, and looked into his own heart at the tomb of Muhammad until a holy angel of light opened the catafalque window: in the tabernacle of light, light upon light, that the voice of assent might resound; present at my birth, he is said to have paraphrased Ibn 'Arabī: *It is a gift as Seth is a gift for Adam . . . the son is the secret reality of his progenitor . . . Every gift in the entire universe is made manifest according to this law: . . . no one shall receive anything that does not issue from himself.* And I still carry that native utterance in my body, for it was to be the origin of my name: am I not persistently called the servant of He who gives? To find I am sealed by my name into the act of giving, here is what leads to excess in debauchery, to squandering of fortune!

Still another family in Fez, settled in Rabat, living in a villa intended as synthesis of forms, resulting in architectural muddle: volumetric principles that share nothing in common with the oriental use of form: enormous entry hall, not unlike the reception area of a hotel lobby, pompous Chinese vases the height of a man, vulgarity of ostentation, disorienting, unsettling: marble, mosaic, decor ruled only by symmetry.

Inspiration? Hotels clumsily built to reproduce an Oriental style: pseudo-patio concealed by a multicolored sliding glass door, living room the size of a supermarket, ceiling in handcrafted stalactites, nightmarishly ugly, fancy benches and poufs, engraved bronze trays with their folding stands in mother-of-pearl inlay, stereo speakers lodged between stalactites, just the thing for a bit of cabaret-style slumming, paunchy Parisian music, furtive gestures, and, already awkward in front of the lady of the house, paragon of Fāsi degradation, emigrants to the seat of power on the ocean's shore.

Husband withdrawn in the face of the lady seeking synthesis of cultures, dressed in caftan, haughty bearing, arrogant beyond measure, proud of her schooling, money, of her pure pedigree, Arab from Yemen, not one of these Arabized half-breeds, purer still than even the noble shorfa, straightforward in her tyrannical affirmation, blind to those things that distort her true style, for could she but see, she would hasten to repair all this ridiculousness. What a loss for history that the heft of her personality has not been used in fiction: ah! if only she could channel Medea's cry!

More than the word of poets or clowns, these portraits provide a history lesson. The stakes lie between this lost soul wandering through the century and the spaces that, out of fear, scorn the new.

And in the choosing, the stale dialectic that privileges some south over some north.

None can match Fez, gathered into the palm of a hand—save Marrakesh, scattered between the index finger of its minaret and the excavations of its quarry. This unrest, city-daughter of the sun, a thousand colors shining mirror reflecting incandescence or turban of snow, between desert and mountain, Kutubīya that troubles the mind, four-sided minaret, each face imposing the secret of difference, shade, water, and flowerbeds, gardens marking borders to various functions, spaces occupied steadfastly by an assertive people, a folk of seasons, music always in profusion.

Not that the southern city is invulnerable—not that it does anything to dismantle the scaffolding of endless bureaucracy erected by politicians and technocrats; but the landscape seems to possess bottomless resources of resistance that facilitate the people's affecting a posture of somnolence and unity that better guarantees survival without deception or hypnosis: in this city, the people are masters of magnetism and of the power that breaks through the repressive asphalt, notwithstanding the residue of feudalism and the archaic pacts that still animate a propensity for the obsequious.

Where else can one find a more peculiar architectural form commissioned a century ago by the Sahrāwi conquerors—pragmatic barbarians, makers of baroque cupolas, only one specimen of which remains, lost among palm trees and russet brick? This Ba'adiyīn cupola, petals brightly salient on the calotte, a play of walls and openings, image of seashell and grape leaf, gathering their compartments into a central stem ending in the cupola faced with volutes, plaster worked into floral patterns, itself receptacle of figures, broken lines, curves and counter-curves, arabesque of line projected into space, perfect Almoravid accomplishment based upon the transposition of the principles of Islamic decoration, flora and planar geometry, to an architecture lending volume to flat motifs, rutilant container, a balance of breaches cleverly circulating blue sky: what uncertain solitude, what southerliness made possible this achievement by interpretation of register, audacity of one who emerges from the desert to impose the notion of unification, to attain an ideal to be formulated centuries later by a Borromini, a Guarini, to celebrate by monument the feast of Catholic power, triumphant propagator of faith after overcoming its schismatic trauma? And what an achievement, succumbing to neither futile gamesmanship nor fastidious demonstration! Just like that, cupola as isolated vestige, lifted onto podium above empty lot, makeshift latrine stinking of urine, one hundred bits of dried, odorless excrement, scrawny cats and dogs; and my solar self, delighted to bear eternal fidelity in love, body swept away imploring a recalcitrant lover.

Tunis: putrescence transmuted by dream, story on the fringes of the real, to be rendered once more exemplary: here, between north and south, the issue is obscured: how indeed is one to choose between Tunis and Tozeur? Oasis, smallish town, unbridgeable difference but pearl of its region, enigmatic remains of early foundations, collapsed tower, ruin in the al-Hadra quarter, a city of clever ancestral occupations of space, clinging, floating up to the canopy, skillful climbers up slender trunks, potheads that no prohibition has managed to deter from their drug of choice, meeting place of old men and nubile youths, grass opening the eyes of the pubescent, arousing precocious papyrus snaking up thighs, souls sold to the most clandestine of brotherhoods, laboring assiduously between groundwater and stream and rootlet, Tozeur seduced by the contemporary and coercive machine that squanders energy, partner to ancient Serjīn, Nefta whose legend points to a son of Noah as its founder, fresh fountain, Eden in springtime, clever Jilāni, between two oases, consummate guide, master of the perilous crossing of the shott, infinite, vibrating salt lake of utter flatness, swallowing up even the most recent traces, imperceptible hollow that vacillates, fragment and metaphor, between sea and desert, salt star whose memory is divided among so many clans displaying what they are not; you, their poet of romantic rhetoric, the bard of the rebellious Jerīd, caught in the web of nationalist fervor, serving that tribe of sweeping polyphonies.

Tozeur, tiny, secretive city, teeming with as many ants as roots, world where an intoxicating sap flows, lagmi, palm wine, stronger stuff than what comes from its orphaned neighbor, Gafsa shouldering the hegemony of the north, ruins and phosphate mines, cops and stool pigeons, trade unionists buried in collapsed mineshafts, militants dating back to the nationalist movement: desiccated remains on the highlands of Metlawī, specters of conspiracy, exiled proletariats never leaving their birthplace, al-Qsar, the permanent suspect, raving between beer and wine, resistance fighter from the nomadic age, herds and seasonal migration, passing from shepherd to miner, recruited as Comintern cadre, knowing no city save Gafsa and Moscow, surreally citing Marx, Lenin, Stalin in the desert, driveling, figures as clairvoyant as a senescent fetish fig tree, ear to the wind, rumbling of ore to extract from down below, a thousand layers underground, lending his language, dexterous handling of contradiction, the veracity of a hermit, of an exile, a man living at the core of archaism and the question of the working class, understanding the threat that continuously surrounds even his most imperceptible exhalation: cousin informers, ruthless northerners, equal to when not worse than the petty bosses of the colonial era, the daily inventory of massacres; tree, man, woman, sand, money, water, the elements drift from their well-balanced interactions: what can you do to dust off the choking August haze among deserts and mines?

Don't denounce but decipher the era of ersatz: rid myself, writing, of an obsession, a nightmare that dogs me, harasses me, disturbs me, inhabits me, that so assaults my sleeping, so bludgeons my waking, that I call it neither-this-nor-that, nickname of the body broken by at least two fractures, spinal column deformed by the attacks of who knows what demon or progenitor.

I need to breathe otherwise, man-eater, blasphemer; negativity obliges, positivity activates—through the flowing current that washes along portraits of cities, men and women, fleeting instants of a life where the border between the real and mere projection is blurred, a host of beings so unlikely to imagine themselves thinking, fantasy and recurrence: I, the teller overcome by the intense need to write, to keep from going irreparably feral, intensely unreadable—an opacity that concerns the body.

Of a character inherited from the father. Channel of reproduction, similarity of zodiac sign, argumentative Capricorn, melancholic, depressive, introverted, fashioned in the cold seasons to represent order, social formality, at times ruthless: commit to a belief in blind imitation of the father in a flagellating fit of anger, supplanting him in rite of violence, ending up helpless, finding I'm suspicious of an outside world that resists the claim to power by dint of primogeniture, having no truck with the energy of rebellion, playing the conciliator so as to fit in socially: impose my own choice of victims when it comes to apportioning the excrement to be consumed, revealing myself a suspended instant of conflicting wills, nothing more than a residue gone in a flash with the first rumble of the reviled opposing storm.

The ravenous memory of white ants was tickling my ankles, sign of life rising from my heels as I strolled on a springtime Sunday down Rue Blaes, Brussels flea market; the city held my attention for the first time out of its wintry bleakness and I skipped defiantly through the Marolles quarter, stumbling upon an old fire station.

Surrounded by two witnesses to my ancestry, borne along by the treacherous silence of one who shared a part of my childhood, he the reprehensible dreg, clear-headed, close to the real, tempted by other people's bountiful tables yet shunning them furtively in a bid to hide his own powerlessness while—mask or no mask—the very effort that seeks to conceal, reveals. Nothing proves that exile, at its basest, is but an exercise in not disappointing his mother by the love he devotes to her through all women, until the sign of paralysis is lodged in his bones: does he not fear the convulsive pleasure that blooms and dies in the eye of a beautiful woman?

Is there more a formidable tyranny than that which goes without saying, transparency of will seeking to domineer through a cunning sweetness? Every word demonstrates tactical arrogance. Not that I feel uncomfortable in this truth. Nor that I'm ready to make a pact with the devil. Not that I justify this tyranny that diverts the celebration of the senses, disparaging the opulence of some other power in exchange for my submission by congratulation or gift. It's just that there are energies whose presence brings out negative ideas that one must pass over quickly, lingering only for the purpose of ultimate exhaustion. Energy of private and solitary pleasures turning fierce the moment you allow them to reveal something.

I rebuff my childhood friend, with his muddied sensibilities and insufferable self-image, his exclusion of the body's possibility, scorpion whose stinger was removed so that it would stop trying to kill the already dead, benefiting from my slim claims to decency, which needn't matter when all players are eye-to-eye, each hoping to make a feast of the other. He who has a finger in every pie surrenders his shadow.

Rubbing shoulders with this presence brings back my migraine. I asked my other companion, the less judgmental of the two, to bleed me by scarifying my forehead, just like that, quick, right here in the middle of the flea market between piles of shirts and rows of dishes. He took out his razor and proceeded with the precision of the Sahrāwi settled in Mitwiya upon return of the clan from Mecca: for decades now their blood has been flowing at the side of the road, in search of fortune and adventure, money or art, drifting, setting off in conquest of the night, generous calm that grasps the heart at its root, nomads who walk with mild vehemence into the night, between vodka and caviar, recalling the primordial incest: the uncle, brother of the mother, seaman, gone for ten years, goes straight for the sister-mother as the laughing child looks on, weighing hugs and kisses and tears; heartbreaking, veiling words: this is what it's like, the return of the tireless seaman, Vladivostok, Johannesburg, sister at work, lady of the house, cooking, waiting, but eyes wide open: a knowing look, willfully naïve, primitive wound that cries out in pleasure and leaves illusions to vegetate in their fallow fields.

The cortege breaks into daylight again as it slowly climbs Rue Sidi Ibn 'Arūs. The crowd bursts into applause at the mummy's weird splendor, three-eyed, dancing stars, steady sway of shoulders. Pastry chef Shāwish, dethroned after servicing the aristocracy, and like his colleague, rehabilitated into a chess buff, is distributing treats to the masses, cakes, marzipan and pine nut, pistachio and pomegranate colors, scented with orange-blossom water, layered in thick diamond shapes, striking the tongue trained to sort out the mix of sweetness, nut flavors, softened with floral essences, to be savored along with the change of name from Confection of Princes to the People's Delight.

After Stanbāli, here are Tibetan trumpets accompanied by tiny cymbals, a mountain sound pouring into the street, borrowed from Asia, accompanying the 'Isāwiya in the early stages of trance but already able to withstand the tests of fire and thorn, rushing their cargo of words through mouths without ever quite conjoining into a single chorus: evil spell, liver and heart, blood of prey, sun, night, words flung like that, solitary jewels set in mouths partly burned from swallowing fire. And the Tibetan trumpets, unflappable, pursue their bellowing equations, some long, others brief. In the midst of the troupe, the lofty green banner dances to the rhythm of the barefoot ecstatics, walking on their hands, glass shards flung about, crunching, bloodstained paving stones, wild cheering of the crowd.

The bard's chant resounds as it leaves the vaulted street, chest swollen, lips moving of their own volition: life is but a dream, a night's reverie, do you know what you were before you were, scarab or bee, go tell it to the keeper of thresholds, he'll show you the way back, choose for your fate the path of the west or the path of the east, that of colored opacity, agate or coral, or that of translucent stones, the limpid reign of diamonds, pyramids one luminosity or the other; and the chorus picks up the refrain, pyramids one luminosity of the other.

The dazzled crowd throws handfuls of rose petals, blue Nile lotus, papyrus from Bahr al-Ghazal, umbels grazing or whipping the nudity of toddlers, cherub musicians, curly-haired, mannered smiles.

And on this carpet of flowers, child acrobats tumble and summersault, upside down, the foot's eye more watchful than palms or toes, avoiding debris, shards, the aftermath of the 'Isāwiya's frenetic passage. Chimpanzees mixed in with trapeze artists and tightrope walkers, rubbing their pink penises as they scurry along looking for little quarrels, forgotten as quickly as begun, provoking the touchy crowd.

Next follows the animal parade, moving briskly along, tortoises, symbol of shadow, walking on two legs, shell at the back, tall as a man, one raising high a tromba marina, the other with a bow playing songs so slow, so discontinuous, so low pitched; a bear dances to a tune imitating the lumberjack's serenade; wild boar, hardened and defanged, less aggressive; tamed panthers that still strike fear into the crowd; serpents with a most expressive hissing—cerastes, the horned desert viper.

Carnival of the eyes, obsessive dream, annunciation of mystical marriage: Mary dressed in blue, kneeling, a ravishing innocent Flemish girl, rosy flesh, braided russet hair, teased by the resplendent light bursting from the radiant face of Muhammad wrapped in a green burnūs. And the hands of the prophet caress the pained face of the virgin subjected crimson to his words; he says to her in Koranic Arabic: you shall be my last spouse, O good fortune! This was heralded to me during my mi'rāj, when I was carried off to the seventh heaven, here he is at last ready for this reincarnation to come to pass! Light and sapience, the scene turns so intense that the crowd looks away, fire and Prophet's beard, scarlet cheeks of the Virgin.

Next follow the women of the Tijāniya, sect ladies adept with the bendīr, frenzied rhythm, a few young girls dancing themselves unconscious, fondled by the ancient mistresses of melody and rage, screaming before fainting in an ambiguous region between orgasm and holy pain, pleasure in open view, freeing the heart, giving wings to girls whose best hope is self-sacrifice, bodies burst.

Exhausted astonishment: Fātima and I, profaners both, taking refuge in the mausoleum of the Murādiyīn, having followed the cortege as far as the marble courtyard, palatine measure of the Hammūda Pasha mosque. Enclosed among the tombs, getting over our initial fright, now exhausted and trembling, my head resting on the ground, Fātima stretched out on the main tābut, cozy catafalque. Why so many animal images? Is there a symbol somewhere, she asks? There is a meaning in this prelude to prophetic nuptials, I reply. Science of emblems in this century of the last gasp of an obsolete power, implications to be deciphered in the papal city, where scattered symbols point to the dissemination of a unified in truth power: the structure respected by all is the vilified spoils to be shared in violence among the claimants, in the absence of dynastic rule.

Perhaps these animals we've just seen express a similar design. The power distributed among the guilds, in search of a unifying tone in which to marginalize chaos and disorder, to make a showing of extreme heresy in order to be done with the figures of the age of prophets.

We might have had to stretch the analogy rather far, but it's a still comfort to see how seventeenth-century Roman popes marked the city with their insignia: a Pamphili becomes pope, Innocent X, and suddenly Rome is emblazoned with doves, alighting or in flight, deployed either as free metope, as in the Palazzo Doria Pamphili, via del Corso, and the family palazzo, Piazza Navona, or imprisoned in the coat of arms of Rome surmounted by its invariable charges: two crossed keys and the papal tiara, signaling in glory the fountain of the four rivers. Let a Barberini, Urban VIII, ascend to the papacy, and an entire quarter changes symbols to match the new escutcheon design: fountains, palaces, churches all parade the bumblebee, whether the Palazzo di Propaganda Fide, the fresco in the family's honor, giant bees swarming the ceiling, the Tritone Fountain, or the one homonymic of the sign, Fontana della Appi, or again the Barcaccia Fountain.

But this dispersal of power comes together once more, affirming unity in Saint Peter's Basilica: on the square itself, colonnade, fountains, and obelisk, the eight-pointed star and the great oak of Pope Alexander VII Chigi triumph, discreet inscription on the façade of Borghese Pope Paul V's dragon, in the nave a polychrome wall painting slips in the emblem of Innocent X Pamphili and by ambiguity, by contiguity, metonymy, dove, peace, Holy Spirit; while the bees of Urban VIII Barberini swarm on the baldachin above spiral columns, a design that captures the monumental radiance of the light pouring through the vault between two calottes, the winding paths of the ascent, the discovery of Rome's eighth eminence.

Dialectic of dispersion and unity, signs are shared by our bodies and the city. We too have our squares and streets designated by a system of iconic inscription: is the chimpanzee not simply a ruse without memory, unafraid of heights, emblem of the trapeze artist, masters of the Hammam Rimimi quarter? The tortoise, whether in creation-myth or chaos, is mobilized as a symbol by the priests who preside over death and who occupy the Qasba, to the west where troops were barracked. The bear, petulant bonhomie, earns honey money for the merchants enclosed in the Turbat el Bey quarter. The wild boar: remote and untamed, wounded animal, refuge of Berber women mourners and singers of threnody, lament that splits the cork oak, Khrūmirī and 'Aïn Draham, come in from the forest, occupying the New Gate quarter, Bab Jadīd, we listen to their chant that our ears might come to know the voices of the dead, energy enough to tear at their cheeks with rough fingernails, lacerations misinterpreted as self-destructive. And what are panthers if not the agile resistance of commandos whose actions mean our survival, who dwell in the Bāb al-Khadra quarter—symbol inspiring pride, hearts at a loss, monuments to build within ourselves so that each of us might overflow his own confines and go forth into unexplored and solitary places, be resolute but not reckless, venture into the space above the river's source, of dangerous repute, bold lair of wild animals to disturb deep in their dens? As for serpents, we know them well, perfect animals sliding meanders all along their bodies, design of the earth, symbol of Gnostics, reminding us that the soles of our feet can turn snakelike on us, causing the vertical remainder of our body to go reptilian in turn, attribute of the Bāb Sidi 'Abd as-Salām, gateway of migration to come. Thus, these symbols that divide up the city and affirm the diffusion of power come together for this parade leaving from the Grand Mosque, temporary Saint Peter's, basilica of the insurrection already underway.

I try to waken sleeping Fātima: it's not yet time for sleep; come, let us prepare to go out again, can't you hear the crowd repeat in chorus the verses of the new Book? What can I do to revive you? I massage, remove negative energy, communicate through electrifying fingertips, sensitized by contact with music and sand, the new circulation that stimulates and awakens various points along the spinal column; I work the cranium, scatter light taps on her cheeks, center in its hearth the fire of the navel, gather up the life principle from the ankles, I shower praise upon her divided body, exploiting a particular flair for its cavities, groping, searching softly for sensitive points, no special technique, just by means of intense concentration.

Fātima rises, head thrown all the way back. At that point, I ask her to think, exclusively, one by one, of the seven colors: white is the hardest to live with, for it seems inevitable that some flyspeck will imprint itself upon the vertiginous gravity of its emptiness; and with this train of thought, my swift and dexterous hand gestures in freefall over her body, from breast to knees, reiterating the movement, furtive jabs, quick and accurate, right where it matters, awakening the sap condensed just above her navel: the body at last refreshed, stirring the very seat of its audacity.

Fātima back in good form, ready to make an appearance, to shout and scream, surrender her whole self, force her way through the procession's flow. The doors open. The crowd squeezes through, pouring through the courtyard, gateway, hall, and stairs looking west onto Rue Ibn 'Arūs and north to Rue de la Qasba. Men and women unfurl slim banners attached to scrolls and read in a steady voice: the saint is no longer manifest; if he is raised up as idol or monument, he will replicate the society of bygone days, he will support both justice and injustice. Our era is based upon the abolition of the saint: how can we delight in sun and moon, yellow and blue, sand and water, wind and rain, olive tree and wheat, gold and silver, air and fire, sky and earth, head and feet, mouth and sex, plain and river, fountain and honey without ridding ourselves of the saints, those menaces, always proscribing of this or that form of pleasure? Let us eliminate the saints, but divide up the spoils of sainthood: that each shall wear around his head a ray of the halo that one saint alone used to monopolize.

Their voices modulate the excessive density of these texts with gregarious intensity. Each listener frozen within himself contemplates his own visage. Fātima steps over those motionless bodies caught up in what they're protesting; following in Fātima's footsteps, I enter the high-ceilinged room, airy and light, slender columns, exaggerated entasis, shaft topped by capital, a typically *Tunisoise* interpretation of composite order, the capital itself topped by a tall impost. Fātima, showing off, climbs up one of the columns and hoists herself above the tie beam that spans the bay in the interstice where the capital and the impost are joined. Soaring angel now, sure-footed tightrope walker, she reaches equilibrium above these slender beams, with each step scattering a dusting of rust. Treading thus, she shouts the text echoing through the crowd. Arriving before the mihrāb where the palanquin and idol have been set down, guarded by those who carried them this far—by Master Mahmūd, who is outraged at Fātima's ridiculous trick; by Ya'qūb, as if stunned by the discovery of the abyss between them; by Saïda, finally taking aside the old preacher of apocalypse, the millennium, the Second Coming.

Attracted at once by the three-eyed idol and by the sumptuous glimmer of the polychrome marble facing, gleaming mihrāb surmounted by a raised arch, dissolved in the centrifugal circle of the monumental arabesque, Muslim signature diverting irrevocably southward this syncretism of Mediterranean architecture, feature of a moment when Tunis, grown wealthy on Corsair plunder, sat at the crossroads between Turkey and Italy, Fātima falls, in pursuit of her own vertigo, in the direction of the qibla, and would have crashed to the floor had it not been for one of the brawny official palanquin-bearers who caught her just in time.

The crowd abandons the officiating gravitas of the text to have a laugh, and a disputatious Master Mahmūd rushes over to rebuke Fātima: this is no time to be attacking the idol, the people have to exorcise themselves by this ritual of allegiance. But Fātima's was not a rational act: reckless, she was tired of self-preservation—a failure at her calling as processionary.

The sun is sinking. The hours fly. Approach of dusk. And the idol is carried outside the mosque, descending the Rue de la Qasba, turning down Rue du Diwān, heading quickly toward Hawānit 'Achūr, the crowd hysterical as we pass. On each square, we are invited to share a farewell meal, opulent feast, white tablecloths, succulent dishes, guinea fowl, quail, pigeon robbed from some coop in Mannūba, plunder from the previous night's raid. Eat, drink, dance, sing outdoors on these lamp-lit squares, flames throwing a reddish glow on this evening's fest.

The present of writing consigns fiction to one of its moments of suspension. Here, writing text that mingles imagination and slices of life, a stage set containing days and dusks, civilized by the word, knowledge as description; not mere fondness for the look of old stone, but willingness to dig deeper and settle in, outside the body in abeyance.

Here, Paris, chosen city of exile, ghurba, way to the west, strangeness, solitude, eclipse of the sun, at the edge of argument, self-taught self-learned, manage somehow to come out on top, illusive acknowledgement, concocted credibility, wrecking of the senses, inanity where so many bodies flounder in their crassness.

Here writing the text in Paris, swapping the anxiety of a vegetative state—progressing extravagantly—for kerria bouquets of text, great golden bunches naming the self, intermingled discipline of questioning, perfected into something other than a string of exiles, banishment, migration; rather, living in search of an excuse to sail off and prosper as merchant in Ecuador, for example, fleeing one's own haunted existence, stating lopsidedly once again the struggle against the impossible, happy not to own up to oneself, namely, a destiny of dullness.

How much bluff is involved between a middle-class social climber and his becoming heir through marriage to a mercantile fortune in India, colonial residence and all? How much between a priest and Buddha? Missionaries will warn not to condescend to the music, not to countenance Japanese sword rituals. I awake to the haunting certainty that no, this is not my land, even if I feel buffeted by the new winds of change; confirmation of the suspicion that my career is but self-delusion, a sediment of adolescent desire to belong to the select few who frequent the prematurely senile painter, Dalí, worldly master of Cadaqués.

Not that intelligence is in short supply. Zhuangzi says: *Too much intelligence disturbs the rays of the sun and moon, wears away mountains, dries up rivers and upsets the natural succession of the four seasons.* One need only read my text, product of chaos, here in the process of writing, capturing the moment, analysis on the sly, for the sudden and salubrious break to ensue.

I am writing here in Paris and something still won't let me leave. Exhaust the landscape, refine it into a distance within. Of course, an idyllic image is lying in wait, the hermit prospering body and wave as the sea draws near. Sharing boudoir and solitude, passionate siestas with a woman infiltrated by the fictitious Fātima, writing in Paris, body on slow quest for self.

Grabbing as I go at impressions and phrases, shadows and cracks, people and paths, recollections, what matters. Latecomer, myself, tricked-out émigré down to my atoms. History manages all comings and goings, arms and hearts. Going home is infection, lays me to waste, forever irreconcilable as I am with friends from the past now in league with the hopelessly hollow powers that be.

Here writing through fever and fragility; the words flow to the metallic jingle of the pinball machine, on the outskirts of the city, Jeanne d'Arc and Patay, at the corner café Le Commerce, waiter, a Ricard, complicit smile, Kabyle drunkard, squinty-eyed chick blowing her nose noisily, high school kids jostling around a game of table-football, a good-looking lady, shy, as if damaged, then another woman, desert tanned, dressed in a range of blues, gold necklace at her breast quivers delight to the eye, legs crooked but pleasant, a curl in the corners of her mouth promising pleasure, in control of her own destiny, a troubled one, I imagine. Obsequious, simple-minded waiter, angling for a tip.

Here writing, heart hitched to nothing, in this city I so enjoy, away from the Oedipal knot, footsteps give way to words: merry May, fine warm days, shuffling along, hunger distant, light, sober, my text in hand—I swear women are more beautiful in this unexpected sunlight—shocked by the need to write outdoors, walking, weeping, laughing, playing with the perilous waddle of babies learning to walk, Place des Voges, something about keys, no I can't come with you, not that I want to work but I want to dissolve myself high on the city.

Me, walking out of the Place, exiting under the archway, stopping at the bootmaker's, trying on a pair of old-fashioned boots, put off the idea by the noonday heat, awakening before a Siamese beauty, not knowing what to do, what to say, post stuck in the ground leaning against the one-way sign; observed, she's bothered by nothing, measuring herself against her shadow; me walking up and down, nothing happening; what to do, what to say, she doesn't speak, only smiles; me dusting off some old tomes in a bookshop dealing in rarities; when I come out, she's vanished.

Footrace, Rue du Musc, out in the square, pandemonium of vehicles, it stinks; the bridge: I hang for a while over the dancing, rocking water, a thousand reflections of the heart on this brackish skin of water abused by solar glare, stones creating rippling grooves that glide beneath the bridge.

Then island, axial street, straight, shop shingles, showcase of the old in a changing city, museum to be preserved, crowds lining up for ice cream chez Berthillon; heat wells up in my body, I seek the cool solitude of the Saint-Louis church; calming down, numbed by the damp, the earsplitting pipe organ, on my knees writing, my lap a lectern, write and tell Tunis daydreamed rebellious in this springtime Paris, here, enclosed, empty pews, organ out of tune. Imagination revives my chilled body, disjointed writing, dislocated story, if only a dense selva or clearing, resulting in a hand itching to write, scribe, the body's implied fate.

Festive May the first. Weather sunny and steady. The bleak trade unionists' parade has nothing to do with our bodies. Mercury graceful atop his tall column: Bastille, the verdigris rises to the heavens. Africans, dancing to the chanted May Day slogans;

Spanish refugees, national colors steering us toward the gates of mourning, ecclesiastic purple, for sure. Nothing left to say, in fact, not even the plebes, bogged down and press-ganged; the organic intellectuals are visibly fatigued, with a poor showing from among the North African stalwarts. And the women: a flowering of colorful vanity; they matter more for the undeniable violence they cause than for their instinct to deflect the mating urge until they come alive to the seasonal call.

Follow the cortege of foreigners: what they say is worth saying, shouting, applauding, smile, courtesy and duty of these people; walking, running, panting, fiercely urging the rebels to take heart, addressing one another in flame and slogan; up and down, whether dragging their feet or rushing about, talking, shouting, breathless, creating a measure of oceanic rhythm; beyond the two gates, on the outskirts of the city, a brawl: to the deniers they respond that Palestine shall be; chance upon a messenger from the south, burnt man of the oases, greetings and embraces for those freshly arrived from Spain, a reddish mop of hair, glowing leonine, moon in Scorpio, consumed by some nameless fire, suitable presence driven whole and of fair abundance, master of his own circle, offers me the little horse-head piccolo to sound the arrival of the itinerant knife-grinders from Spain; dislocated protest march, at the close of Sabbath, dining at Azar & Sons, we eat, drink, sketch, and sing: this outlying neighborhood rivals the bastardized Tunis of the colonial era, Tunis upside down; my leonine friend flips it back upright: a lovely Jewess sings songs of Salīha, of Msīka, call and response, echoing the tune through the subjugated crowd, voices exclaim words of journey, love, footsteps, she-camels, cities, desire for the uncle, brother of the mother, khāl whose kisses are like so many beauty marks.

Lateness of hour and half-moon high in the sky. Taxi driver hails from the homeland, cassette player oozes Umm Kalthūm singing the endless, blissful refrain: *Is there anyone more drunk with love than we two?* We who are off to the Tartar sorcerer who rigs his own architecture into tent, snow, and steppe; our own enchanted ride together, hooves pounding across the cold, icy spume, weeping to the high-pitched music, incongruous guests of an Uzbek tribe.

The day dawns. Outside, light battles the gloom. The square has dissolved, trees seen from fifth-floor vantage, narrow balcony. Traces left behind, children's merry-go-round leaves Chinese calligraphy patterns on the ground; over there, the pointy belfries of Saint-Jean-Baptiste of Belleville; beneath my feet the balcony drops away and I find myself airborne and light-headed, approaching the bell towers, sailing above the buildings, soaring over park and butte, bridge and pond, leaving behind apartment tower and suburb, Saint-Denis basilica, roof dripping green, dropping into the gloom, scattered cedars around Roissy, toward the land of mists. Dawn serenade of the senses, flawless, no notion of vertigo. Take up the pen again, shake off the remnants of sleep, write, type out the text, clumsy two-fingered pecking at work on my speculative rewriting on my Hermes Media 3, staining my fingers on the poorly wound, unruly ribbon. Soon fatigued, out the door again, a morning stroll, only to find myself in the boozy dreariness of Rue Château-des-Rentiers, tramps and welfare recipients, broken bottles, stench and squalor, degradation of the races, morning hue collapsed into the émigré's beer, Kabyle friends keep watch over the street, and I slip into the spectacle, card game on Rue des Cinq Diamants, hallucinating on the whistling glissade of the elevated train.

Here, writing, ally of warmth, for winter is the season of hibernation. Parks, sunshine, and magnolias, ponds and water lilies, sleepy Jardin des Plantes; furtive images each time I raise my head, time for a nap, heat of the day. Peaceful park, like the one in Hanoi, light doubles and masks the heavy heat; little flowers, dry beds; bower and climbing vine, white iris and jonquils, gigantic horse chestnut trees, green punctuated by white garlands, Chinese paulownia trees, bluish-mauve campanula flowers carpeting the ground in color, not unlike a star-studded sky.

Here walking, between zenith and dusk, Friday prayer, throng of believers crossing through the park, blacks from Senegal and Mauritania, white tunics, full and flowing pride of the steppe; Sahrāwis with their far-off gaze, white-bearded, high forehead, sky-blue turban; abundantly mustachioed Turks, a sparrow's perch; Kabyles moving close-knit; Pakistanis frail and unfortunate; Moroccan Chleuhs, red clover flower behind the ear; Arabs and minorities from all parts, North Africans in particular, among those who seem to have emigrated since the mosque was built, but long before the red-headed renegade's takeover. A mixed crowd, mingling trees and dust, uninterrupted flow, a density and heat reminiscent of some land of Islam, Pont d'Austerlitz, Gare de Lyon, Bastille, a flash of bright color sweeping through the striking students' quarter just long enough to mark an astonishing presence, visual turbulence under the sun.

A fine night, moon shining bright for hours now and the stroll is pleasant, Rue Mauconseil, on the corner, Escargot d'Or, glittering sign, retrace my body, median light, the street snakes, all mapping erased, zigzagging under a moving sky, and me, just barely hallucinating to the dance of the stones; my trajectory a half-empty crescent; flat wall, angular and reflecting the moonglow: to each stone its halo.

What is there to add, except that listening sets music free? We are invited up, the place is welcoming, the music a monochord complaint, endless, repetitive, for stoners, for druggies, incisive lyrics vanished in a blink, voice like a brazier, music to lose your mind to: sway to it, or stiffen up, but either way, we fly. Some woman touches down gently, inspires trust. She's been told about so much misfortune that she holds back, cuts herself off, becomes detached, says she's tired, offers to liberate my right foot with Chinese micro-massage. I wash the designated foot, lay down, offer myself up. She lavishes care on both ankles, a foot rub to make the brain bubble, sparks fly and I'm out of body, surprisingly jubilant, no longer feeling the foot in her hands; stroking, striking, pricks and pinches, bones rumpling the skin. Vibrations climb nerve paths from toes upward. Seventh heaven, but she sends me packing with all the others, time to sleep she says, and now I'm clubfooted, with one foot on Venus, another dragging ball and chain; I make my way joyful but uneven. And it's walking through construction sites, housing projects, up we go and down again, turning this way and that, and at each corner, I feel like inventing the sea. Dawn adds to the night some of its nascent light: Rue des Cascades, Rue Savies, Rue de la Mare, Rue des Envierges, mischievously narrow, smell of suspicion in the shadow of these luminous progressions that help me write my text as I walk, strange silence to the credit of the word, carnal abstraction.

Lovely luminosity that no number of hideous buildings can ruin; the place is a wreck, displaced, basilicas of the capital, thirteenth arrondissement in full mutation, money flowing in, migration of workforce, brains and banks, Rothschild and tomorrow's numbers, what's that muralist doing up there, what logic of color is he applying to that blind wall, that visual disaster? High-rise towers springing up, feet lose their bearings as horizon disappears; the dome of the Panthéon floats unreal in the distance, incongruous celestial crown of a dwarfed neighborhood now seemingly rushing toward certain oblivion, visible from here in perspective between the towers, and the central pinnacle of the church, sanctimonious eyesore, Saint Joan, monument heralded by a statue back on Boulevard Saint-Marcel, a patch job and pathetic blend of styles, straight line cut by blue flash flagging the steel gray armature, allegorizing speed—elevated railway.

Not even turmoil at its most intense can prevent us from waking our ghosts, from rushing toward whatever seems most distant, from proceeding down the somewhat warping path of writing with my Hermes Media 3, which at times resists my calligraphic analogy, punching holes through which all its relevance escapes, typing this text from the handwritten original that preceded it, changing it in the process from one sort of music to another; but the paradox is resolved by reading closely enough to pick up on the text's imperfections with patient vigilance. Desperate quest for something ennobled by the body and that ejects us from our normal flow of expression, destinies washed along, cocoons unbound by untimely friction, to uncover the chrysalis, fabled flood that sweeps us away with the alluvium of the world, all of us adrift on bits of wreckage, a deluge of drowning words, pursued by the relentless noise, uneven, intermittent, music displayed as text in the process of defining itself, which won't show a single trace of the road traveled, nor the rhythm that bruises my fingers, brutal as I am with the typewriter, suffocating by increments of the unexpected, or old anxieties repeating.

Fātima invites me to eat and drink. The festive mood continues as the night advances, stars and moonlight. Up and down the street, merrymakers thunder, biting into whole sides of roasted meat removed from smoking ovens, bakers having turned over their premises, requisitioned for the occasion by the cooks' guild: suckling lambs coated russet in a flavor-enhancing saffron sauce, a special delicacy. Several elders with pious pasts, in hackneyed search of redemption in their declining years, decline the robust, sparkling wine that brings tears to the eyes of the mischievous kitchen women, Qmar, Bakhta, Hallūma, Sālha, Mbārka, all ready and willing and sexually adventurous there among the pots and pans, competing to give out the longest screams in serial climaxes seasoned with spices, hands and vaginas permeated with the five condiments: salt, pepper, saffron, ginger, cinnamon, measured out on the tongue in collaboration with sisters gifted in storytelling, invoking poetic license on all taboo subjects, servants of Shahrazād, stale tales to fall asleep by, to dream of princes and treasure, wells and caves, ogresses and demons pressed into service for the festive townsfolk, join in and lose yourself in all the scheming of the women and children who still leave the males with their semblance of power intact, fooled by this apparent nonintervention until they discover they've been duped, victim of opulence itself integral but inefficient as a source of power. We dispatch ourselves undisturbed despite the threat of death, transgression, the bloodbath to come: these miraculous hours of swooning, wine, and mating, joy and propositioning, openly imprudent.

The women are in charge: they ordain and season these pleasures. And the storytelling ladies aren't impressed with their male counterparts, those purveyors of fake tales—if only the artful shadow puppet Karakūz could come to life, satyr's phallus erect as soon as the word *woman* is pronounced, the word *boy*.

Tell you what, says Hallūma. I know an old man who might give us a laugh, marionettes printed on a screen, farce whose truth causes no offense, even in the eyes of a child, invite the boy like a woman to an obscene show, a theatrical sublimation of the abduction urge formerly tolerated.

Oh yes, I know, I say, the bait he used was candy. I wanted to go with the man offering me sweets; he would enjoy stroking my hair, I was only seven, but I suddenly got scared and ran off to lock myself behind the heavy wrought iron and sheet-metal door, back in the garden, shut in, eyeing him from a safe distance, measuring the visitor's potential as ally or aggressor.

Of course the child, focus of abduction, wild wanderer through the city, in search of Karakūz for fun and fright, along with Charlie Chaplin, Tarzan, Zorro, and the Red Pirate, movies at a nickel per quarter hour: but a looming violence made these outings dangerous; among children of the same age, it was an endless brawl: there would be lewd remarks about someone's sister followed by beatings in the latrines, nasty rumors, imitation of the older boys, harassment by pedophiles on the prowl, youngsters obsessed by the threat of rape, a paralyzing fear, that attraction/repulsion, request to offer up your ass, obsessive refusal despite having interiorized the knowledge of one's own beauty as a perplexingly feminine truth in that barracks of a high school where not a shred of such truth remained, where word invented act, consolidating template of the totalitarian model; found myself once at age five on the ambiguously stiff lap of an adolescent hungry for sex, lewdly disguised as a woman in gauzy intimate apparel, on the sly during the siesta; would flee the grip of that provincial mason, bachelor cursing god and men, eyes possessed, making off like a thief; and that colossus with the look of a child, fiddling around with the black domestics, daily signature of blood, foot wound, or face scrape, to ward off the evil eye, gang of kids each weighing his sex in our hands, heavy, enormous; teenager, it was my turn to go on the make, eyeing boy or molesting a little girl, six years old, stroking, rubbing my stiffness against her, simulating love, passionate kiss on the mouth, suffocation, leaving her baffled, curiously frightened, early experience of love's fruit; female servants offer handjobs, vaginas to penetrate, searing heat; then, at sixteen, a fortyish lady, I leave her house, hair tousled, distraught, exhausted, knees trembling, in search of perdition and death, fragile and hollowed out; the cold delirium of tombs resonates in my head; I'm carried away to a deserted shore, taken aboard by the white man waving woman, Reiter's pride, I rush toward the tearing of veils.

Where are our children now that the pact of our revolt has opened our eyes, I ask Qmar: do they stroll beyond the reach of violence or are they in the shadows, somewhere discreetly in the wings? Oh, for us they are nothing but presence; dispel any ambivalence, they can do as they please, play out their urges, which perhaps hold the potential that the world might one day open to their perverse plurality, that they might grow up harmless, beyond the temptations of abduction. One thing only is to be banished from this city while we're still able to make the rules: the fear that leads to inhibition has no more reason to be. Let both sons and daughters sit in their father's lap.

As for the male storytellers, let them learn a new trade, says Bakhta, chewing on the roasted thigh of a francolin hunted by our commandos around Tburba. Hallūma goes further: right, they never take into account the desires of childhood; these men who seem to have forgotten that they once were boys, they bore us to tears! Go ask them for a story to reward the patience of woman or child, and they'll come back with war, fire, and heaven knows what other monstrous machinery!

One of the scriveners takes the floor, talking with his mouth full, insisting on rectifying the statements of the female storytellers and cooks, getting them to temper their grievances. Mbārka is having none of it: sweep away your embellishments with the sawdust of history, she says; we know how you write: enough with the pomposity that clogs up your letters, enough with all those empty formulas, stale models that never varied, even if you had to announce that the sky was falling. Get your fellow writers together and get some reforms started, serve us up something other than clichés. I have no missive to send my wandering tribe down south, but we women are all in search of writers to draw up our accounts, the sum of the proverbs passed down to us, jewels to offer the wise world.

Could you truly provide us a conduit, O scribe—we women, with our mastery of the oral tradition? We don't want those among us who have learned to read and write to betray us by futilely pandering to sterile ideas from outside: no outside can rescue us, we are thriving, clear-sighted, our characters unconcealed: isn't that right, Fātima? Beware, don't be taken in by their schooling, remain with us, where you're a marvel, continue to be a huntress in the half-light, never lose the audaciousness that greens your springtime.

Fātima laughs and says nothing. We change tables, walk along happy, tipsy, warm. A feast of one hundred dishes: a messy affair, we were to learn: eating is a form of exertion, not unlike, as it turned out, the festival of Trastevere—but set, without nostalgia, in Tunis, feeble reflection of Rome. What's missing, other than a further degree of ostentation and affluence, other than the tradition of sculpture and monumental fountains, water music of the Roman nights still dazed by the summer heat, other than frescos and mosaics celebrating on façades the landscape of Myth, celestial Jerusalem, Sodom, conquest of continents? But their overlapping culinary circuits, erotic and spectacular, bear a family resemblance, producing a similar behavior by way of humor, speech, and values whenever words become infested by the taunts of street talk: echoed at Da Mario's, diners at their tables respond at Chez Slah, argument and wit among Hamma, Slīm, Magīd, and the midget illusionist, silky curls, hosts in great numbers inviting people to eat and drink.

Then who should I recognize among those trying to make sure they'll have the most guests of all but a sheikh of my acquaintance, jubilant, beaming, won over by the present revolt, but rigorous in forbidding any transgression of his principles: so many sumptuous dishes, color and aroma in harmony at his table: tājīne, a kind of garnished soufflé; Tunis-style lasagna, eggplant, tomatoes, stuffed young peppers; beef prepared with capers; couscous with aged butter and lamb; country bread soaked in a vinaigrette and topped with egg, tuna, and chopped grilled vegetables; ricotta from Testūr; salted country butter: all delights there to be enjoyed, with the exception of drink—nothing fermented, neither palm nor fig nor wine, no alcohol, blasphemy, for certain tables persist in exuding their Muslim ways. And the zufri friends, day laborers, loudmouths all, still playing the tough guy, tattooed onto the fringes of the city, respect the necessary distance, though an occasional wine-soaked belch might disturb those who persevere in their abstinence from alcohol and invest their desire in the annihilating power of more potent substances, taboo made flesh along class lines. The sheikh nods to me in passing, busy serving those gathered at his tables, swarm of hands, masticating mouths; over here, says the toothless gentleman. Eager to taste everything on offer, two magicians push forward, in full costume, with their stuffed animals, fox tail, chameleon, box of squirming green and gray lizards, and with mouths still full, tout the virtues of aloe gel to help the constipated return relieved to the table. Other readers of the Koran, greedy regulars at funeral feasts, reluctant converts to the bold and disconcerting new text of the revolution: they eat, gluttonous, grasping, as if digging a grave into the table scraps, helpless before the onslaught of indigestion.

The street widens. Around the corner, a rising slope, and the cutting off of side streets allows the water to rise, covering enough territory for nautical jousts. The model scenario to reenact is of the water

festival of the flooded Piazza Navona, a lakelike ellipsis, oars splashing the statues of the four rivers, thighs taut, heads thrown back,
a moment frozen in time. Agility, speed, piercing spears bringing
down the impetuous Moor, robust imposing body emerging from
out of the fountain's waters. Gaudy costumes, boats in the form of
feluccas borrowed from the time of the Aghlabia, when princes dug
vast basins for their pleasure, filled with water that cooled the kiosks
built around them, refreshing winds whipping up wavelets, there on
the fringes of the Al-Qayrawān steppe, where the Sāhib, barber of
the Prophet, apocryphal page in the holy life, left his remains, along
with relics that laid the foundations of a new power.

Al-Qayrawān like a burn, nighttime, skin scorched, running, in pain,
panting, above the town, overlooking street and mosque, room can-
tilevered over the street, glassed in and narrow, veranda in tones of
blue and green, moonbeams, skin on fire, unbearable, incandescent,
after walking for two days, practically naked, between Makthar and
Al-Qayrawān, coming across transhuman shepherds, grazing mete-
ors, never stopping, nomadic, feet bloody, arriving in the city at dusk,
drank water from a well, palimpsest of the Grand Mosque, reddish
paving stones, body recovers its calm, thirst slaked; sat up against a
pillar, in the shade of the central bay, bare skin pressed against the
cool stone, and a woman watching, movements between prayers,
between hours, crying out at the sight of blood; she took me to her
place and tended to my wounds, applying olive oil and herbs, mingling insult and tenderness, daring a caress in the midst of my pain; I
screamed in agony, asked to be left alone with my blistered body, not

knowing what else to do, determined not to curse the sun, nor the brilliance of Venus, the ground a mass of cracks, a canvas of desiccation, a bellicose trajectory travelling the world via the revelation of drought, of wounding, irrefutable star from zenith to nadir.

Nothing but pain; determined to carry on, giving in to the stinging: my hands had stopped shaking, serene alliance with pain, caught up in sentiment; but I couldn't surrender to it entirely. Dawn already, I rose and walked as best I could through the deserted streets; the city gates were just opening, I rushed out and ran to the Aghlabide basins, found a flat-bottomed boat, stayed for two days and two nights in the relative cool of the kiosk, fasting, awake, breathing, ticking away the time; the hot, dry air of the steppe quickly healed my wounds, sparing me infection.

During these silent, torrid, solitary hours, gazing at the great circular pools calling up short-lived images, magnifying and drowning them, enriching recollection of a princess unrequitedly in love who drowned herself in the wild vastness of the pool in the Menara gardens of Marrakesh; gather myself in the slow modification of the body by the water's narrowing effect, presence hinting at the genesis of Venice, from the Via Garibaldi's viewpoint and beyond, toward the immense open-air garage, servicing frigates and vaporetti, fragile bridge leading to this landmark, this extreme, this pole, this white distance evacuated by its faithful for purposes of restoration, San Pietro di Castello, gasoline-scented land's end, whose monumental form cuts short the city's vista toward its egress, its lungs, its bride, its ally: the sea.

The submerged street is host to certain cruel contests. The women tattoo artists board a boat and attack the calligraphers' craft. The assault is launched, music making both sides bold, men versus women; the tattoo artists hope for a quick victory, capturing the master calligrapher—a protean scenery-chewer happy to play any number of roles. We've got you, you're ours, say the women: you may be master of the reed pen, but we ladies gaily engrave pain with a needle: today, on this bed of water, in the middle of our crowd of admirers, we shall tattoo onto your left thigh the formula that your hand never tires of transcribing so eloquently; we shall take as model for our design the words of faith that you lengthened emphatically into a light-oared boat; you shall bear the wound etched into the skin as irremovable inscription: fine motif to be concealed while seducing your lady love; after today's session, you'll return to our shop every morning for twenty days, and forever shall you bear the mark of your captivity in our hands, we Amazons, crafters of words and figures divulged without warning upon the flesh, unmediated, order of blood, lead-colored, gray blackness against a greening plain.

At the start of the tattooing process, the music calls forth tears of pain, then stifles the screams of the tortured man in a monotone andante, a single phrase that the instrumentalists repeat at each new shortness of breath. Master Maḥmūd, secretly inebriated, slipping out of the shadows, advances toward the first rows of the enraptured crowd, steps gingerly into the water, scrutinizes the scene, cocks an ear to the music; disturbed by the cries of the calligrapher, and swaying to the rhythm of the melody, he removes from his pocket an illuminated manuscript of the *Epistle on Music* by the

Ikhwān as-Safā, the Brethren of Purity, opens it with a categorical flair, hoists himself onto the shoulders of a hulking bystander, and starts first to sing, then to orate the text, moving from prose to verse, a dirge in uneven rhythm: *It is told that a certain number of / musicians were gathered for a feast at / the residence of a great ruler who took care to / place them according to rank of / mastery that they held in their / respective arts, when a man of / wretched appearance dressed in rags entered. The master of / the house raised him above / all those in attendance, whose faces showed an / obvious disapproval. Wishing to demonstrate / the man's merit and to appease the anger of / his guests, the master asked the man to / let them hear a sampling of / his art. The man took out / pieces of wood that he had brought, placed them before / him, and laid down some strings upon them. Then, he set the strings astir and / produced an air that set off laughter / among all in attendance, owing to the joy, the / pleasure, and the well-being that took hold of / their souls. He then retuned / and produced another air that made / everyone cry, so tender was the melody, / such sadness it poured into their hearts. He then retuned yet again / and produced an air that / plunged everyone into / sleep; this done, he rose and exited, / never to be heard from again.*

The needle digs into the flesh, the musicians play another melody, Master Mahmūd weeps, the crowd sobs, the victim cries out, the imperturbable tattoo ladies carry on. The music changes, Master Mahmūd bursts into laughter, the crowd does the same, the calligrapher surrenders to this merriment, wriggling in a laughing fit; the ladies hold him down and dig the red-hot needle ever deeper. The black musicians, ghaïta and gumbri, strike up a different tune, and everyone dozes. Then, fearing a premature halt to the festivities, they mix a watery tune in tones of blue, awakening the crowd soaked now in a sensation of wetness; the tattoo ladies resume their work; more music, imperceptible change, in each modality the same musical phrase returns, Master Mahmūd sings lyrics having to do with fire, the persistence of the sun, guarantor of the body's flame, invigorating the blood with a fever that consumes the pain of the calligrapher, now near the end of his ordeal, stirring the crowd into excited movement, then calming things down with a return to the initial adagio, not seeking with its throbbing phrase to stifle the cry of the tattoo victim for, in their eagerness for spectacle, the ladies compress the suffering of the first three necessary sessions into a single attack.

As it moves forward, the cortege sheds its cohesiveness. The night is cloaked in black. Festival fatigue sets in. People disperse. Necromancy enthusiasts gather at Dar Lasram, across from Dar Dzīrī. Inside, images of childhood jostling somehow with the present. The vestibule is long, meandering, high-ceilinged, dark rooms nested together, separate stairways, multiple levels, massive flagstones, masonry benches, antechamber where sharecropping tenants and managers were once made to wait, where peasants paid their due to the city-dwelling lords, a one-sided deal. From out of the shadows, the patio sheds light; foul odors pervade, burning matter on the brazier, the kanūn, acrid myrrh: searching for the effective formula, the sorceresses try out new magic words to accompany the smoke emitted from the burning of dried insects, spiders, lizards, iguanas, locust bellies.

This house that once swarmed with adolescents and women back in times of plenty when the vast tribe had amassed considerable wealth, spacious rooms, beds and alcoves, on platforms or suspended, wooden ceilings painted with flower baskets, betraying the provincial origins of some Sicilian artists taken refuge in the city: garlands of vegetation, mawkish colors against a background of pastel green; hardly the decor to highlight rococo adornments. Several families mix in such a palace, uncles and aunts, brothers and sisters, secondary patios, fine marble. There even used to be a modern apartment within the confines of the building, narrow stairway and roughcast walls painted in a cream color, calling to mind the hybrid style of houses on the farthest outskirts of the city where the pretentiously coated façades, capitals in plaster, flora and fauna, attempt to conceal a less noble substratum.

A lovely, long-haired adolescent girl used to pay visits, and would come to indulge my coquettishly enchanting child's body, cozying up to me, smothering me with caresses, rambling on about the lively and elusive color of my eyes, in the hope of kindling the dormant flame in a cousin her own age, impervious however to her call, proud countenance, chaste Joseph, rising unapologetic from his bed whenever she would simulate a chill to slip under his covers in search of some warmth; he would merely smile and resume his reading, sitting on the divan opposite the bed. Disconcerted, she dared not make a bolder move. I happened to see her years later, found her moping over the lost years of her ardent adolescence, obediently but unhappily married, mother of a brood, wife to a bland barrister.

This was a house where holidays and weddings were celebrated. Our joys came in dreary succession. An air of incurable decadence loomed over the patio occupied by its fragments of female conversation. Our fancy dress at times lackluster, our cuisine just this side of the fine ancestral standard. We children proved infallibly lucid, all hilarity and noise, a sensory adventure, scaling walls and cisterns, up and down before finally reaching a riadh, tiny walled garden that had seen better days, gates padlocked, casual dumping ground, crumpled wrappers, fruit peels, piles of dust and sand, a large well sealed shut.

The house is closed in upon its own history. Once inside, one enjoys its exclusive fragrance. The urban air is left behind. You are elsewhere, symphony of footsteps, death evacuated by the impressive dialectic of levels, parcels, the sharing out of space: Dar Lasram was built to house several branches of the same trunk, each rich in offspring and cloistered around its own cell, complicity of alliances, crossbreeding, self-preservation among one's own. Rare were those who could move about everywhere on even footing, into every nook and cranny, respect for privacy, restriction today lifted as the celebration spreads noisily throughout, reflection of the welcome disorder from outside, free comings and goings, multiple shadows cast as, shoulder to shoulder, the practitioners of palmistry experiment amidst a stifling cloud of smoke.

There do remain venerable old Arab houses, each more spacious than the next, despite the unfortunate tendancy to split them up. Bayt al-Suhaymi, pearl of Cairo, in the Gamaliya neighborhood, Darb al-Asfar, fans out around one central patio, gift of vegetation, behind which lies a garden that ensures there's enough shade to go around, mill and waterwheel, kiosk sheltering the fountain that divides up its water into channels and rivulets, along walkways and flower beds. A walk through this house brings relief to the weary eye. Labyrinth that lightens the oppressiveness squeezing the house's heart, that bruised organ; in the back, a trellis guides a tree, split Y-shaped to climb skyward on either side of a mashrabiya, stark monument.

Rooms follow one after the other, adjacent, separated by three or four steps, each one long and high-ceilinged, but with features all its own; cedar wood, pierced copula filters light, clearstory shukh-shikha and manwar, openly welcoming, enough light that we can decipher the calligraphy of the simple proverbs divided into strips on separate pillars, spatial void corresponding to the suspended empty space of the writing, eye expectantly in search of assonance in the continuity of phrases that intermingle their rhymes; lying down now in the breezy loggia, tea and hookah, conversation, artisan restorer of old pavement and mosaic, pendulous cheeks a camouflage for servile status, head and body mismatched.

Decision by act of will to escape between Bāb Zuwayla and the Ghuriya toward other patches of blue, unifying coherence in the expressive power of void at Bayt Dhahabī, golden in ways my body can understand, manner of organizing a one-way ascent, climbing a few steps to leave the street behind, glare off white patio dazzles the eye while ears attune to the whispering fasqiya, polychrome fountain; climb an angled stairway, come in contact with the sky, sit in the maq'ad, a loggia with spacious bays, continue through a dim passage that only pretends to dead-end, then enter a bright mashrabiya, respite for the eye before moving on to the durqa'a, sunken central part of the room, flanked by two iwan, or side rooms, together a reception hall, feast of light and script, layout of solids and voids, height and constriction, secret ceremony that ends with that perfectly logical enumeration of the elements making up the Arab house, following one after the other in their undeviating functions, a single level suffices, such that a sense of oppression and interior discord emerges, only to be reabsorbed into the general architectural entanglement, a floor plan as reiterative as an ornate polygon, complexity made simple by way of astral metaphor.

The sorceresses keep watch over the idol. Several women whose armpits smell of sweet myrrh come to help enrich their repertoire. Rehearsal of unfamiliar fumigations—beetles, guano of Pipistrelle bats gathered during an expedition to the ancient Roman quarries of Hawwāriya, asafetida—all further fouling the air. The women improvise unheard-of songs, arranged for the occasion, for rituals and the casting of spells: what matters is the protection of the city threatened by the opposing coalition. The enchantment already used to preserve the city is wearing off. Persistent rumors speak of a tightening of the noose, but the people, nestled here among themselves, are not overly concerned: beyond jubilation, solemn joy.

To the crash of cymbals and soaring notes of ghaïta horns, ear-splitting noise, the splinter group of sorceresses persuaded to defend the Zāwiya Sidi Mahrez comes out of its den, accompanied by the doyen of the guild of Moroccans, caretakers of the buildings of downtown Tunis, collectively determined to betray the landlords and join the rebellion. The sorceresses are all different when it comes to sophistication of accoutrement, blouses set off with golden embroidery, fine pearls, glass medallions dangling in their marvelously exposed cleavage, seven-colored face paint turning their faces cartoonish.

They approach the idol, shoving aside Master Mahmūd and Yaʿqūb, old dozing mules, drunken Noahs, decrepit men in rut, inebriated sileni, known to the sorceresses as scornful of their clandestine colloquium. The women now lavish their attentions on the old men, stroking and rubbing, playing with their upright members, tickling them on the bottoms of their feet, under their arms, all right granddaddies, consider our differences resolved. But we have to be allowed to finish up the idol. Mummifying is not in itself sufficient; its clothes are not at all good enough; and you, you women subjected to men, say these sorceresses in chorus, stop chasing after those elusive words you hope to cobble together into spells to save us, as if your ruses were a match for their drunken binges.

Not to be trifled with, these Moroccans, this ocean of knowledge come to us all the way from the Atlas Mountains to supply the herbalists of Souk al-Blāt, and who moldered away organizing monthly collections among their fellow Moroccan concierges—the same ones that you turned into bogeymen, exploiting their foreignness: spectral, lonely presence, indecipherable language, small, bright eyes, well-tailored collars, modest djellabas, wielding their nightsticks, whom you discredited by assuming they were violent, frightening your anxiety-ridden children troubled by their own sexual awakenings during the deserted hours of siesta: sleep, you would say, or the Moroccans will come get you; don't fall for their tricks, don't take what they offer, they'll carry you off, cut your chest open, steal your hearts, lungs, kidneys, and testicles, child organs they need for their magic potions; you take advantage of their marginal status to disparage them, call them despicable and loathsome.

Claptrap, drivel, and nonsense, says the Moroccan phytotherapist from Telouet, hogwash spread by warty old bourgeois ladies, that's what such accusations are worth. We have no need of your children's organs! We use nothing but herbs and plants, birds and beasts. May I suggest some samples of my remedies: I can tell you that sage loosens the tongue, kindles affection; and that hollowed-out aetites stones, when shaken like rattles, then placed on a woman in labor, will make for a quick delivery; likewise, rose of Jericho, macerated and then taken in liquid form, can also ease delivery for those of you ladies looking to bear children; donkey and horse hooves will likewise make birthing far less arduous, without exhaustion or excessive strain.

Secrets jealously preserved, slough of snake, molted skin, fox flesh, we need only these, along with a drop of afyūn, the milky sap of the Egyptian black poppy. As for those of you who would rather prevent the fruit from ripening in the womb, may I advise crushed cabbage seeds to abort: no sooner consumed than your troubles are gone! While those who suffer from constipation need not place their trust solely in aloe and colocynth: instead of croton, try a dose of myrobolan and tragacanth gum.

And what about me? asks the blind musician and singer, voice straight from the gut, raspy throat, playing somewhat crudely on a poorly tuned lute, singing of gloom and sinking sun, as far as the eye can see—love of a people whose history is bound for pitch darkness: death to this kind of blindness.

For you, says the Moroccan, may I advise bile of crane mixed with honey and fenugreek sap: ten drops of it every morning in each eye; and one day you shall see, the obscurity that veils your eyes shall vanish. Then shall you sing the world of light, cast your eyes upon the people's victory, you shall discover perhaps what by gaining sight you have lost as you comprehend secrets in this new light and you shall say: now I know: the blessed tree is the olive tree, and of its fruit, of its pit, of its oil, you shall anoint your body, and your breast glistening in the sun shall blind you like a bolt of lightning, and in that instant of memory shall you discover the true meaning of blindness. A shiver up your spine, and you shall laugh!

And what about me? asks the other, I who am weary, so drowsy I'm about to drop, though I want to assist you sorcerer women in your bid to instate the idol? Yes, what about me? he repeats, exhausted, drunk and feverish, while clever Fātima starts by disinfecting the air, expelling the putrid fumigation by tossing onto the hot coals something to lend fragrance to the atmosphere: labdanum and frankincense.

For you: cola nut, remedy of kings, something not only to dispel drowsiness but also to awaken an irrefutable erection, to the delight of many a female; it will also sweeten your breath and soothe the body; wakefulness shall grip you as a falcon's talon grips its prey. And for the joy of your nostrils, let me offer what I have just gathered from the Adonies, tiny suspended gardens, flower boxes on the terrace, parcels signed *woman* on the roofs of the Zāwiya Sidi Mahrez—here, smell these sprigs of hyssop!

We have to flee the city, say the sorceresses, far away, in hope of another life of great expectation, a desert to swear our allegiance to.

What remains of life for us here is but the timely circumstances to bid farewell to the city, a tomb dug for us. Let us seize the moment, our hours are numbered. Relieve the city of its law before abandoning it to the fury of our enemies who by slaughter will seek to exorcise this space in which the true nature of their intentions has been, at last, supremely expressed.

And you, calligraphers, cease shedding tears over your master's wounds and make yourselves useful by talking some sense into the gullible fools who continue their trance-inducing spins, bearing their sackcloth and gut-wrenching hunger into the courtyard of Sidi Brahim ar-Riyahi, age-old ascetics in search of ecstasy, believing that by assuming some position—pure fiction!—they'll encounter God; go write on the catafalque of the saint in your finest archaic kūfi script—a frieze in gilded letters against the green covering—the following precept that has come from the land from which we have so much to learn, blurred proximity to China: *Defiling rough wood to make out of it utensils, such is the crime of the carpenter.* In that way, they shall perhaps understand that our turning toward timeworn values and the reemergence of the dying craft guilds do not constitute a return to the way things were, nor the fantasy of a weak imagination . . . no, we are neither backsliding nor simplemindedly well-intentioned when it comes to tradition. We are more modern than you may think. We are readying ourselves to galvanize the as-yet unthought. Let us strive to shake up what remains of this city, until we exhaust the ancient principles—the next stage of our development shall bear the mark of an inaugural wisdom, rising out of despair and ruin.

Let us renew our ties with desert, mountain, a retreat outside this history whose final cataclysm is still liable to take us unawares. And to seal this pact, these areas chosen for our wandering, let us cast at the feet of the idol the skins or symbols of the animals that will be our exotic familiars in our remote, future retreat: shrew, mongoose, ibis, jerboa, fennec, zorille, oryx, bubale antelope, ibex, bighorn mouflon, screw-horn addax, gazelle—beasts to weep over, to consume, to admire, to sacrifice, to look after.

And each sorceress removes from her bag a sculpture or some animal remains to cast theatrically all around the idol, votive offering as embellishment. One of the sorceresses grabs hold of the palanquin set right on the ground and begins to cry in the manner of a wounded animal: O final return of the gods who nearly fooled these good people, who, liberated from themselves, thought they were capable of reviving what had preceded their enslavement; O enlightenment of we sorceresses who will lead these throngs with foolish hands toward the discourse of the dead: how many tears shall unite us!

And in the middle of the patio, emerging from a trapdoor in the ground, a girl, misshapen family shame, monstrous, hands knotted and deformed, on her left arm a right hand and vice versa; green eyes, dull and lackluster, deathly pale, bowlegged, ribcage sticking out; bony, disjointed chest; kept on a leash by her mother: woman in traditional dress, tight blouse, navel and flabby belly exposed, skirt of long flowered cloth wound around the waist, tight at the legs. Two sorceresses immobilize the mother and free the girl, mute monster who only cries out in sharp little barking noises. She approaches the idol, removes amulets from her little cloth sack one by one to be hung on the still-damp wrappings of the mummy: a golden Egyptian djed pillar, a carnelian earring, a golden sparrow-hawk, a moonstone necklace; *Wedjat*: an eye of Horus in emerald, a smooth, gleaming soapstone.

Meanwhile, the two sorceresses gag the mother with an ecru scarf in raw silk that she'd been wearing over her bottle-blonde hair. She is led away, captive among her enemies rotting in half-flooded underground chambers, moaning in their chains.

Lastly, the girl exhibits a Uraeus, golden cobra, neck swollen in anger; she can't manage to hang it on the forehead of the idol, above the third eye. And it is the trembling hands of a drunken Master Mahmūd that serve as her stool to hoist her up to set the jewel in its place, to complete the cycle of the eye.

Then the young girl turns toward the sorceresses, vague smile, a bit distraught, distracted, mouth gaping uncontrollably wide so that drool flows down her chin and onto the white lace collar of her yellow dress.

Musicians and sorceresses blessed by the Moroccan's acts on their behalf now supplant a number of other forces that had always believed themselves destined to rule uncontested; the musicians strike up a melody in the mode of fire, having surpassed the mode of silence, invented during the mourning period following the execution of a Barmaqi vizir in a Baghdad filled with anxiety. The sorceresses accompany this music with their voices, in a song declaring that the outsiders, and the women who watch over them, shall have the last word.

After dances and speech-making, serpents wound about bodies, the sorceresses carry the palanquin and idol outside. Street dimly lit by the luminescence of the misty dawn, still marked by the color of disseminated dew, tinfoil on the pavement where feet, creaking or cracking, shod or barefoot, are reflected.

And Saïda, the sorceress considered a traitor by her peers, manages to convince those women who deride her to follow the logic of her preferred itinerary: idol to be set down not next to the tābūt of Sidi Mahrez, patron saint of Tunis, but instead facing it, inside the eponymous mosque, so that, by a radiating effect, the idol's presence will permeate the architectural forms that surround it, that its image might shine radiant on the face of the world, near and far, gilding the monumental dome of the mosque, centered in the manner of Sinan, the most impressive silhouette in the city. Argument finding favor among the sorceresses, who acquiesce.

Swift as abduction, while a number of other bodies hope to take advantage of the dawn to catch an hour or two of sleep, the sorceresses cross the short distance. Climbing the steps proves difficult, and help is required to prevent the palanquin from becoming a runaway perambulator.

After courtyard and gallery, the idol rests in the center of the cubelike mosque, protected by the four square pillars paneled in blue tiles from Izmir, massive base to support the high dome, half sphere whitewashed and without blemish or crack.

The sorceresses are off once again, deliberating now in the crypt, an older structure that opens onto the street. Fātima and I stay to keep watch over the idol. Silence and lingering in this dawn that preceded us. Fātima dozes, stretched out alone near the mihrāb; as for me, I walk about, small steps, determined to triumph over sleep by way of controlled breathing. I'm gnawed at by thirst, speak to no one. I talk to myself in secret, enumerating the effects of these times, meditating so as not to perish from wild dreaming, from seven-glint colors.

Over the course of their difficult passage from manuscript to typed draft, the words sometimes mutate, due either to my slowness at the keyboard, to my discovery of a better word, or to my integration of a typo, slipped first letter of a word that evolves into another word, the right one, splendid, joy at being spared the drudgery of reaching for the bottle of white-out and painting over the offending letter of the solitary word from the original manuscript; a text is not immutable, but open, carrying events and words along in its stream picked up from both lived experience and fiction, and in this anxious moment, weary of my typewriter ringing obsessively in my ears, detestable Hermes Media 3, desire to rip its rusty guts out, its sticky metallic branches that so often cross, dueling, obstructing the void that separates the letter from the space it is destined to imprint, not to mention the blank interval that separates the words.

Abandon the Hermes Media 3 and get out into the street, just after midday, diving into Barbès in search of faces mirroring mine: not a city in all the Maghreb contains such a dense crowd, variation on the twenty ethnic types usually more dispersed in their natural habitat; enclosed now in a male mass, jostling to get to the brothel, pastry shops packed to the gills, grocery shops redolent of back home, street music, Goutte d'Or, feeling carefree, rootless, stepping lightly toward Rue Myrha, Rue des Gardes, Rue des Poissonniers, Rue Labat where couscous is served, hard to swallow in this summer heat, veil of haze on the city and body, vocal Kabyles, fruits and vegetables, Muslim butchers advertising sale of halal meat, card players: black loses red wins; chance and roll of the dice, measuring the misfortune of the naïve fool caught in the snare set by neighborhood crooks that never allow a cop anywhere near the most exclusive part of the extensive Arab ghetto, though blacks get safe passage; heat and sweat, language of desire, shouting matches, austere threats as they exit the seedy fleshpots that get forgotten the rest of the week as body is given over to the workplace, a few female faces lurking beyond the stench of public urinals, waddling about in gaudy djellabas purchased chez Tati, cross over into Marché Saint-Pierre where mixing of populations is profitable for all, exercising a form of covert kleptomania, here, I've just pinched this almost-silk scarf, it's yours my lovely, dark eyes questioning in return. Haunted by these faces encountered so soon after leaving the text, after having walked through cities within the city, but Barbès, bodies and music clashing, stands out: city highly organized around an offshore Arabness, where the day is not divided between female territory and male terrain: here they don't play mother, and out of violence alone the bodies on sale forget themselves just long enough for a mirage of hunger, available men.

Beyond the portico, a flawless sky unveiled, vanquishing residues of rapidly dissipating mist. Reflecting upon names gives me reason to follow this thought as it integrates the body, tempted to penetrate, serene or disturbed, the world wrapped about us during sleep.

Where are you from? asked a man with a preacherly voice, face beaming light, as I sat down beside him on the curb, shady Rissani souk, town of Tafilalet, cradle of oligarchs and shorfa. Tunis, I answered. And he, smiling, touched my head: city of Sidi Mahrez, he said. He stared at me with a look fit to penetrate both objects and men, a translucent gaze, and told me that I would later learn the meaning of his allusions: there are, on the one hand, the admirable child and the shrewd old man; there are, on the other hand, man and woman; an isthmus separates the ones from the others; he who treads upon the territory of the other will be goaded like a heifer is by horsefly. Meditate upon this, and you shall find your fighting spirit and reveal to yourself, by means of your own enlightenment, by the meaning of your present civil name, and then of your symbolic name, your own death and gravestone.

The name spells me: of the first name, servitude expressed already as gift, nothing further to add there; not that you're tight-fisted or an outrageous spendthrift: your eyes alone ferment the gift despite your introversion and sudden melancholies.

Your family name, however, is another matter: originally Mu'addib, schoolmaster, teacher, prescriber of knowledge for its proper usage in society, dispenser of adab, a purveyor by name of good breeding and official culture, for the training of scribes and other executives of Arab power.

But language slips in usage from ritual purity toward demythologized dialect, the genealogical real: thus, Mu'addib changes into Middib, a phonetic fate that's not at all trivial, because the meaning shifts—the task of education becoming that of nursery-school teacher: the middib is the one who, with the Koran as excuse, teaches children to read and write.

Deconstructing your name, we shall perhaps discover emblems and symbols: mid, morpheme in Arabic designating the action of giving, of bearing, of extending the hand, instrument of mediation, percept matching the features embodied by the name: gift/give: another morpheme, dib, is given a form that, slow and genial, may be likened to a bear, emblematic animal, alliance with the émigré Orsini captured by Jean Fouquet in that same solemn posture, bear emblems surrounding his head in the background.

The French transcription of your name, stigmata of colonial intervention, claims to lighten its load with a new spelling, municipal duty, respecting neither the phonetic resemblance nor the logic of transliteration, Middib becomes Meddeb, quirky habit of altering spelling and sound ascribed to some Corsican civil servant, some Alsatian brigadier.

Keep the letter *mīm*, that of gift, and you get *Mulay*, master, to exert sovereignty of the self in all ways possible. Thus begins the new name, worn as new and positive body. Second to see: Hanīf, Abrahamic word, predating things Arab, rousing the pagan body. Of the letter *ha*, that of *hāl*, or state, fullness of the moment, heightening the flash of certainty, distancing you from the man of doctrine, of *maqāl*; of the letter *nūn*, emphatic graph extolling *nūr*, light to incorporate, to bequeath, to enlighten the self, not simply to confront its reference to the sun, think in terms of the Verse of Light and its commentary by Al-Ghāzali, *The Niche of Lights*, which has recovered its rightful place in the hierarchy of Enlightenment, by Mazdaist contribution, by Suhrawardian incandescence; of the letter *fa*, to say *fā'l*, good omen, unique to each, for every person is in the world an irreplaceable herald, an idiosyncrasy of sex, of being, of death, of text, of idiolect, the self observed, outside the convergence of interests; there you have it: superpose Meddeb Mūlay Hanīf, supported by the master of extraordinary light, and, by the name image, you will designate the body that will translate his passion within the real.

To each name its desert. Nothing if not that part that no name can begin to cover, nor self-defense, nor struggle, nor appeal of saint, nor derangement of the senses. By derivation, history completes the name, but uproots it just the same; I celebrate myself, more void now than before I was born, less determined by heredity, ruffling the genealogy of the name, of the organs, symbolic of recollection, veil disclosed as irreconcilable difference that nothing names, to harmonize as before, sufficient unity of hermaphroditic body from before the split. Name as body label: for want of body, how does the name take effect? Again this word body, restored but as distinct from what lurks around it: it is in itself nothing but exactitude refusing to magnify the way out through the word: redemption, protection, snare that many a tradition has exploited to express its promise.

The body on which a name is affixed moves forward and labors silently in its own vacuum: it is but chaos, disorder. Hygiene of course is the moral base, but death lurks everywhere. Breathe, eat, love, sleep, keep vigil, be lavish, dream, think, feel, see the world from upside down, be to oneself the wrong side of the world, careful not to bother the right side of the world, use up its colors, its emotions, get to the heart of its fragile representations, patch up this or that crack, work at it, displacing inspiring accuracy to certain wandering parcels of the body, impervious to its unitary permanence.

Body as vigor, sap, running, copulating, to reserve for it that basic boldness that allows it to enter where another body calls. Not that one ought to display the body, play the exhibitionist, genital display, in the hands of Salome, of Judith, women who think with their sex, reinvent evil that they might reproduce us as something other than we are. The body offers its services, decomposed dreams of annihilation.

Let the body follow the trail of Mercuro and Dora, descend into the burial vault, woo Mercuro's Dora, a love's labor lost, evasive responses, imagining myself flute-playing Pan, and after the curious music, anxious and unfinished, of this musician of absolute vocation, was it not Mercuro that nothing could save, not even the speed of his wit, coursing through the actual body of my sleeping state in the incurious company of Dora, India eyes, and Mercuro, winged heels, sunken spirit, on the edge of a precipice allowing the ocean to overwhelm me with unaccustomed iodine, face violet, singing so loud as to subdue the rival fury of the wind, watching the sun sink, out there at the foot of the Pyrenees, ocean of inconstant color, blues and greens, spheres black and luminous, instantaneous rise of the crescent moon, a warrior's red saber, scythe and death succeed the igneous contours of the sun, wonderful seething waves of fire, by wind become infuriating, decapitating, startling, ripping from my voice the madness that carries me away across the vast stretches of sand.

Lost descending into the ravine, near invisible path, discovery of the enchanted couple seized by sickness, reason for shutting all their anguish into something dual, gnawing pain sharpens unity of both bodies in distress: orphans and parents one of the other, a need for petty name-calling in reciprocal aggression, mutual challenge and baiting, threatening vengeance one way or another, while the music of insult flows toward the Basque side of the mountain. Meanwhile, admiration and disturbance of the feasting raptors, hawks and buzzards descending upon a badger, tearing it apart with excellent technique, flesh from under flesh, pecking at the slightest smidgen of meat so that only an immaculate skeleton will remain, set apart from its unwanted hide.

So I play the troublemaker, the contrarian, not understanding the compassion of the others in the face of so much destruction, so much considerate scheming, not knowing how to handle this constantly shifting balance, one's own reality, body and feelings apart from what one would insist on being.

Eating by night in Saint-Jean-Pied-de-Port, chilly April, listening to the Nive flow by, feeling more involved in a Serbian night than a Basque one, steep streets, singing outside cafés, church and midnight Mass, drunken brawls, exquisite full moon dispersing clouds scudding by high in the sky, ballade of the stars, while I, acting on Mercuro's advice, was sampling a pigeon conserve, shivering in this late-coming springtime in the confines of inaccessible mountains that thunder with the enigma of separation, of borders.

Hungover Sunday in Cambo, scrawny bodies, emaciated old men, satyrs fleeing the sanatorium for the day, recollection of the seminary; Mercuro speaking of a priest he'd befriended, adolescent body and insane man of the cloth not daring to approach the heat of pubescent youth, troubled by the vainness of it all, even as a source of favors given in exchange for such tender attentions. Sickness was circulating among us, threatened as we were by the mountain's chill shadow and by the approaching twilight, watching the ewes and rams graze, smell of dung; fragile, vulnerable lambs; a parable sprang to mind, such easy prey for the taking.

Heartbreaking music in Pamplona, sad circus strains, clownish, subtly poetic and comical, passage of Easter procession, Virgin in flowing blue mantle studded with stars, statue ascending into the dark heavens, hands contracting, eyes full of wonder, adoration of the Son. Crowd falls into silent respectful prayer, O sacrifice! Children of dismal Sundays, colors like the weather, outfits where the dominant color is the black of widows, the gray of bureaucrats, the dark blue of uniforms. Clarinets, tinny and invasive, gong and bass drum. So mucky, so messy, I'm going to puke, ready to cry, what's with this old jalopy, said Mercuro, exasperated.

To end up there, having run out of dreams, by way of absence, body gutted, no privacy, for the self or shared, solitude of footsteps, hotel on the main square, toreadors' purgatory, chipped paneling, faded luxury, carpet dusty and moth-eaten, disemboweled chandeliers, rattling old elevator, vestibules painted in honeymoon blue, beds faded and creaking, faucets dripping on your nerves through the night, spent half in, half out of body, not even that dense, forced sleep never taken for granted.

Comings and goings, and the mosque alive with activity as the morning progresses. Some movement around the idol, and I, barely awake, meditating and remembering, having entered the perilous gloom of recollection. One of the sorceresses speaks out, provacative: the time has come to unveil the surprise; those who wish may follow me. She nimbly descends the stairs, crosses the street, and enters a bathhouse they call Hammam Dhab, neighboring door in circles of silver, edged in white, red, yellow, and green, filling arcs and extending branches, contained profusion that catches the eye without spinning it dizzy.

Apodyterium where women and adolescent girls shine, beauty assured, prey ravished the previous night from beyond the medina's boundary, in the new quarter, Rue de Serbie between the central market and the train station, behind the French Embassy, hair salon for well-born ladies, mistresses, and high-society insiders, antechamber of the State, orgiastic pleasure palace, sex without despair, consume now, pay later, hairdresser as madam, inventing new couplings then undoing them, cashing in, or not, on the goodwill of bodies, we merge into sex for sale, soft bed for softer breasts, finding mother in woman, ignoring her fervor, offering ourselves up as products of exchange: generosity that reifies what little remains of the body, experimenting with the self as other; backsliding patriarchs, recalcitrant Messalinas: get back to the vengeful Bedouin Eros, squall that leaves nothing behind but a body now neutralized; women, split from your new alliances, surrender yourselves as demons even more debased than your city-dwelling sisters, take on the roving eye and daring of men: woman is an other.

Here are the enemy women, says the sorceress. What treatment do they deserve, you who are absolute masters here? Hammam invites nudity of both sexes; without equivocation, the circle of water is drawn: let the bodies enter it, splash around if they want, and let the games begin! Make these women your own or banish them, the choice is yours between sperm and blood.

The music thwarts its own lordly origins and quickens our craving, limpidly testing notes in an aquatic mode. The supposed female victims enter with us into the baths, moving from cold to hot, *frigidarium, tepidarium, caldarium.*

Those with less patience or greater appetite welcome each other to love with open arms. Others, going too far, whip the bodies of their choice, in defiance or ecstasy. There are insults. There is love and death. And death sends a shiver of love through the steam that clouds the room with its basin of blisteringly hot water, where the fearless hurl the bodies of these enemy women; they scream in pain, to the delight of the few men and women now losing their inhibitions.

Two slaps knock down one intimidated lady of means, hand hiding her pubis, recognized by the violent sorceress as her former employer, back when she was servant to the wealthy, jealous of her mistress's righteousness which always managed to conceal her perverse ways. Her heaving sobs grow wearisome, repulsive mawkishness: hardly the right background music for these altercations, these scandals.

Ridding myself of memory, blank absence. Not that our collective nudity is particularly disenchanting or disconcerting, as we crawl across the warm flagstone floor, reptilian sliding. The princely perfumes of these bodies claiming to be victims facilitate the exchange: to each an odor, flavorsome spice enhanced by the heat reputed to be an offensive obstacle to be overcome, whereas, in fact, it stimulates!

What's there to lose? Putrescence, decay, decomposition, nauseating memory: that hammam in Marrakesh as it was when I passed through and grew accustomed to its sense of mortality, its unclean bodies, stringy clumps of filth on the floor, gray with grease, slippery stones shiny with it, streaming water carrying along hair, razor blades, and bits of conversation between cops and athletes, side stalls for shitting, grunting with pleasure, doors half open, walls mottled with excrement, offerings and choephori, inevitability of death in this coprophilic ecstasy, knowledge of bodies brought back down to the messiness of sex, sphincter worn out, anus injured by the efforts of constipation.

Like the time in San'ā, at the close of an evening of qāt, relaxing mafraj brightened by polychrome windows, leaving at dawn, garden, circular openings, rings and acroteria, lacy cornices, walking to Hammam al-Maydān, dome and cistern, spray of water falling into concentric traces of itself, pool receiving reflection of sunbeam. Stone permeated by the heat, powerful odor of men, heavy fatigue and skinny bodies, only metaphoric nudity bearable, whining as soon as a man undoes his belt, drops his dagger, janbiya, metaphoric member.

Or again, of a space where we build the body of death, of love, odor and odium, colors to reproduce in inaccurate fantasy, strictly historical, such as the splendid Seljuk dome rising circular above the basin, itself circular, near Bursa, Hammam Eski Kaplica, constructed to make use of the hot spring, sexed symposium of high civilization, men pushing the bounds of urbanity, old men and youths, taking advantage of the heat, vapor stripping bodies, preparing them for their end, scraped clean for burial; upon return, my sex rises in reference to an unattractive, middle-aged woman, a bit cross-eyed, who I find irrepressibly attractive, perplexed by the excremental odor that keeps my sex at bay, waiting, magnificent, to expend and recharge.

The smell of cum grows intense between forest and bath; crushed fruit, to chew with pleasure. Here's a woman in tears, called bitch and cunt, treated like whore, let me bury my big red cock right there, addressed to a pale pink ass, pussy unplugged, disgorging semen, insatiable, this sucked flower, this skin inhaled, this fragrance, dazing even the most dissolute. And the woman laughs and cries, gesticulating and wincing, crouching with hips in constant motion, here and there, full pelvis, uncontainable bulimia, quivering redhead, violent caresses, uncontrollable screams, long moans, sobs, suffering and howling; tongue clicking, flesh wiggling, bites and blood, sucking the next available woman who is bringing to completion the pleasure of some man who is also howling like a woman, yielding only in ejaculation. Roles are reversed: now it's the woman running after the man, squeezing his swelling member, drawing screams of refusal and pain. He recants calling her cunt.

Other women attack with sickening joy, lewdly nimble, isolated in small closed cabins, oaken doors warped with water, huge gap between stone floor and door allowing full view of bodies colliding, propulsive energy, stroking of legs, moaning of virgins, fondling fingers wandering tearful over skin, lingering, hardly moving, ants in a trance, hair by electric hair, clitoris sending out its spout pleasure, fiery sap, scroll of nerve endings: man, be in your pleasure woman with woman.

Thrilled, certain women abducted the previous night now declare aloud their allegiance to the insurgent city, thereby traitors to their station, quick to yield: is it possible to erase the past without consequence? They reply that they are ready to offer themselves up, having found their bodies less self-sufficient than before, now beyond mere routine, a sexual burning within, a thawing of vision, sorceress's legs spread, motionless in display of her fleshy, greedy vulva, primordial sign, next to a splendidly erect phallus, monument of admiration, belonging to a solemnly smiling blacksmith: the *frigidarium* reconciles bodies in its coolness; once inside the chilled chamber, bodies mate more serenely; the smiling woman receives the deep thrust of the man's burning member, tamed and thoughtful, calm breathing that delays climax: fully experience the heart of one's own dissolution, beatific flash, timeless duration further than the determinism of orgasm.

Bodies emptied, the nuances that follow pleasure, beating of hearts against trickling of water, rivulets and fountains, sprouting from the Sphinx's teats, concert of liquid music ingeniously original, falling water, jet or drip, sound intensified by resonant echo, metallic percussion, ghaïtas suddenly unleashed in the muffling mists of the bath, curving architecture, stifling the music's deafening reverberation.

Myself aroused, between my teeth the carnation and tulip of union, deeply penetrating the body and gaze of a lovely lady, like a pomegranate bursting, a little girl teasing from between the posts of a garden fence, hurrying past, gaze haughty and limpid, teasingly distant, slow to conduct herself more liberally, proving here demanding and self-assured enough not to fall prey to any Pygmalion.

One of the sorceresses asks the imprisoned women to prove their allegiance to the insurrection by allowing a bit of ear—lobe or cartilage—to be severed from each, choosing between seeing blood spilled and this secret sampling of flesh that will seal their abandonment of their own history, that will make manifest a sign of their new belonging. Few of those who claim to be on our side accept this ordeal, however, hallmark of confidence signed in blood, symbolic amputation borne on the tangible face of the body. But an era of new decisiveness has dawned for those rare individuals willing to give of their blood in suffering: it is decided that they should be initiated to become bold sorceresses themselves.

Though past their prime, some men remain agile, found to possess a most worthy phallus, tiny in position of repose, but impressive in state of erection: once asleep, now it is awakened for hours by this woman, eyes rolled back, pleased to breathe life back into dormant instincts, spiriting her ithyphallic prey off the scene, copulating in the vestibule near the latrines, odor of urine mixed with the quest of desire over the threshold of moist warmth. And it wasn't long before screams and panting were heard: never has there been a more surprisingly ardent lover, such indescribable pleasure?

Slippery stones, interstices of hot earth. Balqīs, splendid, almost gets her transparent robe wet, dragging along the ground, believing perhaps that here too the floor might be of crystal, as in the palace where she succumbed to the snare, yielding, declaring her love to Sulaymān, before whom she nearly failed to recognize the false throne, in every way identical to the true one, saying: by the gods, it looks exactly like my throne! Admitting her ignorance after being fooled by the double simulacrum, she gave herself to Sulaymān: mistaking crystal for water, lifting the hem of her robes, she bares her legs, already a sign of yielding the body. How she insisted on not repeating her show of docility, haughty woman that she was, appearing dressed among our nude bodies! But reversing the situation doesn't right the wrong: she would have undressed to our great relief, already a Koranic figurine, boldness debasing her gender if for no other reason than to display her power, if only—and here's the point—she had entered speculum-like into the excavations and other anfractuosities, allowing us angles inaccessible to the eye, instruments of the heart that project for us the cavities to be transcribed into fleshy landscapes.

Yūssif, having returned, perfect body swaying with feminine grace, seeing him makes the eye overflow with desire and fear, Dionysian phallus, bees and honey, curls touching his shoulders, radiating energy, smooth and sleek skin, color of bronze, a smile of absolute openness, passing through the *tepidarium* where disarray still reigns: cracking bones, cries, pleasure; upon his arrival, the chaos settles at once, like a land dropping to its knees in respect at the moment of the sun's sinking into what can no longer be represented as only a temporary death, the interval of night. And men as well as women, seeing him, gnaw at their fists until blood flows, and from their sex as well, some thanks to knives, others releasing their monthly due. And no one is caught off guard by the pain, the hurt, hot taste of what seethes in the body, idling, blighted.

Yūssif has some paints—but how to capture them in writing, how to deliver them accurately transposed into words? How does this text treat color and odor if not as approximation, abstraction, setting aside stereotypes that only name what glistens in the eye, what nourishes the nostrils? But paradoxically, despite convention, be we casual or literary, none of us calls colors or odors by the same name his neighbor does: which doesn't surprise us, which can't save us, which in no way guarantees the sincerity of these sensations— so impalpable, so unspeakable.

Yūssif has some paints, then. Pigment and palette: he coats the western wall of the *caldarium* where heat stifles a thousand capacities to resist it; before the first brushstroke, he calls all the bloody fingers and groins to come dry their wounds or flows on the heat-softened wall. Lay down thus a foundation of crimson that he circles in one stroke: vast serpent devouring its tail, eye of keen appetite; and beyond, two arms of black Hercules girding the upper half of the serpent-circle where he paints the profile of a nude woman, eye like a heifer's, heroic arched brow; woman seated, knees tucked under her belly, gazing at herself in a mirror, as if looking glass in one hand, scepter in the other. Left foot extends just beyond the circle's edge, representing the moment of movement; she is leaving her place, body red with blood; the painting as a whole resting upon a *bucranium*.

And Yūssif says: we are no longer under the yoke of Pharaoh; be seers through the waking night; do not take revenge upon the malice of your brothers; let the great love of fathers live on, far from you; the stallion can only be chaste for the sake of its body: to serve, first one must know how to be one's own master.

Pursuing, he says: let us each exalt our sex, let us be swift men, and you women, take the initiative, be hospitable; let us recover sound judgment and calmness that we may be worthy adorers of the rising sun—in us, womanhood is lost if it does not declare itself. Sun, woman of our days. Man invented the sun. It is not the sun that beams toward the eye, but the eye that imprints itself upon the sun. Stare at the sun, and the eye is blinded. Look at the rays that pass through the skylight to dry the fresco. Our painting restores our childhood. At the bottom, the bodies are exhausted. By fire, all is transformed. Color is fire to the eye. With water comes the greening of life. Odor carries away what grows on the surface of the world. From Ephesus, Heraclitus declared: *the sun is every day new*. Let us keep silent when the words grow thick and dense. Let us not be wandering bodies. Let us not close society's gates to our excremental values. May our accumulated odors open the way to a death consummated by the newness of the sun; we are not to flee its incandescence by reproducing underground landscapes; rather, let us contemplate bodies playing in their flames, newborn sun.

Yūssif surrounds himself with scribes. He calls the young girls, Fātima included, to his side. They seem ready to play their parts, cheerfully confident, as though seasoned by the debauchery that preceded the ceremony. They have pulled themselves together, effectively deflecting any attempt to sap their energy. But they wish to erase the sign of anxiety they still bear in the hollow of the soles of their feet. This has them giggling nervously at memories of school and family. The scribes are wearing short tunics, color of cinnabar. They order the scriveners to scent their fingers before kneeling on the marble stage, facing the circular pool overflowing with boiling water.

It requires an enormous effort for the body not to be overcome by the intense steam heat. Sex is the path to the grave. In one intense instant, the hammam is enclosed in the weight of rocks assembled into a gigantic pyramid atop the narrow space of the underground chamber. Nothing remains but steam and heat. Already, our breaths are colliding, intruding on one another's space, extremities grow numb from increasing scarcity of air crowded out by the accumulated mist.

The reference to Dante is unavoidable here. I tried to get away from that reference, to get out of the stifling atmosphere. But nothing can save me now: I find I'm facing the now walled-in entrance, between *apodyterium* and *frigidarium*, calling vividly to mind the famous opening:

All hope abandon, ye who enter here.

Turning around, discovering myself walled into a Cairo-style villa, bay window separating me from the veranda, dust and dead leaves, living room full of furniture covered in white cloth, renovation underway, painters and masons walking along wooden scaffolding, refurbishing the crumbling Ionic capitals. Outdoors stretch the sandy streets of Guelmim under a crushing sun; a Friday and a crowd of a thousand tunics in the same hue: purple, mauve, lilac, burgundy, crossing through streets on their way to the mosque if only to seek some shade, to perform the cooling ablutions—not for prayer. All the town's shops are closed. Only the bakery remains half-open, run by missionary nuns, livid Catholics.

Deserted streets. Fātima screams endlessly under the whip, bloody bitch, falls to the ground moaning, in tears, near the fountain. A strong odor of sperm mixed with acrid-smelling paint permeates the living room, nostrils nosing about for base scents. A few drops of plaster coating seep through the gaps between scaffolding planks, splashing down onto hieroglyphic parchments.

Stretched out on a sofa, Hādī, drowned ten years ago now, a face revealing his obvious Pharaonic ancestry, smiles at me, arms wide open, beckoning. I draw near, reproaching myself for having waited so long to see up close, if only out of servile curiosity, a living example of the mummifier's painstaking labor. He takes me by the hand, announces that he's been working here ever since his death, that he acts as a kind of ferryman to lead us into the cool room, where the body doesn't suffer but simply vegetates, and that the chance of being reborn animal, vegetable, or mineral has nothing to do with the hierarchy that humans establish during their lifetime, giving preference to one or the other of the three kingdoms.

A chill wind sweeps through the immense frozen space. I don't know what to say and feel a case of alexia coming over me. Though I feel a vague anxiety, it's only a fit of shivering that causes me to flee so quickly from these painted scenes of my life—in halftones, unfinished. I'm obsessively eyeing everything around me, outside the furnace. The cold burns and the icy ground tortures my bare feet. Gradually, the light fills out the space, shadows of massive columns, ballet of arms and twisted fingers. A woman extends her arm, openhanded, ready to give and receive. A man closes his hand, hounded by a haughty onanistic smugness.

I am as lightning-struck by the eye each time it gazes on me. The eye is both sun and woman. Eye of the falcon. The gaze is empty, relieved of nose and mouth, which would usually facilitate access to the eye. The ankle, which among the living acts as tense articulation, vital and fragile, disappears among the dead. The order given by the falcon head, Horus, meets an army quick to obey. I'm taken away before I'm able to react. The seahorse, the bee, the lotus surround the solitary eye, flaming owl. The power of death plunges its scepter into my head, excavating; out of it spring plundering arms, touching the stellar ceiling, dusky blue studded with stars circled in red, golden branches.

Passing through the warm room, a less spacious one, carried off by Horus's army, leaving Hādī behind, we come upon the scavengers, birds with a taste for the dead, squawking and squabbling, dust in suspension and feathers flying: royal falcon, vulture, buzzard, kite, several species of owl. Further along the way, less quarrelsome, impotent and silent, sit the ravens, quails, hoopoes, pigeons, swallows, passerines, orioles. A little stream barely flowing is muddied by the splashing of waders: kingfishers, magpies, ibis, spoonbills, plovers, herons, cattle egrets, and the occasional phoenix preaching among ducks, geese, teals, pelicans, cormorants.

A monster of a man, half ape, half human, walking along the wet sand, blowing molten glass, a bubble at the end of a blowpipe, translucent unevenly contoured sphere; hands it to me that I might better see the eye separated from the eagle, distorted through the glass: eye in eye, to a degree invisible to the naked eye. In search of the elusive eye, where could it be hiding, while the voice of the monster assures me that it's within view. Why this concealment—enigmatic gaze that uncovers other worlds? I offer you my glazed eye that so many humans loved before its color faded. In my hand, the eye jumps and slips through my fingers. I find it, almond-shaped, yellowish pupil that hides behind the hand likewise taking the form of an eye. Between the eyes rise crescents, gaze of times past. My light still present receives by blood the lunatic memory of the eye.

I know where to find the eye that remains impervious to saying, to seeing. The bull's eye, as if pampered in the shade of its own power. Impressively thick neck, stubborn muzzle, the eye, despite an emphatic expression, maintains its bovine air, a sleepy rage. The eye is concealed, then revealed, like an ironically coy smile. Predatory eye, are you a flesh-eating fish that sees nothing without voracious thoughts? The eye dances, then bites.

Eye of mischievous satisfaction well matched to Asian mouth, or African, more fleshy, chin small and fine. The eye slumbers: empty boat and beauty, white place without pupil, thin little sun, lukewarm but still looking at me.

Slave eye, captive, repeated, different: shackles weigh down the arms, swell the breast, orbit the eye marked by submission.

Pupil that wanders idle, starting geometrical, future labyrinth.

In the depths of the eye there collects potential energy, hands tight, pitch-black hair; the eye is in the shadow of a gratified mouth, a pout too faint.

Beside the eye, the pupil, in the service of the eye, the eye's fear, for the eye is always watching: barely sensing nuance, it is nightmare, it is unity that changes imperceptibly. Insect deforms, eye informs: the scarab in the eye decomposes.

After heat, warmth. Stifling listlessness, dense humidity. Crowd packs in to admire the sun painted by Yūssif, garrison where scribes are quartered along with Thoth, master of writing, of the word, of thought, reigning figure in the territory of magic, ibis-headed, lord of the moon, male counterpart of Seshat, goddess of writing, himself a scribe, measurer of destinies, generous, bringing Horus back his eye, Set back his testicles, this arbiter to whom complaints are addressed as long as scribes chronicle lives and Thoth measures the weight of words with the scale of the eye, handling paintbrush and palette, registrar of *psychostasia*.

Fātima calls me and invites me to attend the weighing of hearts. Yūssif, sitting peacefully on the floor, seems distant as he contemplates the tree of finality. Anubis is busy ushering in the dead. I disrupt the proceedings and beg Thoth to initiate me into the secrets of writing, to deliver me the stone tablet, to school me in the quality of words, sole route to recovery, to self-reproduction, that I might be reborn a cohesive whole within the unstoppable continuity of history, without my rebelling against its inexorable march. Am I to possess the tablet of writing, correspondence of the word, desert of the body, writing as raison d'être, to finally reveal it, to retell instincts and reinvent others, to delay the lowering of the barrier that imprisons the secret each time that one thinks he has sufficiently mastered it to hand it over unharmed? To write without the word standing in for being, but rather as food for those who hunger in a broken world.

You see, Thoth, as a schoolchild, I didn't want to learn to read, to write. My whole body resisted what it considered a useless form of relaxation. School was an ordeal. I sought revenge by filling the classroom with eau de latrine: farts, urine, feces, scatophiliac gestation, enough to grow worms and flowers, to water the classroom with piss so that I might blame the blond, foreign schoolteacher's dog. I would chew on the collar of my pink smock with white fringe, uniform with name embroidered over the heart; I would swallow paper, chew on chalk, drink ink; I loathed the schoolmistress's whip, and leaned with all my might into its suppleness, to counteract its weight. Thoth, grant that I might walk the range of writing whence you draw your perceptive power, extending your influence over the body's persevering desert. Thoth, I call upon you, do not push me to rebellion's point of no return, now that, regressively, I am prospering in the great beyond.

Dive deep, he says, after administering me a dose of ambrosia and henbane, you will see only what you are capable of seeing: your faculties of discrimination will not become any sharper. You need only cross over the serpent's circle, to push aside Lady Sun, to reach the far side of her visage, and you shall break through the wall and discover a nostalgic elsewhere.

And what should I see but time and space compressed, moving yet immobile, effect of a ship at the end of Rome's Isola Tiberina, river flowing foamy, rolling auspiciously muted, forget the analgesic odor of the hospital, flee the ether and septic cotton thrown about on the shore, decipher the spaces and messages, illegible scrawl of imponderable meaning. Why am I ejected into Rome, exiting from the Cloaca Massima, the greatest sewer, pestilential return to history, via swampy *Romanité*? Why does a wave of queasiness bear me away to the Capitol, to breathe more easily, muse upon the autumnal twilight? How else to answer but the instinctual urge for continuity of transcription into myth?

Dona Colonna awaits me at the entrance to Chiesa del Gesù: we contemplate the glittering Name of Christ lettered in light, golden glint. Michelangelo wept over me, she says; he's said to have blamed that chaotic, deliquescent fresco spilling out of its frame: such perverted architecture, hardly the place for my funeral mass to be celebrated. You want to know the real story of how the master composed his *Rime*. What can I report, except that he was tormented, perpetuating the spirit that animated stone; if you would like to understand the genesis of those sonnets, you need only read while thrilling to the emotion that vibrates inside the stones.

On the road to Bologna, by donkey, veering off toward Fiesole, bending over to clear the beam, solar clock, tabernacle, *Qui patitur vincit*, entering the home of a shepherd who offers food and drink, dry peccorino, fava beans, recognizing from the back the silhouette of Dante, frenetically composing. He turns toward me, smiles, the look of an ecclesiastic, and says: write the spoken word; the word rehearses the idea; style is but an exercise for taking power by its baby toe, a knave's business. Words command men, would fill the walls of churches like the blue frescos of Giotto or some other master of hell, torments, cauldrons. But what can writing do in the face of plagues and pestilence except submit yet again to Providence— that is, recite the Scriptures?

From Itéa, on a scrubby ascending road dotted with olive trees, goats grazing, hemp seed, birds' delight, following the dry riverbed, approaching the rugged uplands, like a wall fashioned into a temple by the hand of man, echoes of the Pythia, contours forming various signs not unlike writing, trembling voice, message decoded, Delphic charioteer about to speak, endowed with the capacity of imitation, shield with hieratic figures, symbols of woe and war, Delphi finally comes into view, enclosed inlet, site of assembled treasures, sustaining wall below esplanade, hot spring whose vent denounces silence, thread dividing the mountain, Hölderlin, ever seeking the occult, Apollo in wait; only stones upon stones now, tiny edifices bereft of their sculptures, archive for those able to grasp what's hidden from view, promising aftereffect of verbal magic; astonishing Hölderlin who with words made shoots and shrubs tremble, chanting the poem passed down in memory of the ancient standard, pastoral desire, the need to know that one might mourn one's fate, to endure if only in stone the words of the God of Light:

Delphi sleeps, and where does great Fate resound?

You claim to transcribe the wisdom of the gods, I remark wryly to Hermann Hesse, referring to the unfolding of his text, he exhausting himself in his demonstration of the concordance between Western and Eastern gnosis, pitting a Muslim talisman against a Romanesque sculpture, detail in the choir of the Basel cathedral, pair of dragons clashing, each biting a loose knot, intertwining from between claws of the left-hand dragon, but which nothing can untie, a tangle transfixing the gaze, everything is in everything, dragons borrowing head of fish and mane of horse. I reiterate that Klee, with steppe, sky, sea, architecture, carpets, jewels, ravished the country of its signs, which he was then able to repossess and transfigure, revealing by color and rhythm, by line, tension, and grid, controlling saturation or dearth, Sinbad between two seas, more credible still than the tunics and togas of the wealthy collectors with their libraries, cabinets, and file drawers, publishing accounts of such pathetic little voyages.

Voyage: are you not the writer's theme? Transporting the body, life and death of words? Let us follow Tangiers-born Ibn Battūta, between Rayy and Mashhad, cursing Asia the beautiful for its inedible rice, failing to celebrate the ordeal of blood that is remembered as the tragedy of Karbala; on the journey home, telling tales of India's riches, the splendor of her palaces, of her royal fortunes, her armies, raving on, facts and figures at hand, narrative megalomania boasting of the swiftness of his account, faithful to what the eye saw, the ear heard. Leaving traces in Tangiers itself, unlimited sense of wonder, stories of monsters laying waste to the shore, peddler of stories, a passion for the affairs of the world, advising the powerful how to choose sides in conflicts, to resolve problems according to his insightful instigations. Writing consists of rejoicing at one's own falsehoods, putting order in the real through the imaginary, its faithful scrivener, marveling, sliding toward the territory of fable: to chronicle one's voyages only further confuses imagining and living—thus establishing a lawful entrance into writing as a form of reconciliation with whatever sort of hell the body is hatching.

Ibn 'Arabī speaking in the mosque in Damascus that would one day house his own ashes: these days, you're mistaken about the written word! Writing is neither vomiting nor pleasure nor giving birth: it is the death of the self; upon returning from the east to attend a synod in Morocco, I urged my African colleagues, whose languages are still mostly unwritten, to be mindful of this: seek enlightenment before changing the spoken to the written, perpetuating speech, stars and mages, from upon the mountaintop, through the pass, view of the ocean. You, I would add, for whom writing is of multiple implication—levels and stages, wandering and halt, departure and return? But in a certain tone, it remains as much symbol as sign. And need I recall for you the saying of Mansūr? *He who does not grasp our allusion does not comprehend our expression.* To write is to reflect energy as it opens up to you. Arouse it. Contemplate it. Delight in its richness. Renew your vigor. Inscribe your experience upon the mirror of the world. Project yourself as fragment of the archetype. Reside at limit's edge. Gather the *I* as part of *Self.* Do not dilate your experience by the use of *we.*

To each text its gloss. In the commentary on my poems, I said nothing of heresy: I had a text to defend, to preserve from the malevolence of learned men, for I do not advocate any experience that provokes the law, nor indeed for the repression of impulses, for submission. A matter of cloaking one's ideas in secret language. Those who can read shall read, and leave commentary to the others. To the first, joy is limited to reading, deciphering the sign; for the others the satisfaction and nourishment of their intelligence is achieved beyond: by interpretation, by unveiling, kashf.

She says: I marvel at this suitor
whose beauty derives from flower and garden.
I say: marvel not, for the one you see is
but the mirror reflecting your own image.

The commentary interprets the feminine of this poem as the divine presence—but without denying the primary meaning. Presence always takes on a body, an image. Here it is embodied in a Persian woman, great love, my ascension taking form, and myself as the form of her assumption. Do not turn away from the body: it is the place of experience. Love women. In their pleasure, your night journeys.

What to say to Cervantes, man of glass, strolling through the streets of Salamanca? Laugh at him? No, but question him, make his parable easy, his low-down sarcasm, fabled vehemence owed to the masochistic abuses of Iberian tradition, which so fiercely endeavors to obliterate its Arab, Berber, and Jewish centuries, invading locusts, decimating the bamboo screens along Andalusian streams at their low-water mark. The text, he says in mime, faithfully records the hand that undertook to transcribe it by referencing misplaced documents, unknown to the official archives, taking advantage of chance encounters, talkative Bohemian woman, Shahrazād in tatters, Arabic manuscript ending up as wrapping paper, walk the streets, put leather to pavement, ever vigilant. One's intelligence grows sharper the less one frequents, deferential, the erudite masters of recited commentary, polyglot pleasure, of Ximénes de Cisneros, along with the severity of Ignatius Loyola's exercises among the conquering propagators of the faith throughout the world, a race to shape minds according to the most obscure definition of obedience.

Can continuous coitus—coiteration—shape a fertile matrix for writing? I asked a recanting Casanova, tripping over the warped mosaics that tile the floor of San Donato, in Murano, as he had just taken leave of Sister Maria-Magdalena. A most evasive answer from this bed-hopper, mistrustful given my accent and insistence, holding in one hand his purse full of gold ducats, clutching in the other his navaja. What are you insinuating, then? Haven't you seen for yourself that my memoirs abound in philosophical remarks and debates, implying that I have at the very least learned my Humanities lessons well and that writing is rather too serious a matter to be left at the disposal of scoundrels?

Cavafy of Alexandria, seated, rumpled, cane in hand, little potbellied personage of questionable respectability, spacious Greek café, stern matron at the cash register, past her prime, Greek profile, selling inedible confections: the best in town, he tells me. How does this man, who has never left this square, ear attuned to the sound of wagons and donkey carts, to the faraway rumor of muffled waves protected by the bay, this man who makes the trip to the corniche only with supreme effort, negotiating step by step with his body the project of reaching the far-off, whitish silhouette of Fort Qaitbay, how did this man manage to depict out of sheer idiolect such spot-on characters across time and space, to render the olive trees more true than at Skopelos, to rethink its decimated convents and ruined temples, to navigate, marine ephebi, to approve of me by subtle hints, sex swollen to bursting point, deformed, twisted, self-discovery, self-description, flashback to reality, at the very instant of my frolics and embraces with Bérénice, Parisian of Greek origin, a Byzantine Madonna's chin, occasional muse, embodiment of evil in the noonday heat under the olive trees to the crickets' incessant trill? Cavafy sips his coffee, invites me for a drink and garrulous begins talking about the world outside poetry, the quality of coffee beans, the best way to roast them, to flavor them, Eden of the heart, counting out the months.

Praying before the tomb of Imām Shāfi'ī, monumental splendor in wood, gigantic ribbon of calligraphy unfolding as if to strengthen the base of the dome, I awaken Ghazālī, who says to me: I only just fell asleep. But, in patience and love, I shall respond: writing is a matter of temperament, a gift. I retreated from the world, fled society, did not write for ten years, wringing dry my solitude; but some force called me to write, to refute, to illustrate, to comment, to counsel, to rectify, to conciliate, to reproduce, to prescribe. But one more thing: how will you understand what I mean if you yourself do not write? I had a friend who was impotent; one day he asked me what an orgasm felt like; I told him: I thought you were merely impotent, but now I see you're also an idiot. There is knowledge that is incommunicable, there is a knowing-how that requires experience, a bodily initiation.

The teachings of Plato give us the Idea. He perceived the meaning of love, but perverted its rule by abasing bodily contact. From India to China the matter was more effectively dealt with: the wise men conjured up the spark that flares within us, we beings of clay, kindling us, either masculine or feminine: rendering sacred the principle of love, the upwelling of the soul.

The Christians, obsessed with deadly transgression, gathered the corrupting clay from out of the Platonic text. Then, they denied the body. Out of that neutering error was born a second front of compartmentalized thought: Aristotle seeks to reflect the real through accidental flaw, from the pug nose to the cleft foot. You will therefore understand my criticism of the Arab Peripatetics and especially those who obscure the light of vision with the veil of thought! How can one be confined to speaking the body in isolation when everything calls out to think it, to live it to perfection? The same goes for the written word: I contest any writing restricted to describing things as they are observed, as nothing but fixedness, without grasping the implications that transfigure them.

Pack of feral dogs tearing tenfold into the corpse of a mule, exploded carrion fouling the vast, slow mouth of the Guadalquivir. Wearing a coat whose sleeves extend below the fingertips, Genet warms himself, small fire, shifting flames: I believe the wandering beggar that literature has embellished. I find that the warmth of rented rooms lends itself better to writing, luxury hotels more so than dives and fleabags. A nomadic life, changing hotels as often as lovers; stop at a museum, my eyes go ripping through the paintings like those famished dogs back there, unprincipled, unreasoned. And I don't care for design furniture, the indulgence of avant-garde musicians; soon as my ass makes contact with those curved chairs, I find myself saying whatever I think, and I collect—I beg—for money for the Palestinians, future diplomats. My writing: what is it if not literature, delving into a place that abhors the sedentary, ritual violence: to write, in French, *écrire*, contains "rire" and "cri," laughing and crying. Add sex to say, perfecting the cry.

Why do you, among the living, come speak to me in this gallery of ghosts, beyond quarrels, ancient or modern? Because I often die and return to ejaculate my preciously archaic style. Because we don't write unless already dead. Only words spoken by the dead endure. My writing wears funereal colors, mourning and wake: banquet and gladiolus, violets, emerald, bishop, amethyst on bruised finger, swollen hands from prison to kitchen, from tomb to altar, from brothel to canteen, from urinal to port, from crime to widower, argot that roots me beyond redemption in history.

Or what remains of the souk of Grenada, rushing to find the final footsteps of the Moor, sighs and tears; discovering nothing left of consolation save the memories of underground tunnels that link certain patios; impatient, I'm lured into the trap and lose my way thanks to a fleeting visit to the Alhambra, deserted, whispering expanse of water, without wishing to get up close to the damp walls plunging vertiginously downward, citadel overlooking the city, ceremonial room, on this dark summer's night, Ibn Khaldūn, counselor in the shadow of dynasties, mastery, betrayal, exclusion, observe and formulate the laws of history so unlike the elusive ones governing power, premonitions of decadence, theorizing repetition, determining its cycles and phases. I needn't analyze further what's so obvious today, he says. The historians of your present are unenlightening. Esprit de corps and tribalism are still the engines of Arab powers. Yet, it is imperative that you modernize, you Arabs of today, that you master the progress that has eluded you, that you assimilate the rupture that has dealt a blow to history's customary march, that you defend yourselves by adopting the same machinery that the West possesses. And don't start raving, for it's well known that you're given to endless talk. I urge that you build a nation-state, a subject for contemporary writing if there ever was one: then theorize the State, slander anarchy, banish excess. Remember, the only writers are those who think in systems. But alas! and as ever, the politicians do not follow suit: they can't be counted on. And it is history's great misfortune that they exclude thinkers from power, forcing them into a collusion whereby they must equivocate, betray, bargain, and bend to the inconsistent will of the politician.

I don't know how to reply. I turn over twice, bed of embers, taken in by risk, violated by the speed of this century that has turned the heads of so many ardent worshipers of the State, God of Modern Times, on a quest for progress; Italy lulled by fascination for manufacture, signing pacts with flash-in-the-pan figures who ransacked their revolutionary period: sucked into the trajectory of bolstering the State and corrupting it in the process, creativity abandoned in sinecure and prebendary to set off in discovery of the proletarian era, with its canned announcements, lunar conquests, poetically inspired factories, how far we have drifted from that initial project that with millions in voice and deed made the country tremble, now returning to dissidence: Malevich, Mayakovsky, whose images and words capture oblivion, injecting us, in proletarian zeal, with the elixir that will purge us of our mystical vanity.

Among wild cherry and *pêche de vigne*, ardent Ardèche, summer heat. No, no, I can't stand the sun, I hate the countryside, I feel like going back where I'm from, where I scream from, Black Forest, Bavaria, says Ferdinand, redhead reddened, skin scorched. Screaming only suffocates him further; I refrain from insult, he calls me and keeps me from writing: you have nothing to say, don't think about writing anymore, just write the quintessence of speech, don't go beyond your own discontinuity.

I don't defy writing, vomit, or excreta. He opens the window, smashes the table, has no more interest in existence, shatters the glasses that he had once painted before filling them to the brim with milky plaster, then inserting wrinkled figures, deer heads, fashion nudes, newsworthy presidents. Dressed in black, solar target, he who abhors the heat, fiddling with the annoying sound of a siren, cops and ambulances, in this drought-stricken landscape, crickets and blackberries, whinnying mares, he listens, disturbed, panting even, to Schumann's *Kreisleriana*, at the cruising velocity of *Schnell und Spielend*, Ferdinand weeping, he on occasion capable of providing voluptuous presence, bone to suck on, gnaw at, tearing off the last scraps of flesh and fat still clinging to its rigidity, suffering from the disease that eliminates the pretense to write, getting back up to the home country on foot, then carjacking a ride, devouring the kilometers, tires squealing around bends, following the Rhine so closely as to forever be lost in its icy depths, finally voiceless, corpse corroded by acid runoff.

See Konya at dawn. And in springtime. And apple and apricot blossoms swaying in the wind, that non-shape giving shape to things that circulate in elusive temporality, breeze that makes flower and foliage quiver, inner music and flame. Encounter with a tekke, whirling with the dervishes; in the distance we hear the shehnai

flute of a Sūfi sama' session, dizzying circles gyrating around themselves, like so many tops spinning in white circumference. The light
soothes faces. And the minaret, monumental pencil, multifaceted
mass ending in a fine tip to inscribe its message across the expanse
of sky: beneath, the tomb of Rūmī, mawlānā of incisive, edifying
thought: what matter is writing to me? he says, for it was not I who
was writing, but Him through me; I was sun, and by writing was to
enlighten the world; in doing so, I found neither pain nor pleasure.
My verse is given me, whirling upon itself until delivering ecstasy
to whomever transcribes it; and I in turn give them to you, out of
solar duty. When writing, I am in my place. I wrong no one. But
I prefer speech, I enjoy teaching, disclosing disciples unto themselves, commenting upon hierarchies and wringing out of morality
its alibis: a fire suddenly summons me to compose verse and to say
what favors or hinders the spectacle of the world.

> *The crooked looks straight to the crooked.*
> *If you were to tell the squint-eyed man that the moon is one,*
> *He would reply: "No, I see two of them.*
> *I doubt that the moon could be one."*

Exiting the Araboglu mosque in Karaman, awakening to myself,
nomadic traveler's body, Yunus Emre, such distance lies between
us now! I write nothing, I compose, he says, offering verses to vil-
lages that welcome me, those for whom I am a guest. And then, the
verses have a life of their own, enriched, transformed, lengthened,
rectified by those who recite them, repeat them, as echo engenders
echo; I sometimes hear my verses chanted, the ones on Unity, on

Fusion, on Love, but I don't recognize them; yet upon rehearing them, I say to myself, that's it: this is not apocryphal verse, I might even have composed it myself.

Mountains above Tūnfit, hard to reach qusūr; after climb, the verdant valleys, sun and cultivated fields, chaos of rock, ring of mules below Aït Slimān, in these times of submissiveness, during an evening of Tibetan lucidity, the animals turn, spurred by man, golden straw sent flying, powdery; what remains after threshing if not the grain, to be gathered once the chaff is removed by the endless motion of animal hooves at work?

Akoray takes leave of the peasants; whipping of mules. Indiscernible face, one-eyed, mouth grandiloquent: come have something to eat with me; you're my guest. Arriving at his home at an hour of rarified daylight, I gaze out from the terrace at the winding valley, its center the pure water that rushes through.

Akoray unplugs a hole in the earthen wall and removes a delightful honey into which black bread is dipped. He accompanies himself with an old violin beyond tuning and declaims lengthy poems in a language whose truculence is conveyed to me by a Chleuh friend, translator for the occasion.

My themes issue from our daily life, says Akoray, but I also compose verses to the glory of officialdom: I do have to earn this pittance that the mokhanzi brings in. I don't know how to read or write. It takes me weeks and months to memorize what I create. And once the text is etched into my memory, nothing can intervene to alter it. It is sign engraved upon the face of the world, glinting off the smooth quarry that shines on high, grayish and brownish effects even by moonlight.

But I don't make my living off these official compositions. I work the earth. I keep bees. I obtain their honey. And I laugh at it all, myself a mirror to be shattered, to think of myself as other than a packet of words to be broadcast: but since I am under obligation, I play the sleepwalker, deaf, vast echoless cavity, dry gourd, playing on my self, the transport of words, from lips to lobes.

Only revelry reconciles me to the chaos of my verse, echoing against boulders to be shaken free, rockslide crushing the lost bodies of lovers secluded on the slope sheltered from the east wind. Discover myself the lord of language perforated by light, blinding those in attendance, the curious or voyeurs. We are told that with each new encounter, the world changes. Go see whether they are still weeping over there where the child shepherd calls out to his sister in a song of my words. If you are not offered drink, that will be the sure sign of breach. Do you find the water salty to the taste? You must be on the wrong shore, then, you the scribbler who seeks to revive the traces of lost words, footsteps absorbed by nakedness into no other height or mountain than where the goiterous proliferate, to whom words are but an exhausting respiration whence the winds of fierce expectancy blow.

Might I be back to break up this bickering over buckets? The dense steam makes the ovenlike bath even more stifling, now stripped of the staging that brought it to life via my journey into the saying of writing. To write the people while so far removed from them, with writing that does not transport lived experience in the raw. This is the coherence of the speaker of foreign tongue. Writing that is self-perpetuated stillborn. This is said, but the people, concerned hero, shall not repeat it. Theirs is another language. They aren't the least bit interested in lingering over fictions that do not embrace the cause of their history. Write yourself as discontinuous, passion that embarks upon a visit to the dead, rediscovery of myths.

And I meditate transfigured upon this loss of the popular canon, dissolved in the masses, losing none of its claims and qualities, nor the radiance of its lessons. No longer able to be the equivalent of Homer or any pagan poet, Raphael painting his holy scenes for everyone, including the most narrow-minded of bigots. Laugh it away, orphan of the body, how could I be anything other than one more link in the chain of orphaned writing? I gather up by fragments the eclectic book for those who swarm among the gods, in the burial ground of the fathers.

And no wind comes to disturb our desire, vacuum of the body, writing with no ulterior motive, giving a full account of our collective yearning, without in any way diminishing the accomplishments of the loner who resists the *we*, no longer among his people, swept up in the turmoil of revolt.

Might it be bickering over buckets? Hearing women meddling and laughing, then shouting in the less crowded hammam, steam around my sickly body, numbness setting in, drowsiness that reveals an unmistakable reality.

And you have nothing to teach me, I hear Fātima shout violently, ire aimed at the senior woman of the group—Fātima a more versatile sorceress now, seeking to pillory the hackneyed phrases of her elders, to paralyze their poisonous mouths. No, I have nothing to learn from you; have been dropping my panties since age twelve and have seen a thing or two over the years: have experienced the pinnacle of pleasure, an all-powerful virility, carried away blissfully carefree, idealizing bodies as they plug away, animal thrusting; have swapped partners, experienced screams, collective nudity, trivial coitus, smack, aphrodisiac nectars, ears that burst and bleed, the thrill of a scorching caress; have stagnated, then revived, nimble and ready to experience new pleasures; dancing and weeping to complete my delight; have shared beds with sisters and men, with old lechers and young men my age, some awkward, others more skillful; no, I have nothing to learn from you, and spare me the dazzle of your young boy-gods and lovers, silence of fish, the itch of sex thwarted by society's projected image of women's position, one of theatrical passivity, a ravishment from the very start, prepared as offering sealed in blood: mark my words, all sensual pleasure delves into my solitary self, killing, dying in oblivion to the self in this insatiability that comes over me periodically, intoxicated, as much as the body can endure.

What a laugh, seeing you thus edified, O my attentive sister! What were you seeking, then? To stigmatize me? To put me to the test? It's not fatal, you know: Ah! if you had seen me at fifteen, how every male organ in the city used to stand at attention for me, how my firefly eyes would shine, by day and by night, lips white amber, how they would make a man of the most timorous, how men would fantasize, replacing their partners with my nubile image. What do you think? That you can get beyond sex? You cannot, no, you traverse it, transexually if it suits; by guiding the foreplay, I delay my moment of succumbing; by imposing withdrawal, little death plays out sans consequences, pure pleasure. To bear one's own vulgarity without the dissimulation of hatred, that's how we come to terms with the slaughtering instinct that lies dormant in our men: arms that by day engage in butchery serve at night to move lips to song. Sister peers, be no more mistaken, and do not forget that my words are like euphorbia; though preserved by their milky sap, they will turn unhesitatingly black as soon as they exhale their venom—as you look on, horrified.

Words that rouse me, magnetized, from the litter of my own corpulence, ensnared by the will of Fātima, feminine plural that pulverizes any stray impulse to respond, I imagine myself a slashed clearing, tyrannical undergrowth, little habits fitted out as weapons of power. Contaminated by the unforeseen blind eloquence of Fātima, I get gradually carried away, trying to filter out my emotional tendencies, borne by a bidding that is neither sermon nor harangue: so, what will it be, I demand, daring the sorceress to use the exact word: you thought that through trial and tribulation you would do away with the fear that intimidates us? I see the fire burn, the iron red-hot; Fātima and I bound and gagged to stifle the scream, simulacrum of wound, but only a knife cooled in flowing water touches the skin streaming in sweat, ready to receive the glowing ember; and this cold contact, eyes blindfolded, brings out the most atrocious scream, representation of burn: so you thought this is how a new people is born, thankful and relieved that this time at least, the threat proved idle, so that we stay subservient out of gratitude, subjugated to the power of your sect!

Do you not hear, asks the gasping sorceress Saïda, the beating of the kūs heralding the imminent attack of the enemy, bent upon taking the offensive now to break their ineffective state of siege? Put an end to your foolish bickering, let us return to the procession and be done with it in haste, so as to allow us the time to flee and escape reprisal. Wash yourselves, then, and return to the mosque to carry the idol into this final stage and put it behind us.

The faces of certain eminent scholars and sages reappear on the scene, and much energy is spent contesting their unexpected liberation or escape. They are allowed to follow as spectators the cortege lead by the sorceresses, out of the Sidi Mahrez and into the square emptied of its cheese vendors, taxis, shoeshine boys, and other black marketeers of exchange, safe deposit of foreign currency, florins, francs, dollars, lira, pounds, showcases of stolen jewelry. Grouped by twos or scattered among the crowd, the sages are reluctant to criticize the crowd's excesses: faint-hearted reproach or allusive prescriptions falling on deaf ears.

This is unacceptable, Tahar finally exclaims: in my day, I defended women, I sought scrupulously to integrate them, I called for their liberation, but when I see what is happening in this lawless city, I am staggered by the scandal of it and cannot help but vigorously protest and disapprove of such depravity, particularly when coming from the weaker sex, these raving females, they who in our tradition are described not even as a negative pole, but as absence, degree zero, a thing that need not to be taken into account: remember the war of the camel and 'Āïcha, daughter of Abū Bakr, favorite of the Prophet's wives. She was brought to her senses when 'Alī, peace be upon him, granted her a golden retirement provided that she cease meddling in affairs not meant for her gender: politics and history were thus made off-limits to women!

We have nothing to say in response, reply the sorceresses in chorus, not even an insult! Let us continue our march. Let us make our way into the meat district, repulsive odor of all the animal flesh on display, sides of beef, sheep heads with bunches of parsley hanging from their mouths, calf heads swinging among bicolored lanterns, green and red, blinking on and off against the marble slabs, garlands of merguez, gold-toothed butchers, bloody meat hooks, no talk of prices, kidneys, livers, fat, offal, lungs, hearts, testicles, udders, meat to be divided up among the families and sects milling about in the wake of the sorceresses, some of whom are bearing along the wobbly idol, the others struggling to rein in the sacrificial bull, an angry Apis, white coat with black spots on the forehead, neck, and back.

Master Mahmūd, at odds with 'Abduh, bursts out laughing despite the respect due to the sheikh of the nahdha who denounces our scandalous relapse into savagery: what will civilized people say about us? We called for a cultural rebirth by returning to our pure origins, to the fundamentals of our religion, to a more righteous age; we proved, through a series of concordances, that our Book already contained all the technical miracles that transformed this century! We advocated for the unification of all the judicial schools, for an end to meaningless rhetoric, for an effort to make the acquisition of modern science a pious duty, to assimilate the boldest of inventions so that we might rekindle our golden age, our grand tradition, our contribution to world civilization, minarets, monuments, cities that made the desert bloom, to urge the nomads to abandon their turbulent existence and to settle into more sedentary lives, to commit ourselves as unwaveringly civilized, to transform the fabricated void by erecting shadows of repentance, to strengthen and defend our bygone principles. And what do I see here? The worst debauchery, the most disgraceful disarray, the mortifying spectacle of Arabs in an all-out attack on civil reason.

And Master Mahmūd laughs all the harder, calling the sheikh an old coot who thinks that defeat means error, that excess equals a fall in prestige. You share not even a handbreadth of our origins, replies the furious Master Mahmūd, his tongue no longer tied by respect. We are drunks and blasphemers, we will not give ourselves over to idle speculation; we took part in the abduction of the black stone; who do I see around me if not Zanj and Qarmatians? This hasn't been an attack but an exorcism; we are haunted by history that spirals ad infinitum, carrying us toward apostasy; such a trove of energy is not squandered: exertion has taught us new lessons, and we are rousing the people of the steppe to form new cities. We shall be leaving this city to prosper elsewhere; and surprising though it may seem, the story that has triumphed for two millennia will not last forever. Our incursions and deeds will not go down in history as a revolt against the rational side of the State; we represent neither its reverse nor its double. Understand that we are other: generous and long-suffering. Those of your ilk, people of god and of reforms, are to be crushed.

And a burst of applause from the crowd for the inspired arguments that flowed from the lips and down the beard of Master

Mahmūd, garrulous, almost sober now. And the crowd in choral repetition of the hemistich transcribed by the hand of the tattooed calligrapher, intoned by the bard, chanted by that mix of criminals and wordsmiths: we are Zanj and Qarmatian. The phrase spreads by word of mouth, and the determination of voices stifles the throbbing, deafening, obsessive echo of the kūs, sign of our obsidional delirium.

Meanwhile, the astrologer wanders through the crowd shouting to anyone who will listen: after the layāli, nights black and sleepless, after the chilling rains, after the tilling of fields, after the sighting of cranes, after the return of storks, after the coming of spring, after the arrival of swallows, after the grueling husūm, hardest days of all, after the grafting of trees, after the equinox, after the nightingale's song, here come fierce winds of the west, of the north. See how Jupiter and moon tease each other in Aries. The moment is critical.

The sorceresses move swiftly. The musicians strike up allegro. Skin shining, the dancers gesticulate on the fringes of the march. Wrestlers spar with imaginary opponents. The smell of grilled kebabs wafts through the air, reviving appetites. 'Allāl, pedantic collar, fez worn at a tilt, words uncompromising, attempts to harangue the crowd, to repeat 'Abduh's babble, searching for some precious teaching that guided the great men of history, upbraiding like naughty children those devoted to the commonplace, nostalgic, archaic, and dangerous practices that deviate from the true religion, based upon reason and law. It rebukes the politics of instinct, relating it to the immoderation of peoples without history, culture, or civilization: to Negroes, Amerindians, Berbers of the uplands, to idolaters and man-eaters. He brashly suggests punishment for the few leaders who have been sowing discontent among the naïve and pliable masses!

He appeals to reason, asks that people return to their homes and not lose heart, not opt for the revival of certain traditions, not dream impossible dreams, that they abandon the notion of utopia; he promises clemency for those who have been misled as soon as things return to normal: reuniting of slaves clinging to the desperate desire to see their master dead. He boils it down to essentials by advising passersby, lured by other speeches and spectacles, to sift through their history and once again revise their judgment, to gather concordances of values, of parables, and of mysteries that demonstrate the intrinsic scientific qualities of the civilization that is ours, which through no fault of its own has found itself relegated to the margins, disinherited, ranked among countries fit to be colonized.

But the crowd, feeling its strength in numbers, scorns such nonsense. Still, a few do stop to at least listen to this reedy voice, breaking under the strain, but everyone else is busy taking part—eye, tongue, mouth, or hand—in the imminent sacrifice. A kid strolling past says out of nowhere that this discourse is the consequence of the teachings of a certain Lyautey, nostalgic aristocrat who believed himself sufficiently strong-willed to shape after his own fashion an impossible history, evacuating its violence.

Bashīr, who made his fortune in the medical business, feels the same outrage as 'Allāl. He goes over to console him: we are helpless among these hordes; how are we supposed to educate these louts, these pigs, with their bestial instincts? And yet, we did what we could to set them on the path to civility. What more can we do? We undoubtedly need to denounce the primal pagan urge still rife here. Along their route, they sacked the Khaldūnia, venerable institution we had the honor of creating after bitter battles with the occupier—concessions, in order to bring modern knowledge to the sterile Arab, lulled by musty, head-emptying medieval scholastics. Weep, O brother! It's enough to make one want to change skins, change races; we shall remain the dregs of the world so long as these masses continue to agitate—impassioned, empty, destructive Arabs.

The cortege reaches its terminal point. Halfawīne, inhabited by its bygone days. Fencing around the square has been torn down, the grass trampled, inadequate water fountain shut off, its basin turned into an altar. The sorceresses lash the sacrificial bull to it and a sturdy arm plants a knife into its struggling throat. Spurting of blood. The crowd cries out, haunted by the vision of red. The bull splashing about in it. Avid mouths attach to the mortal wound, drinking in the warm blood. Roaring in fury and pain, eyes on fire, the bull gores the altar. The sorceresses decide to release the dying animal. The bull lifts itself back on its feet, weakened and stumbling, wavers, attempts to bolt, falls again, gets back up. Men and women are chasing it now, while others cling to the neck to drink in the gushing blood, dip their hands into it up to the elbows, soak their faces in it, lips, cheeks, neck, and forehead.

It is the hour of blood on the public square, the pale green grass daubed with clotted streaks. The square breathes in solemn joy. No more is the square incongruous within the city; it has been redirected, back toward its origins, by the people. Is there no instrument more appropriate to examine modern Arab regimes than the idea of the public square and its by-products? In the beginning, the people, using their brains, discover they are backward; they feel threatened by colonization; certain voices rise and advocate westernization, sole remedy against uncontainable conquest. A tempting rationale, but one that didn't get far.

In the beginning, there was a king and a city, Khedive and Cairo. The first Arab garden square inspired by western urban planning is thought to be the Azbakya, located near the Opera, inaugural *Aïda*, equestrian statue of the brother of Fu'ād, Ibrahīm, frozen upon his clumsily immobile steed, looking out upon Maydān al-'Ataba al-Khadhra, formerly Muhammad 'Alī Square, between blue café where the big names of the nahdha would meet, propagators of fundamentalism, and the Hotel Parliament, its name reflecting a desire for a constitutional framework, as if history did not always involve, ahead of any transient democratic experiment, ruptures and dethronings. And today, everything looks terrible, in ruins, not even a picturesque façade round the front of an immense covered market strewn with trash, great sides of buffalo meat spattered with the purple ink stamp of officialdom.

What is a square if not space developed in order to demolish any location steeped in popular word and deed? What is Azbakya if not a gate closing in Sidnā Hussayn, song of the people, cloistered edifying narrative, mystical dance, ecstasy and excess, trance and abandon, bendīr and flute, gate opening onto the misery of modernity transplanted to riverbank and desert's fringe, people as furtive pilgrims on the move, dipping their trembling bodies into the waters once again, confronted with their unmentionable origins, kept alive in the wisdom of their ghetto?

Djāma' Fnā, unalterable din, undisturbed by the presence of tourists, even they have been adapted to, a square wholly unlike Azbakya in its vernacular resistance: remedies for all the body's ills, for all fears, breaking of spells, dancing snakes, clownish gnawa, tightrope walkers, trinkets, storytellers, voices eschatological or humorous, sebsi hash pipe circulating freely, lovely ladies with come-hither looks and quick hands, madmen like shooting stars, idiots with famous punchlines, horribly made-up effeminate youths, raising the stakes with their Spanish accents.

Halfawīne was comparable to Djāma' Fnā. Circles floundering in endless stories, movie segments shown under tarpaulins. Lubricant tank turned into resonance chamber for a tight-lipped storyteller's makeshift violin. Snake charmers, childhood friends of the old gentleman who used to walk us to school in single file, vendors of all sorts, of herbs, plants, engravings, drawings, decorative planks, bodies, slaves, monkeys, gold chains of mythical proportions, lions' teeth to be worn to ward off slander and death curses. But the era of independence remembered Cairo's edifying precedent: what could not be carried out in the nineteenth century was finally executed in the second half of the twentieth. A city like Tunis, disgraced bride, rid itself of its popular locales along with its colonial statuary. To celebrate her newfound freedom, she decked herself out in public squares *made in Cairo*, fully assumed modernity, reconciliation with a presentable *Arabité*. Parterre of flowers in the shape of a monumental clock, to amaze the simpletons, not unlike the scene changes that regularly disrupt the former Place de France, currently Place Muhammad V, in Tangiers: the sign there is unstable: one day, you're passing under a tossed-together triumphal arch, the next day it's flowers that take you in, and later it's a clock or a gigantic portrait. The rising classes are dazzled, their historic entrance onto the scene authorized by the rhythmic spray of a fountain, light and color, tinny music, the Spanish-inflected square of Tetouan oddly Arabized, roundabout where avenues converge.

Halfawīne recovers its original destiny through rebellion. The bull lies dead in the neighborhood's heart. The fresh meat is shared out after the animal is skinned. Music is in plenary session on the square. The storytellers set aside their quarrel with the women, who wish to challenge them to a narrative contest.

The Sahib Ettaba'a mosque, shadow of the past century, shows that borrowed motifs can be enriched by making detail yield to the integrated whole: and that a pulpit reproducing gothic idiom remains, beyond its minbar decor. Mosque with gallery opening onto Place Halfawīne, forum evacuated by those who live, weep, eat on the square, now occupied by the learned men, recalcitrant traitors. Tāhar, Bachīr, 'Allāl, and 'Abdūh have been joined by the venerable blind man Taha, sarcastic, caustic humanist, whose words are recognizable among a thousand others, whether spoken or written, if only because it can be likened to the blind man of Ma'arra's, master wordsmith and writer of fictions; to calm all this agitation, says Taha, we must introduce the teaching of Greek and Latin, thereby allowing our peoples to settle down by assimilating the ternary progression: they will realize that they are floundering in archaism, that they must attain balance in a classical period before finally declining into the baroque and perishing for good! And such teaching is like mathematics: it is not so much acquisition and retention of knowledge that counts as the exercises that help to shape the mind.

Serendipitous presence of 'Abdul Karīm among this inopportune elite: the insurrection has met with failure inside the city, he says. For the city secretes a web that tames revolt, revolt cannot endure there among peasants and marginal women. Fez, Tunis, Cairo: these are, at varying scales, cities to be remade. The Prophet said: prosper on this land, build cities. But the cities we build will be located on the edges of deserts, of mountains, cities subservient to the capacities of these two spaces, surge of fire. And of ancient cities, we shall tend only to Marrakesh and its peers: Biskra, Tozeur, Medīna, Najaf, Karbala . . . And we shall rebuild the San'as of this world, the Tinmels.

The other learned men find nothing to say in reply. Some acquiesce out of politeness, considering the leader's prestige, precursor to subsequent maquisards. But they disapprove on the sly, a way of insinuating that the founder of the Rif republic is now in his dotage.

Meanwhile, the kūs thunders on furiously, though forgotten amid the other explosives crisscrossing the sky, rockets, cannonballs, grapeshot, crossbow bolts, and an avalanche of arrows. The attack on the city proves deadly, but the crowd is not inordinately restless. The sorceresses place the idol with its palanquin on the dried blood that discolors the pink granite of the basin. Ya'qūb, emerged from his private journey, heady cavalcade, soaks the mummified idol in gasoline, and it is Fātima who sets it alight, flame taking instantly, sudden crackling, charring the reconstituted corpse, desperate search for the third eye, horror of face eaten away by fire, dust and smoking ash scattered by female handfuls, carried away by cold blasts of wind that sweep the square, blinding the remaining attendees who must choose their fate at the crossroads of history, not knowing whether they should die as mad warriors, a determined decision made by a few among the insurgents, or else flee in order to propagate elsewhere the values of the impossible and excessive.

The first to hide, then to give away the keys to the city, are the learned men, dressed in their loose embroidered tunics, their perfect turbans, lofty cupolas.

Massacre and rape, plunder and theft: the Spanish attack from the east, advancing on horseback, lancers, infantry, archers, armored and shielded; they besiege the Zitūna mosque, camp in the outer court, turn the main prayer hall into a stable, smell of alfalfa, hay, horsey warmth, steamy breath, laughter, and soldiers making the sign of the cross; gouged eyes, numerous tortures, moaning of the wounded, soldiers mortally injured and then finished off under the Christian auspices, occult gesture cleaving in two the territory to be blessed by priestly honors.

The French, triumphant army come over from Algeria, violent resistance, warriors strewn on the ground, muskets against chassepot rifles and machine guns, storm Seagate, *Bāb al Bahr*, renamed Porte de France, pushing and poking, invective and abuse, military music, signs of victory and temporary submission, striking up bellicose tunes, parading its power beneath the arcades, military club, bleak presence, aggressive uniforms, arrogance interiorizing racial superiority, bombs of resistance exploding beneath the feet of military columns, perpetrators turned victim hunted down and tortured.

The Turks, nonchalant and brutal, enter through New Gate, *Bāb Jedīd*, moustaches and insignia, words and formulae, heartfelt recitation of the credo of belonging to the same community, to the same law: few of those in the resistance oppose their forward march; on horseback, the corps of Janissaries, uncompromising, cruel, rapists of women and children. Nothing impedes their advance, save perhaps the reference to the Name that sometimes helps mitigate the acts of vengeance wrought upon a city that dared oppose the affixing of the seal, Sublime Porte, emblem redeemed by blood.

The clan of village folk attack via Green Gate, *Bāb al Khadhra*, in an attempt to revive the memory of Independence and to once again recruit the masses to celebrate victory, cortege imitating the spontaneity that shook the city on the day of return and declaration of freedom, inflation of symbol, trite theatricality; no one cheers; the order to charge is given, truncheon-wielding thugs attack the rebel houses, aided in their effort by foreign informers, relentless in their pursuit to uproot the weeds that have lately proliferated and prospered in these untamed, happy quarters of the city. To fight back against this barbarity, to ponder a feasible course of action, would merely confine us to the most predictable response, to engage the enemy on its terms. Our attack on history would only serve to further the notion of nation as sole guarantor of legitimacy, an unimaginative political logic in thrall to so-called universal standards of power.

EPILOGUE

A great many sorceresses and other obstinate forces, along with us,
have taken leave of the city. Hijra, voluntary migration, in the foot-
steps of Hājir, Hagar, beyond defeat, into retreat: orphans all. We knew
that we lacked persuasive authority, that it would be a while before we
made known the ritual that exorcised our age-old submissiveness, a
past to be resumed as we head out toward the desert, exiting the city
through the Sidi Abd es-Salām gate, passing by the dairy plant and
brewery, by the cemetery, the stadium, and the decommissioned army
barracks, through the Cité des Oliviers, until Jbel Lahmar, red moun-
tain, where we are welcomed by a knowing populace who give us water,
dried meat, hash pipe, ululation, embraces. We are greeted as if mem-
bers of the tribe, offered a hideout. But we cannot linger, and as soon
as night has fallen, we are off again, leaving in small groups, setting
our meeting places along a string of nomad encampments, remaining
pockets of Berbers, as we head south. We negotiate forests and fields,
woodland and underbrush, thirst and heat. Everywhere peasants take
us in, recognize us as their own, come to our aid, understand, though
poverty-stricken, eager to see us succeed in our southbound retreat.

Reunited, we are more than one thousand, exhausted, eyes caked
with dust, each of us bearing desert within, in contact with the star
that descends to our feet, offering to divine the unfathomable; nights

endless and exquisite in the deepest darkness, walking all the way to the mountains stripped and arid that overlook the desert's edge, walking in silence toward the secret land of minorities; vanishing pockets, moribund with illness, anemia, eyes out of balance, field mice and wolves, leprous, cast-off humanity, exhausted from excessive clairvoyance and the knowledge of vain truths.

Reorganize space, bring the bald mountains back to life, hollow out the slopes, read their stars, tame their raptors and serpents, take stock of rare plants and herbs, collect fossils and stones, meditate like the cave-dwelling recluse, refuse to go down to the plain.

And thus pass the months: hating intensely before loving, cutting ourselves off from Mediterranean habits, sharing afresh sense and sex, rising up lords of beauty, stripping ourselves of the act of exchange, caravan, commerce, until the group, worn and weary, on the verge of internal strife, decides to disperse, to split in two.

Fātima leaves with those whose objective is to revive the pagan spirit of the Banī Murra, people buried deep in sands of the Arabian peninsula, the most arid of deserts, the Empty Quarter, passing on their way through the land of the Nubians, source held back from history.

As for myself, I join those bound westward, taghrīb and not ghurba, to gather the scattered forces of nomads, Sahrāwis and Touāregs, to extend the capacities of the desert, Rio de Oro, Sāguia Hamra. Woman: music and verse; man: camel driver's pace, tea burning hot; full-bodied dates, milky, sap and succulence, sun, could I be other than taste of passion on virgin's lips, O claws of the basilisk, nest of the Anqa bird, sepulcher of the first man, in search of lacustrine aftereffects, flowers that bloom and fade in one day, stones that signal a millennial presence, skin burned, twice baked, mobile gaze itself desert, back and sand where footsteps are written then erased by the constant winds.

Ephemeral crossing by igneous flow, mouth full of oases large and small, at times regressing, curious emergence of my former life, Laure in Paris, comfort and decorum, winter remedy for Venetian flu, Adda Francesca, colors of Rome fleeing then rushing back into my arms, encounter with dogs, wandering hunted, France, Europe, beguiling prey, pursuing us in our retreat, coursing through our veins, lifting us up without denial, images and flavors that vanish beneath the intense gaze of the sun, nothing but man among sand and stone, waiting to break our fast to the rustle of palms, where fate will carry us empty toward the arm of the sea that extends into the desert, mist and pink flamingos, mirage not far from furious, fish-filled water, we shall feed ourselves on mullet and meagre, presenting ourselves as unimportant enigma in the hands of the old man kept as guardian of the waters, patching together a fishnet to facilitate extraction of our meal, then digest the rectitude of a history off-center, for as long as it takes to silently repudiate this journey, derisory death.

I compose myself here, repeating the words of Nietzsche:

The desert grows: woe to him who harbors deserts!
Stone grates on stone, the desert swallows down

We have confided through writing, but without giving you a foot-hold, have strained your eyes with our arabesque of words, have recommended the circuits of our journey, have warned you of the fissure in all that meets the eye, have unsettled you on high moral grounds, have ruined among you the most robust constitutions, have dusted myself off, vanished into thin air, have found my way inside you through the least perceptible slit; text like dust to be read as the Book in reverse, a text replete, where four or five ideas repeat, in the tawdry play on difference, having despaired of any law, interleaving experience where, through my I, the living might find mutual recognition: put down in writing, dreamed in reverse in the Book, dearly departed allograph that disoriginates a sated sensibility, transcribed left to right while body and eyes follow their meditative course in the text from right to left, in the same horizontal continuity the inverse direction becomes clear: words of exile, sun concealed, man disappearing, from the here to the there we wander between concealed and revealed, sunset to sunrise, favoring blood-red fall over luminous rebirth, genesis of the ephemeral, stealthy sundown: maghreb; beyond veils, reappear to the pagan yes through the text as long as the days are shortening, to affirm its presence on the trail of abandonment, by antithesis and physically inverted graphic, by return to themes that withstand no words: body, pleasure, death, desert; all unutterable and transformed into moments of uttering by way of the language of metaphor, rendered archaic even to oneself, old as the world, to repeat that the light to brighten our lands shall come from women: by the planet Jupiter, by chrysolite, by Venus, by hematite, the female will make fertile the beds tread upon by male readiness; and by this new suffusion may the divided body recover its orphaned other.

MARCH 15–JULY 13, 1976
REVISED OCTOBER 1986

TRANSLATOR'S NOTES

p. 58   Hayy ibn Yaqdhan is a character in a twelfth-century novel
          from Islamic Spain written by Ibn Tufail, after a similar work
          by Ibn Sina (Avicenna). The philosophical tale involves a
          feral child raised by a gazelle on a desert island, and who
          discovers the world on his own through reasoned inquiry.

p. 105   Succession of ruling powers over what is today Egypt, from
          the Arab Caliphate in the tenth century to the Ottoman
          Turks who ruled loosely through nineteenth.

p. 188   A deformation of French common to non-French-speak-
          ing North Africans of the term "les ouvriers," meaning

"laborers." The "s" of "les" is pronounced like a "z," and the letter "v" does not exist in Arabic, and is heard as an "f," resulting in "zufri" for "les ouvriers." The word is often used as an insult.

p. 245   Tahar Haddad (1899–1935) Tunisian writer, scholar and reformer, an early promoter of women's rights and trade unions.

p. 246   Muhammad Abduh (1849–1905) was an Egyptian social and religious reformer.

p. 247   The Zanj were East Africans taken as slave laborers to Mesopotamia, where they eventually staged three separate rebellions between the seventh and ninth centuries. The Qarmatians were a Shi'a sect in eastern Arabia that founded a utopian republic in the ninth century. They are known for their revolt against the Abbasid Caliphate, during which they sacked the holy sites of Mecca and Medina, stealing the black stone of the Ka'aba and holding it ransom. The names Zanj and Qarmatian are synonymous with revolt.

p. 248   Muhammad Allal al-Fassi (1910–1974) Moroccan politician, writer, poet and Islamic scholar. Founder of the Istiqlal party that led Morocco's independence from the French Protectorate, he broke briefly with that party to join armed revolutionaries that opted for a campaign of urban violence rather than a diplomatic solution.

p. 253   Bachīr Sfar (1856–1917) Founder of the Khaldūnia, Tunisia's first modern school (1896); modernist reformer who believed that western education could coexist with local cultural values.

p. 253   Taha Hussein (1889–1973) Influential Egyptian writer and intellectual, figurehead of the modernist movement in the Arab World.

p. 254   'Abdul Karīm (1882–1963) Moroccan leader of an armed resistance movement against French and Spanish colonial rule in the Berber area of northern Morocco, the Rif.

Though he has lived and worked in Paris for many years, ABDELWAHAB MEDDEB was born in Tunis in 1946. Meddeb has written some dozen works of fiction, but is best known in the English-speaking world for his outspoken essays condemning religious fundamentalism, *The Malady of Islam* and *Islam and Its Discontents*.

JANE KUNTZ has translated *Everyday Life* and *The Power of Flies* by Lydie Salvayre, *Hotel Crystal* by Olivier Rolin, *Pigeon Post* by Dumitru Tsepeneag, and *Hoppla! 1 2 3* by Gérard Gavarry, all of which are available from Dalkey Archive Press.

PETROS ABATZOGLOU, *What Does Mrs. Freeman Want?*
MICHAL AJVAZ, *The Golden Age.*
The Other City.
PIERRE ALBERT-BIROT, *Grabinoulor.*
YUZ ALESHKOVSKY, *Kangaroo.*
FELIPE ALFAU, *Chromos.*
Locos.
IVAN ÂNGELO, *The Celebration.*
The Tower of Glass.
DAVID ANTIN, *Talking.*
ANTÓNIO LOBO ANTUNES, *Knowledge of Hell.*
ALAIN ARIAS-MISSON, *Theatre of Incest.*
IFTIKHAR ARIF AND WAQAS KHWAJA, EDS., *Modern Poetry of Pakistan.*
JOHN ASHBERY AND JAMES SCHUYLER, *A Nest of Ninnies.*
GABRIELA AVIGUR-ROTEM, *Heatwave and Crazy Birds.*
HEIMRAD BÄCKER, *transcript.*
DJUNA BARNES, *Ladies Almanack.*
Ryder.
JOHN BARTH, *LETTERS.*
Sabbatical.
DONALD BARTHELME, *The King.*
Paradise.
SVETISLAV BASARA, *Chinese Letter.*
RENÉ BELLETTO, *Dying.*
MARK BINELLI, *Sacco and Vanzetti Must Die!*
ANDREI BITOV, *Pushkin House.*
ANDREJ BLATNIK, *You Do Understand.*
LOUIS PAUL BOON, *Chapel Road.*
My Little War.
Summer in Termuren.
ROGER BOYLAN, *Killoyle.*
IGNÁCIO DE LOYOLA BRANDÃO, *Anonymous Celebrity.*
The Good-Bye Angel.
Teeth under the Sun.
Zero.
BONNIE BREMSER, *Troia: Mexican Memoirs.*
CHRISTINE BROOKE-ROSE, *Amalgamemnon.*
BRIGID BROPHY, *In Transit.*
MEREDITH BROSNAN, *Mr. Dynamite.*
GERALD L. BRUNS, *Modern Poetry and the Idea of Language.*
EVGENY BUNIMOVICH AND J. KATES, EDS., *Contemporary Russian Poetry: An Anthology.*
GABRIELLE BURTON, *Heartbreak Hotel.*
MICHEL BUTOR, *Degrees.*
Mobile.
Portrait of the Artist as a Young Ape.
G. CABRERA INFANTE, *Infante's Inferno.*
Three Trapped Tigers.
JULIETA CAMPOS, *The Fear of Losing Eurydice.*
ANNE CARSON, *Eros the Bittersweet.*
ORLY CASTEL-BLOOM, *Dolly City.*
CAMILO JOSÉ CELA, *Christ versus Arizona.*
The Family of Pascual Duarte.
The Hive.
LOUIS-FERDINAND CÉLINE, *Castle to Castle.*
Conversations with Professor Y.
London Bridge.
Normance.

North.
Rigadoon.
HUGO CHARTERIS, *The Tide Is Right.*
JEROME CHARYN, *The Tar Baby.*
ERIC CHEVILLARD, *Demolishing Nisard.*
MARC CHOLODENKO, *Mordechai Schamz.*
JOSHUA COHEN, *Witz.*
EMILY HOLMES COLEMAN, *The Shutter of Snow.*
ROBERT COOVER, *A Night at the Movies.*
STANLEY CRAWFORD, *Log of the S.S. The Mrs Unguentine.*
Some Instructions to My Wife.
ROBERT CREELEY, *Collected Prose.*
RENÉ CREVEL, *Putting My Foot in It.*
RALPH CUSACK, *Cadenza.*
SUSAN DAITCH, *L.C.*
Storytown.
NICHOLAS DELBANCO, *The Count of Concord.*
Sherbrookes.
NIGEL DENNIS, *Cards of Identity.*
PETER DIMOCK, *A Short Rhetoric for Leaving the Family.*
ARIEL DORFMAN, *Konfidenz.*
COLEMAN DOWELL, *The Houses of Children.*
Island People.
Too Much Flesh and Jabez.
ARKADII DRAGOMOSHCHENKO, *Dust.*
RIKKI DUCORNET, *The Complete Butcher's Tales.*
The Fountains of Neptune.
The Jade Cabinet.
The One Marvelous Thing.
Phosphor in Dreamland.
The Stain.
The Word "Desire."
WILLIAM EASTLAKE, *The Bamboo Bed.*
Castle Keep.
Lyric of the Circle Heart.
JEAN ECHENOZ, *Chopin's Move.*
STANLEY ELKIN, *A Bad Man.*
Boswell: A Modern Comedy.
Criers and Kibitzers, Kibitzers and Criers.
The Dick Gibson Show.
The Franchiser.
George Mills.
The Living End.
The MacGuffin.
The Magic Kingdom.
Mrs. Ted Bliss.
The Rabbi of Lud.
Van Gogh's Room at Arles.
ANNIE ERNAUX, *Cleaned Out.*
LAUREN FAIRBANKS, *Muzzle Thyself.*
Sister Carrie.
LESLIE A. FIEDLER, *Love and Death in the American Novel.*
JUAN FILLOY, *Op Oloop.*
GUSTAVE FLAUBERT, *Bouvard and Pécuchet.*
KASS FLEISHER, *Talking out of School.*
FORD MADOX FORD, *The March of Literature.*
JON FOSSE, *Aliss at the Fire.*
Melancholy.
MAX FRISCH, *I'm Not Stiller.*
Man in the Holocene.

My Life in CIA.
Singular Pleasures.
The Sinking of the Odradek
  Stadium.
Tlooth.
20 Lines a Day.
JOSEPH McELROY,
  Night Soul and Other Stories.
THOMAS McGONIGLE,
  Going to Patchogue.
ROBERT L. McLAUGHLIN, ED., *Innovations:*
  An Anthology of
    Modern & Contemporary Fiction.
ABDELWAHAB MEDDEB, *Talismano.*
HERMAN MELVILLE, *The Confidence-Man.*
AMANDA MICHALOPOULOU, *I'd Like.*
STEVEN MILLHAUSER,
  The Barnum Museum.
  In the Penny Arcade.
RALPH J. MILLS, JR.,
  Essays on Poetry.
MOMUS, *The Book of Jokes.*
CHRISTINE MONTALBETTI, *Western.*
OLIVE MOORE, *Spleen.*
NICHOLAS MOSLEY, *Accident.*
  Assassins.
  Catastrophe Practice.
  Children of Darkness and Light.
  Experience and Religion.
  God's Hazard.
  The Hesperides Tree.
  Hopeful Monsters.
  Imago Bird.
  Impossible Object.
  Inventing God.
  Judith.
  Look at the Dark.
  Natalie Natalia.
  Paradoxes of Peace.
  Serpent.
  Time at War.
  The Uses of Slime Mould:
    Essays of Four Decades.
WARREN MOTTE,
  Fables of the Novel: French Fiction
    since 1990.
  Fiction Now: The French Novel in
    the 21st Century.
  Oulipo: A Primer of Potential
    Literature.
YVES NAVARRE, *Our Share of Time.*
  Sweet Tooth.
DOROTHY NELSON, *In Night's City.*
  Tar and Feathers.
ESHKOL NEVO, *Homesick.*
WILFRIDO D. NOLLEDO, *But for the Lovers.*
FLANN O'BRIEN,
  At Swim-Two-Birds.
  At War.
  The Best of Myles.
  The Dalkey Archive.
  Further Cuttings.
  The Hard Life.
  The Poor Mouth.
  The Third Policeman.
CLAUDE OLLIER, *The Mise-en-Scène.*
  Wert and the Life Without End.
PATRIK OUŘEDNÍK, *Europeana.*
  The Opportune Moment, 1855.
BORIS PAHOR, *Necropolis.*

FERNANDO DEL PASO,
  News from the Empire.
  Palinuro of Mexico.
ROBERT PINGET, *The Inquisitory.*
  Mahu or The Material.
  Trio.
MANUEL PUIG,
  Betrayed by Rita Hayworth.
  The Buenos Aires Affair.
  Heartbreak Tango.
RAYMOND QUENEAU, *The Last Days.*
  Odile.
  Pierrot Mon Ami.
  Saint Glinglin.
ANN QUIN, *Berg.*
  Passages.
  Three.
  Tripticks.
ISHMAEL REED,
  The Free-Lance Pallbearers.
  The Last Days of Louisiana Red.
  Ishmael Reed: The Plays.
  Juice!
  Reckless Eyeballing.
  The Terrible Threes.
  The Terrible Twos.
  Yellow Back Radio Broke-Down.
JOÃO UBALDO RIBEIRO, *House of the*
  Fortunate Buddhas.
JEAN RICARDOU, *Place Names.*
RAINER MARIA RILKE, *The Notebooks of*
  Malte Laurids Brigge.
JULIÁN RÍOS, *The House of Ulysses.*
  Larva: A Midsummer Night's Babel.
  Poundemonium.
  Procession of Shadows.
AUGUSTO ROA BASTOS, *I the Supreme.*
DANIËL ROBBERECHTS,
  Arriving in Avignon.
JEAN ROLIN, *The Explosion of the*
  Radiator Hose.
OLIVIER ROLIN, *Hotel Crystal.*
ALIX CLEO ROUBAUD, *Alix's Journal.*
JACQUES ROUBAUD, *The Form of a*
  City Changes Faster, Alas, Than
    the Human Heart.
  The Great Fire of London.
  Hortense in Exile.
  Hortense Is Abducted.
  The Loop.
  The Plurality of Worlds of Lewis.
  The Princess Hoppy.
  Some Thing Black.
LEON S. ROUDIEZ, *French Fiction Revisited.*
RAYMOND ROUSSEL, *Impressions of Africa.*
VEDRANA RUDAN, *Night.*
STIG SÆTERBAKKEN, *Siamese.*
LYDIE SALVAYRE, *The Company of Ghosts.*
  Everyday Life.
  The Lecture.
  Portrait of the Writer as a
    Domesticated Animal.
  The Power of Flies.
LUIS RAFAEL SÁNCHEZ,
  Macho Camacho's Beat.
SEVERO SARDUY, *Cobra & Maitreya.*
NATHALIE SARRAUTE,
  Do You Hear Them?
  Martereau.
  The Planetarium.

SELECTED DALKEY ARCHIVE PAPERBACKS

FOR A FULL LIST OF PUBLICATIONS, VISIT:
www.dalkeyarchive.com